STO

Minn.
218 - 864 - 5430
Linda = work
1 - 460 - 3100

THE GOOD SPIRIT OF LAUREL RIDGE

Books by *Jesse Stuart*

The Good Spirit of Laurel Ridge

JESSE STUART

Sז915g

McGRAW-HILL BOOK COMPANY, INC.

NEW YORK TORONTO LONDON

Published by the McGraw-Hill Book Company, Inc.

Printed in the United States of America

TO ED KUHN,
friend and editor

THE GOOD SPIRIT OF LAUREL RIDGE

Theopolis Akers, six feet tall and broad-shouldered, sat on the sty where he had rested so many times after climbing the winding path from Fidis Artner's with a coffee-sack load of supplies. For the first time in his life, he had been led to this sty. He remembered every curve in this path, every rock and tree. He sat listening to the water, nearly a mile below, pouring over the rocks in the river where he'd fished ever since he had been a child. He had often thought of the Sandy River as a big vein in his body. The water in the river was his blood. And the path down to the Sandy River was something that belonged to him, although he wasn't the only one to travel it.

Many times, fox hunters had climbed this path to Laurel Ridge where they could sit in one place and listen to their hounds chase the fox all night. They didn't have to move from where they built a fire on the ridge road under the tall yellow pines, for the hounds ran the fox down under all night. The fox circled around the slopes on both sides and across the long ridge. The music of the barking hounds never faded until they went down into the deep hollows on either side.

Beginning at Six Hickories, Laurel Ridge formed a great arc of more than a mile in length. This giant perimeter was so perfectly arranged around the Sandy River Valley below that the Creator of the Universe might have shaped this one spot of earth for His Own. Down in the arc was a deep gorge with many little tributaries flowing into the main stream which tumbled over rock ledges down the steep, rugged slope to the Sandy River. In this gorge were giant rocks, lying over the earth like scaly monsters sleeping in the sun. Many of these rocks were now resting in the shade of the giant yellow poplars, yellow pines, oaks, beeches, and sourwood trees.

If the rumors, passed down through succeeding generations, had any foundation in fact, General Morgan, leading his Cavalry on a raid into Ohio, had been forced to flee from this point. When scarcely an able-bodied man was left in this hill section of Kentucky, not serving in either the Southern or Northern armies in the Civil War, a band of old men and boys armed themselves with rifles when they heard General Morgan was coming. They hid behind these rocks and when his cavalry covered the full arc of the ridge, they opened fire, shooting the horses first and then the men. General Morgan and his men in their hurried retreat carried away the dead and wounded men on horseback. He was forced at this point to postpone his invasion into Ohio.

More than a century ago, Laurel Ridge road was the main artery of highway traffic from the county-seat town of Honeywell, directly south into Looten County. This was the time when Laurel Ridge was dotted with log shacks, along the backbone of ridge, on the steep slopes and down into the deep valleys. This was the day when there were seventeen iron furnaces in Looten County, when men came from states beyond to dig iron ore from the hills and to cut the great forests into cordwood. The cordwood was hauled by oxen to pits and, after being burned to charcoal by colliers, was used in the furnaces.

Now, after more than a century of change, the great forest had returned to cover Laurel Ridge. Leaf-rot loam, from successive years of falling leaves from the new forest, had covered the foundation stones where more than a hundred shacks had once been. Piles of field stones had flattened, and sandstones had disintegrated where small chimneys had once stood. The lumberjacks, miners, ore diggers, and colliers disappeared with the ore and timber. The Laurel Ridge road had been closed by an order of the Fiscal Court of Looten County, since it was no longer traveled. The old road along the ridge remained where the wheels of thousands of wagons, buggies, surreys, hug-me-tights, and express wagons had left their marks. Heavy-wheeled ore wagons, drawn by twelve yoke of oxen, had rolled slowly along this Laurel Ridge road. Tanbark and cordwood wagons, charcoal wagons with high wagon beds. But that was a century ago.

Now, one man, Snake Blue, owned all the east side of Laurel Ridge. He had inherited it from his father, Little Johnnie Blue, who had squatted on these worthless acres, after the coal and ore were mined and the timber was cut. Snake Blue owned, in addition to this ridge, more than half of Little Whiteoak Valley, which lay east of Laurel Ridge. Fidis Artner, whose father, Moses Artner, had squatted on the rugged terrain between the Little Sandy River and Laurel Ridge, had inherited all of this land and had divided it into four farms for his children. All of Laurel Ridge, where civilization had once been, was now a forgotten segment of Looten County. Only the ghosts remained. People, for a century, had reported seeing the spirits of the men who had been killed there. Ghosts digging ore with picks in the night had been seen by the fox hunters. This tradition had been passed down until Laurel Ridge, with its perfect arc and its great beauty, had become the ghost-infested, forgotten wasteland of Looten County.

I'd better take a bite of my calamus-weed root fer my blood pressure, Op thought, putting a big calloused hand into his pocket. Lutie'll be a-comin' soon to lead me to the cabin.

Theopolis Akers was a big man and powerful, with muscular arms and blunt fingers gnarled and curved. The long hair on his head which he seldom cut was tousled as a cluster of saw briers.

The heavy beard on his face he kept three seasons of the year and only shaved when the days grew long and hot.

"The air is so much better to breathe up here," he said to himself. "After the bad air in that hospital, it's good jist to breathe on Laurel Ridge. Jist as shore as my name is Theopolis Akers, I'll never darken the door of another hospital. It's the first time I ever went to a doctor in my life and it'll be the last time. I'll stay on Laurel Ridge and use yarb poultices and breathe the air of home."

Would he ever see again? he wondered. Would he be able, when the bandage was taken from his eyes, to see the Sandy Valley? Would his sight be restored before the dogwoods and the redbuds shed their blossoms on Laurel Ridge? Would he see the whippoorwill flowers, the May apples, and percoon down in the deep coves beside old rotting stumps and logs? the bracken, the lace fern, and the lichen on the rocks? the great green clouds of leaves that rustled in the wind? leaves so thick above his head he had often walked yards before he had found a hole in this green roof that he could look through to see the blue sky!

2

"Dad, have you had a good morning?" Lucretia asked.

"Wonderful fer a blind man," he said, his voice soft. "I believe I'll allus be blind. I oughtn't to've gone with ye to that foul-smellin' hospital." He stopped chewing his calmus root. "Anyway, how do I know ye're my daughter? I've never seen ye. Stop callin' me 'Dad'! I don't like it!"

"But I am your daughter," the girl said firmly. She was as much of the city in appearance as Op was of the hills. The old

12

man's face was dark and the back of his neck burned and wrinkled. The girl's complexion was smooth (because she'd worked to keep it that way) and her brown hair and high-cheek-boned face were nice to look at. Only, Theopolis had a white bandage over his eyes and he wasn't doing any looking. "I am your daughter, Lucretia Akers," she went on, "and I want to call you 'Dad.' Let's don't go over all this again. You were already blind when I found you. And now you'll have a chance to see again. You know Doctor Turnbo said you might get eighty per cent vision in this eye. And if the operation on this eye isn't successful, you have another eye to operate on."

"I've never been ust to anybody a-leadin' me," Theopolis grumbled as Lucretia took his hand. "I'll never get ust to it. I don't like to be any trouble to anybody."

His brogans whetted on the pine needles along the path. Little stems of wild wood grass caught in the laces of his shoes and left tiny seeds. He walked with the rhythm of a steady wind but slightly bent forward as if he were always climbing a hill.

"I've been a-doin' some thinkin'," he said. "If I don't get my sight back, at least I have a lot of things to remember. A lot of people have never been able to see at all. I'm better off than they are."

"Of course you are," Lucretia agreed.

"I'll remember things," he said. "Without my eyes I can still see 'em. The trees, cliffs, the big rocks in the arc. The Sandy Valley and the snake bends in the Sandy River. The wild flowers in their seasons, the white and black walnuts. I like to think of 'em in autumn when I ust to take a coffee sack and gather nuts. I'd come in with a sack stiff full. These are the things I like to remember. Huntin' in the woods with Jerry. I'll miss these things this fall. Gettin' the' 'simmons and pawpaws after the first frost."

"But you'll get them after the first frost this year," she said.

"I'll go along with you to see that you do. Don't worry about gathering them."

"I'm not so shore that ye will," Op said, suspicion creeping back into his voice. "I'm a-goin' to haf to know more about ye."

"But I am your daughter!" Lucretia's tone was positive. "I know you think I'm not, and it's so silly of you!"

"But ye wouldn't have come back fer my sake," he told her. "Ye never have. My gal young'un was taken from me twenty years ago. Old Will and Corrinne Day come back from Dayton to Beadie's funeral and took 'er. I didn't want to give 'er up but they threatened me with the Law. Said they could prove I was an unfit father who laid flat on his back in the huntin' woods filled with the sperets of 'simmon and pawpaw."

"Well, were you an unfit father, Dad?" Lucretia asked.

"I might've been," he replied. "Since then, I've never had any use fer old Will and Corrinne. I never went to see 'em in Dayton! They took Lutie but left Jack. They thought he was teched in the head 'r they'd 've taken 'im. I've allus thought they raised my Lutie up agin me and that's the reason she's never come back."

"That's how it was," Lutie said. "I heard a lot about you from them."

"I'll bet ye never heard anythin' good, either."

"No, I didn't," she admitted. "They said you were a—well—drank too much."

"I did ferment the 'simmons and pawpaws and made my brew," he admitted. "But 'simmons and pawpaws 're put here fer a purpose. I ust to think brandy was the purpose. I s'pect old Will and Corrinne did give Lutie a purty good home."

"They did, Dad," she said. "But I always wondered about my father back in Kentucky."

"When Beadie died and they took Lutie, I left Ironweed Holler," Op told her. "I come up on Laurel Ridge and built my

14

cabin. I fetched Jack, and Laurel Ridge has provided fer us ever since."

They walked along without talking, the girl gently leading the older man. The dog Jerry ran along the path in front of them, wagging his stubby tail.

"Ye seem to be happy this mornin'," Op said, breaking their silence. "I could hear ye a-singin' at the cabin while ye worked. And ye were singin' when ye come to get me. I heard somebody talkin' to you, and a man laughin' too!"

"This morning when I went for water, I met a Ted Newsome," Lutie began. "He was sitting on the big rock near the spring. Had his back toward me. I spoke to him for I thought brother Jack had come back, since butterflies and bees were working on the blooms. You know we've been talking so much about Jack's coming back to Laurel Ridge since April's here."

"What kind of a lookin' man was he?" Op asked, stopping suddenly.

"He was handsome, Dad," Lucretia said. "Honest, he was! He was wearing khaki pants. He had blond hair and . . ." Lucretia stopped short.

"That's John Newsome's Ted all right," Op said, after waiting for her to continue. "He served in the Army in World War I, and come back here and was bushwhacked."

"But, Dad, he was a real man," she said. "I talked to him and he talked to me. He carried two buckets of water up the hill for me. He wasn't a spirit!"

"Lissen, young woman, I was a boy when Ted Newsome was a young man. Ye saw the Ted Newsome I ust to know. I went to the Freewill Baptist Church with 'im many a night. That Ted Newsome was a handsome man with blond hair and the bluest eyes I ever saw. About six-feet tall, with purty teeth and a square-set jaw."

"Don't tell me that, Dad," Lucretia interrupted.

15

"I don't want to skeer ye," Op said. "But there's been a lot of ghosts seen on Laurel Ridge. Did ye ast Ted Newsome where he lived?"

"I tried to find out where he lived and he said different places on Laurel Ridge."

"Which way did he go when he left?"

"Out Laurel Ridge road."

"That's in the direction of the Freewill Baptist Churchyard," Op told her. "That's where his grave is. That's his long home and it wouldn't surprise me if Ted was a-headin' back to it!"

"Dad, I don't believe in ghosts," Lucretia said.

"It's because ye don't want to believe," Op told her. "I thought first it might've been ornery Hootbird Hammertight a-hangin' around tryin' to spark with ye. But I don't believe Hootbird would give ye a different name, he's allus been so proud of his own. But ye said this man was blond. Hootbird is, too. Was he wearin' a big Texas hat?"

"No, Dad, he was bareheaded," she said.

"Then it wasn't Hootbird, fer he allus wears tight-fittin' pants, flowered boots with high heels, a belt studded with ornaments and a big Texas hat," Op laughed. "Hootbird has a hankerin' fer wimmen. Tries to talk to every one he sees. I've been plannin' to warn ye about 'im. I think the man ye saw was the Ted Newsome I ust to know. Ted Newsome, I'm shore, is a good speret. And he'll be harmless around wimmen!"

The girl shook her head and sighed, obviously regretting having brought up the subject.

"There's a reason why he's back here," Op told her. "I think sperets come back on earth to the places they love. I've never told ye all the things that's happened on this ridge."

"Listen, you can't scare me," she laughed. "I don't believe people come back. I don't believe in ghosts."

"Young lady, many a night I've heard the sound of hosses'

hoofs a-poundin' this Laurel Ridge road," Op told her as she led him down the ridge. "I've jumped up from my bed and run to the door, opened it in a hurry and looked up and down the road and never saw a man or a hoss. I know who it is a-ridin' past in a hurry. It's General Morgan and his Cavalry. Back there at that arc on Laurel Ridge, down behind the big rocks, the old men and boys stopped 'im onct and made 'im turn tail when he was a-goin' to raid Ohio in the days of the Rebellion. My father was one of the men behind the rocks. Bones of their hosses were left to whiten the ridge. Hoss bones can be found there now if ye dig down into the leaf-rot loam, rib bones and thigh bones of Morgan's hosses. But Morgan got out of that deathtrap in a hurry. Carried away his dead and wounded. Don't know how many of his men were kilt. Don't know where he buried his dead. But they come back here now and ride this ridge and worry me since I'm the son of George Akers, who hid behind a rock with a long rifle and helped stop 'em. I know the riders that I hear a-goin' by in the night are Morgan and his men.

"Looks like that would scare you," Lucretia said.

"They don't skeer me," he told her. "I'm ust to 'em. Ghosts are on this ridge, but I've never heard of one walkin' around in the daytime but onct. One Sunday, back when Teddy Roosevelt was President, old Doc Burton drove his two-hoss surrey out Laurel Ridge to see Mort Doore who got blood pizen from runnin' a rusty nail in his foot. On his way back, a young couple walked outten the Six Hickories Church House. Doc Burton didn't know the young couple who flagged 'im fer a ride. They said they were on their way to Honeywell. The young woman was dressed in white and was carryin' a armload of flowers. She told Doc Burton her name was Rinda Stevens. The young man, dressed in a blue suit, white shirt, little bow tie, and a red rose in his coat lapel, told Doc his name was Tom Kitchen. Doc said he never let his fast-steppin' bays stop trottin' till he got to

Honeywell as he was in a hurry to get back home to a Sunday dinner. Said he talked to the couple till he started down Seaton Hollow into Honeywell where it was downgrade all the way and he had to do a lot of brakin' and guide his team too. When he stopped talkin', they stopped talkin' to 'im. When he drove into Honeywell and turned to ast 'em where they wanted out, they were gone, nothin' but the flowers on the back seat."

"What did Doctor Burton think?" Lucretia asked, amused.

"Passed out cold as a cucumber, and him a doctor, too," Op said. "I've heard 'im tell it many a time. When he told the story in Honeywell he larned that back in the days of President Garfield, Rinda Stevens and Tom Kitchen, who had planned to get married at the Six Hickories Church, were drowned while swimmin' at the Sandy Falls. Reckon their sperets had come back to the Six Hickories Church and got married.

"It was either the Ted Newsome that's dead and gone," Theopolis explained as Lucretia helped him upon the porch, "or it was Hootbird Hammertight a-givin' himself another name. Hootbird Hammertight ain't as good a-lookin' man as Ted Newsome. And Hootbird always wears them flowered boots. I believe ye saw the Ted Newsome I ust to know."

3

After Op and Lucretia had eaten their evening meal and she had washed the dishes, put a clean cloth on the table and a fresh bouquet of wild flowers in a bowl, they went to the back of the cabin to a wooden bench. This bench was a log Op had split in halves and had put four strong legs into the deep holes he had chiseled into the log. He had smoothed the upturned split with his double-bitted ax and had shaved it to smoothness with pieces of broken glass. This was the way Op made ax and hoe handles. The bench was directly beneath the entanglement of horsehairs among wooden pegs on the cabin wall.

"If we get a wind," Op said, "we'll have music. I've heard a lot of purty music out here at night sittin' all alone on this bench, a-watchin' the moon come up. I can't see the moon tonight but I can hear the music."

"There's a new moon, Dad," Lucretia said. "It's like a silver sickle in the sky."

"Then I've waited too late to get my taters in the ground," Op told her. "I've allus planted 'em in the dark moon in late March but my eyes have kept me from a-doin' it this year."

Lucretia looked at the new moon, which seemed to be just across the Little White Oak Valley and down under. Sitting on this bench, in their back yard, she could look down into the many tributaries of Little White Oak and their deep green valleys. When they sat in the front yard, she could see into the deep Sandy Valley, as the cabin was in the center of Laurel Ridge, the backbone of upheaved earth that separated Sandy River and Little White Oak Valley. To the west of the cabin was an acre of flat ridgetop that Op had cleared years ago and had planted in garden. He had fenced this acre with palings he had riven from white oaks with his froe and wooden mallet. In the corner of this garden Op had built a log smokehouse where he kept his tools, dried his wild roots in summer, and kept his animal pelts in winter.

"Lissen, Lutie," Op said. "Hear the music. The wind is a-risin'. We're a-goin' to hear music tonight. Ye've been a-laughin' at my hosshairs on the cabin walls. But wait till ye hear the music on a night when the wind is right, not too slow and not too fast."

There was a soft, crying sound. The wind was blowing from the west, across the Sandy Valley and through the horsehairs on the north and south walls of the cabin.

"It's mournful music, Dad," Lucretia said. "It's like somebody crying."

"Stop callin' me 'Dad'!" he said. "I don't like it!"

"Like it or not," she replied quickly, "I'm going to call you 'Dad' because you *are* my father. You can't get cranky with me."

"I sit out here and lissen to it winter, spring, fall, and summer," Op said in a subdued tone. "And when I go to bed, it often sings me to sleep. Sometimes when Jerry hears it, he lifts his head and howls to the stars."

Lucretia watched the new moon pass behind the top of a tall pine on a finger of a hill that separated two tributaries of Little White Oak. The pine needles were caught against the small, thin moon. Op sat listening to the crying wind in his network of horsehair.

"Fidis Artner thought I was crazy when I ast 'im to save me the hair when he sheared his hosses' manes and tails," Op said. "He said to me: 'Op, what on earth do ye want with hosshair?' And I said: 'Fidis, I want to lay 'em in the water fer nine days and see if they won't turn to snakes.' 'Snakes!' Old Fidis shuddered. 'If I knowed they'd do that, I wouldn't give ye a single hair. I've heard they'd turn to snakes but I've got my first time to see one. I've heard people say they'd turn to snakes if ye'd leave 'em in warm water fer nine days.' 'No, I got a purpose fer 'em, Fidis,' I said. 'I won't put 'em in water and turn 'em to snakes, fer the woods are too full of snakes now and I don't like a snake any more than ye do. I'm allus a-jumpin' every time Jerry leaves me in the huckleberry patch and I see a bush move.' Then old Fidis laughed and laughed. 'Ah, come on down, Op, and get the hair Monday afternoon,' he said. 'We're a-goin' to shear both teams. Will give ye black hairs from the span of hosses with black manes and tails, and flaxen hairs from the span of big gray hosses' manes and tails.' Now, Lutie, that's how I got the two different colors of hair on these walls. When Fidis sheared his hosses I was right there to get the hair."

"Dad, how did you ever go about putting the hair over the cabin walls?" Lucretia looked curiously at the old man with the bandage over his eyes.

"I had to cut and season my pegs and bore the holes into the walls," he explained. "I had to cut little slots with my pocket-knife into the pegs to hold the hairs. Put the pegs in the holes and lace the hosshairs through the slots and tie 'em. It was a job but it's paid off. And let me tell ye, Lutie," he continued, "once old Fidis was up here to see me when he was squirrel-huntin' on the ridge and we were a-sittin' in the front yard. The July wind blew from Sandy Valley and it was the purtiest music a body ever heard. 'What's that I hear?' Fidis asked. 'Harps of the angels,' I said. Fidis looked quair at me as the music went on. He jumped up from the porch in a sweat. 'It sounds like harps all right,' he said as he started lookin', and then he found the hairs. He started laughin'. 'See what ye wanted with the hoss-hair that time,' he said. 'Didn't think of a man a-havin' a crazy idear like this. Looks like this strange hosshair music would run ye crazy at night a-livin' up here by yerself.' 'That's why I have it, Fidis,' I said. 'Even my dog loves to hear it. And I go to sleep at night and have a pleasant dream if the wind blows jist right and the music is good.' Old Fidis never could get over what I'd done."

As the wind rose higher, there were many strange sounds on the cabin walls.

"A body can hear fiddles a-playin' if he lissens." Op leaned toward the wall. "He can hear mandolins, geetars, dulcimers, and harps, too. Hear 'em all a-playin' together."

"But all these instruments are not in tune," Lucretia said, smiling.

"I know they're not allus in tune," Theopolis admitted, "but sometimes I've heard 'em play a song. When the wind was low, I've heard 'On Top of Old Smokey,' purty as ye please. When the wind's blowed hard, I've heard 'Cripple Creek and Sourwood Mountain.' I could sit here fer the next hour and tell ye tunes I've heard played on these cabin walls."

"After what you told me about ghosts," Lucretia said, "this music gives me the creeps."

"Ye jist don't want to think the young man ye saw wasn't a real flesh-and-blood man," he said. "But ye saw Ted Newsome's ghost all right."

4

"Listen, Dad," Lucretia said. "I hear something."

Op and Lucretia sat breathlessly silent.

"Hear somebody whistling 'There's a New Moon over My Shoulder,' " Lucretia whispered.

"I hear it too," Op said. "Sounds like somebody comin' out Laurel Ridge from toward the sty."

"I don't believe it's anybody coming out the ridge," Lucretia said. "It stays in one place."

"So I believe it does," Op agreed.

Then they sat quietly and listened until the whistling stopped.

"I've never heard whistlin' like that," Op told her. "I know all the people around here who whistle. I know the tunes they whistle too."

Lucretia and Op sat in silence except for the weird sounds of wind crying on the cabin walls.

"That might've been Hootbird Hammertight out there a-doin'

that whistlin'." Op shook his head. "But I've never heard 'im whistle so good before."

"Why wouldn't Hootbird come to the cabin?" Lucretia asked. "I'd like to see his flowered boots and Texas hat."

"I never want ye to think about meetin' that feller," Op warned her. "If ye're my daughter, or even some strange woman, I never want ye to get tied up with that fambly. I've seen a lot of famblies among these hills but I never saw one like the Hammertights. I'd hate to see ye fall in love with a boy like Hootbird. Old Ben, his pappie, is like an ape. He's got long arms that come to his knees. He walks slow and swings his arms when he walks. He thinks slower than he walks. He's married to a little tiny woman that keeps the paths hot to Honeywell. She sets up an uproar among people wherever she goes. She has a pizen tongue, old Doshie does, and she's a dangerous woman."

"Stop talking, Dad," Lucretia said. "I hear a guitar! Listen!"

On top of Old Smokey,
All covered with snow,

a voice rose in song to the music of a guitar.

I lost my True Love
From a courtin' too slow.

On top of Old Smokey,
I went there to weep,
A false-hearted lover
Is worse than a thief.

"Oh, Dad, listen to that voice!" Lucretia spoke excitedly. "That's the prettiest voice I ever heard."

"If that's Hootbird, he's been takin' lessons," Op said. "But it might be Ted Newsome. He ust to play on his geetar and sing the old songs! Sounds a lot like Ted!"

For a thief he will rob you
And take what you have,
And a false-hearted lover
Will send you to the grave.

The grave will decay you
And turn you to dust,
Show me a girl in ten thousand
That a poor boy can trust.

She'll hug you and kiss you
And tell you more lies,
Than crossties in the railroad
Or the stars in the skies.

On top of Old Smokey,
All covered with snow,
I lost my True Love,
From a-courtin' too slow.

"I've heard 'Old Smokey' sung by many different people in my day and time," Op said, "but I like that singin' the best of any I've ever heard."

Then Op rose from his bench.

"Come out to the cabin and sing fer us!" he shouted.

He waited for an answer.

"Is that ye, Hootbird?" he shouted again.

Again Op was greeted by silence.

"Is it ye, Ted Newsome?" Op paused. "If it is, don't be afeared. Come to the cabin and sing and play fer us. I know ye're a good speret."

There was silence except for the wind in the horsehairs on the cabin walls.

"He's not going to answer you, Dad," Lucretia said. "Let's wait and see if he'll sing some more."

Op sat down on the bench. "Ted Newsome ust to walk Laurel Ridge and whistle and sing when he's a young flesh-and-blood man on this earth. He ust to play the fiddle at the square dances too. That singin' and playin' is a little too good fer Hootbird."

Theopolis and Lucretia waited until the night grew chilly. The new moon had gone down and the bright stars twinkled in the blue sky just above Laurel Ridge. But all they heard was the wind in the yellow pine boughs sighing overhead and the wind in the horsehairs making strange sounds.

5

The next night Lucretia carried two chairs from the cabin to the front yard. Then she went back to the porch where Op was sitting with his feet hanging over. She took him by the hand and led him to one of the chairs.

"In seven more days," Op apologized, "maybe I won't haf to be led to my chear. I hate to haf to be led every place I go. Ye lead me to the sty and back. Even when I come out onto the porch, ye fetch me by the hand. And maybe somebody'll haf to be a-leadin' me from now on." Lucretia helped him down in his chair. "I've never wanted to see so much in my life as I want to see right now. I want to see what kind of a lookin' woman ye are. I want to see what ye've done to the cabin."

Lucretia said, "You'll see that I've done plenty. I won't stay here unless I can clean it up and rearrange things."

"I didn't send fer ye," Op grunted, kicking the ground with the blunt toe of his brogan.

"I didn't say that you did," she replied. "But I'm here and I'm going to stay."

"If I'd had half sight in one eye, I'd a-slipped out there on the ridge last night to've seen who that was," Op said, to change the subject. "I've been a-thinkin' about it all day. Purtiest whistlin', geetar music, and singin' I've ever heard in my life. And I've heard a lot of it in Looten County. Back when Teddy Roosevelt was President, there was a dance someplace every night. There was allus someplace to go. I've heard fiddle playin' and singin' at parties, bean stringin's, and corn shuckin's, but I've never heard anything as purty as that last night."

"Maybe we'll hear it tonight," Lucretia said. "I've hoped all day that we would."

"Lutie, I've never heard ye hum and laugh since ye've been here like ye have today."

"I've never been so happy, Dad," she told him. "I don't know why. But I feel like something good is going to happen. I feel like I'm going to meet the man I heard whistling last night. He might be Hootbird Hammertight or he might be that Ted Newsome you talk about."

"Hootbird's the most triflin' man alive," Op grumbled. "He won't work. He walks this ridge with a gun. He's been a-larnin' how to play a geetar, so Penny Shelton told me. When they's up on the Wince Leffard Gap above Hammertight's one night a-listenin' to the hounds, they heard Hootbird a-playin' the geetar and a-singin' down there at the shack. Penny was mad about it. He said all the racket Hootbird made turned the fox from his crossin' and made the hounds lose the track."

"Maybe Hootbird will sing tonight," Lucretia said.

"I hope somebody will sing," he said. "We don't have much wind; so we won't hear my music among the hosshairs."

Then a hunter's horn blew a long, mournful note. Two short notes followed the long one.

"That's Penny Shelton's horn," Op told her, a note of excitement in his voice. "The fox hunters are on Laurel Ridge tonight. We might hear a different kind of music."

"Where was that horn, Dad?"

"Out near Six Hickories," he answered. "That's where they allus start the fox. Foxes den there under the rocks in the arc."

When the first hound barked, Op turned his face toward the sound and put his hand behind his ear.

The hound barked again and again.

"That's Penny Shelton's Blue Boy," Op said. "Best cold trailer in the woods."

In a few minutes, Blue Boy's barks were faster.

"He's got the fox a-goin'," Op bragged. "We'll have a fox chase here tonight. This is a good night fer the hounds to run. They're out a-fox huntin' in these woods most every night in April."

Now Blue Boy was barking most every breath.

"He's a-takin' that fox toward Wince Leffard Gap," Op said. "Lissen fer more hounds to open up! Every fox hunter on Laurel Ridge'll let his hounds loose."

Op just finished speaking when more hounds started barking.

"Hawgie Cawhorn has turned his pack loose," Op said. "I hear his Gunpowder, Fleetwind, Jet, and Shootin' Star! Lissen to 'em, won't ye!"

The music of the barking hounds seemed to come from everywhere.

"There's Penny Shelton's Brown Boy openin' up," Op said. "There's Jimmy Torris's Drum and Dollie."

As the hounds entered the chase, Op called them by name. The pack went down into Little White Oak Valley.

"That fox will go down Little White Oak," Op explained,

27

"but he ll cross Laurel Ridge about three hundred yards from this cabin. He'll come up Shinglemill Hollow, up the fox path from the old pasture field, and cross the ridge right out yander. I know the way the foxes run here. Lissen to the music of them barkin' hounds!"

They had gone around a high hill and were coming up Shinglemill Hollow.

"That's not music to me, Dad," Lucretia said. "Not like I heard last night."

"But, Lutie, when ye get to know all the hounds, it's music," Op told her. "When ye know their barks and know who's in the lead, it's sweet music. I don't own a hound. But I own them all like I own this land. I get to hear their music same as the hunters that keep and feed 'em."

Jerry stood near the paling fence, barking and growling.

"Hush, Jerry!" Op scolded. "Ye'll turn that fox. Let 'im cross out there on the ridge so Lutie can hear the hounds come up and over the ridge."

Op silenced Jerry as the hounds started up the hill toward Laurel Ridge. Then a shot rang out that echoed over and back across Shinglemill Hollow.

"What was that?" Op asked. "Was that a rifle?"

"Sounded like one."

"Somebody knowed where the fox crossed," Op said, as the hounds kept running up the hill. "We'll know if he kilt the fox if the hounds stop barkin' and go to fightin'."

When the pack of roaring hounds topped the hill, for a minute there was a lull. Then there was barking, growling, and fighting. Hounds whimpered and howled.

"Somebody kilt that fox," Op said, excited. "We'll hear about this. The hunters've heard that shot ring out. Now, a lot of dogs will be bitten in the legs a-fightin' over the dead fox and won't be able to run agin fer a spell."

"Who killed it? I don't understand," Lucretia said, as the hounds continued to bark and growl.

"I don't know who'd do a thing like that," Op told her. "I wouldn't want to be accused. I'd be afraid my cabin would go up in flame and smoke, and ye a strange woman in it with me."

"You scare me when you talk like that," Lucretia told him. "We're not afraid of being burnt up alive in our beds at night in Dayton. I thought Laurel Ridge was a quiet place. I didn't dream of anything like this."

"But I know the fox hunters," Op explained. "Josh Kenton was accused of pizenin' foxhounds onct after they run through his green terbacker and broke the leaves. Somebody put the pizen on fried taters. That fall, after Josh had cut his terbacker and housed it in two big barns, one night both barns went up in flame and smoke. Everybody around here's afraid to kill a fox even if one does eat yer chickens, carry off yer lambs or pigs. This will cause trouble on the ridge. I don't know who's brave enough to stand on this ridge and shoot a fox when the hunters are in the woods. I'll bet whoever shot that fox is not one of our people."

The hounds had stopped fighting now. There was silence on the ridge. Jerry barked and growled and ran to the front-yard gate.

"There goes a white-and-black-spotted dog on three legs," Lucretia said. "I see it limping toward the sty."

"There'll be more than one on three legs," Op told her. "There'll be chawed-up hounds with their throats cut and their thighs slashed. Hounds are bad to leg one another when they're a-fightin' over a fox."

A hunter's horn blew two long notes and one short.

"That's Hawgie Cawhorn's horn," Op said. "He's a-callin' his dogs."

Then Penny Shelton blew a long note and two short ones.

One after another the horns kept blowing, calling the hounds from the chase.

"The hunters know what's happened," Op said. "They'll find out who fired that shot. I don't believe there's a speret on Laurel Ridge that would do it. Last night we had strange music. Tonight we had a fox chase and somebody kilt the fox."

6

Theopolis was sitting on the porch with his feet hanging over, enjoying the afternoon April sun when he heard men's voices. He heard footsteps and the clop-clop of horses' feet on Laurel Ridge road. He heard swearing and threatening voices from the direction of Honeywell.

"Right out here's where old Op lives," one said.

"But old Op Akers allus liked a fox," another said. "He'd never bother one."

"He ust to stay all night with us and lissen to the hounds," another said. "If he shot that fox, he's lower than a snake's belly."

"Boys, it happened awful close to the cabin," said another.

Op thought the last man's voice was Hawgie Cawhorn's. As they came closer to the cabin, they talked in softer tones. Lucretia heard them and hurried to the porch.

"There's old Op sittin' there on the porch now," one said. "What's the matter with 'im? He's got a bandage over his eyes."

"Howdy, Miss," said a beardy-faced hunter. "Howdy, Op!"

Theopolis greeted them. Lucretia counted twelve men walking, and three on horseback. The men on horseback were older. Six of the men were carrying shotguns and rifles.

"What's the matter with yer eyes, Op?" one asked. "Gone blind since that fox was kilt?"

"My father isn't blind, I'll have you know," Lucretia retorted. "He had a cataract removed from his eye. And he didn't kill your fox."

"Jist a minute, young lady. Don't get on yer high horse." One of the hunters stepped forward.

"I'm Penny Shelton, Op," said one. "I've come to see if ye know who kilt that fox up here last night."

"No, Penny. Lutie and I were a-sittin' here in the yard when the rifle cracked," Op explained. "We were a-lissenin' to the chase, and I was a-tellin' her the names of the dogs and who they belonged to, when it happened. We heard the rifle crack as loud as a cannon. Heard the dogs run up on Laurel Ridge and start a-fightin'. I told Lutie whoever shot that fox knowed where the fox path crossed the ridge. And I said he must not be one of our people. I don't know of anybody around here who would kill a fox!"

"Who's Lutie?" Penny asked.

"She says she's my daughter," Op sighed.

"I didn't know ye had a daughter, Op," Penny said.

"A lot of people don't, Penny," Op answered. "I don't know if she's the one, since I can't see 'er. I haf to take 'er word fer it."

"I wouldn't be here unless I was his daughter," Lucretia snapped.

Then the fox hunters talked to one another in low tones.

"Even if ye could see, I don't believe ye'd shoot a fox, Op," said a big man. He was carrying a rifle across his shoulder.

"That's ye, ain't it, Hawgie?" Op said.

"Yeah, it's old Hawgie, Op," he said. "Reckon ye'll be able to see when the bandage comes off?"

"I hope so, Hawgie." Op shook his head. "The slippery-elm-bark poultices and the juice from the pokeberry roots didn't bring my sight back. The fog got thick and then thicker and Lutie took me to Doctor Turnbo, the eye specialist in Auckland. I won't know fer five days whether I'll be blind or not. But I got another eye to be operated on. It's kivvered with a cataract too."

"We're sorry about that," Penny Shelton said.

"Ye know now I didn't shoot yer fox," Op told them. "If I'd a-had two good eyes, I wouldn't have gone up there and shot that fox."

"We didn't think ye'd shoot it, Op," said a man sitting in the saddle. "I'm Plack Rivercomb."

"Thought I knowed yer voice, Plack," Op spoke softly.

"It's a-gettin' so we can't have a fox chase on Laurel Ridge any more," Jimmy Torris grunted.

"If we find out who's a-killin' these foxes, Op," Penny said, "we've got the rope with us and there's plenty of oaks with strong limbs over Laurel Ridge road."

"Have ye seen any strange men around here, Op?" Plack Rivercomb asked.

"Op can't see," Penny said, turning to Plack. "He's jist said he was blind as a bat and might never be able to see again!"

"No, I ain't seen a man on this ridge road fer months," Op replied. "Day before yesterday, Lutie saw a man."

"What kind of a lookin' man was he, Miss?" Plack asked.

"Well, I didn't see him very close—"

"Go on and tell the boys," Op said.

"Yep, we want to know," said a small man with a black mustache, carrying a rifle across his shoulder.

"Well, if you want to know, find out the best way you can!" Lucretia looked straight at the fox hunters without batting her eyes. Her lips were trembling a little.

"Did he have a gun on 'im, Miss?" said a big red-faced man

sitting on a gray horse. "Most likely he's a dangerous man if he's not one of our people."

"Is that ye, Turkey Maddox?" Op asked when he heard the voice.

"Yeah, this is old Turkey," he said. "Can't ye get this gal of yourn to talk, Op? She's purty sassy."

"If ye're my daughter, Lutie, I wish ye'd tell my friends about this strange man," Op begged her. "Show 'em we've not got anythin' to hide."

"Well, if you insist, Dad," she said in a softer tone of voice. "He was a little short man who didn't come to my shoulder and he had a head of bushy black hair. He was dressed in a blue suit, a white shirt, and red tie and he wasn't armed. He said his name was Ted Newsome."

Theopolis squirmed in his chair. "Lutie, that's not . . ." Op started to say.

"Ted Newsome," one of the fox hunters interrupted. "I don't know of any Newsomes around here. Did he say where he's from?"

"I asked him," Lucretia said. "He told me— He wouldn't say exactly where he lived."

"That's strange," said a small man with a double-barreled shotgun across his shoulder.

"Which way did he go when he left?" Plack Rivercomb asked.

"He carried two buckets of water up from the spring for me and put them on the porch," Lucretia continued. "When I turned around to look for him, he was gone. I looked everywhere for him. He'd vanished like thin smoke in the wind."

"Jist like the twinkle of an eye, he was gone," Op interrupted. "Now, let me tell ye somethin'. When Lutie told me about seein' this feller, I thought she might've seen Hootbird Hammertight and . . ."

33

"But we've been to Ben Hammertight's place to see Hootbird," Plack interrupted Theopolis. "And we don't believe it's Hootbird a-killin' the foxes. Hootbird's got a twenty-two rifle but this feller's usin' an army rifle. We've found the empty cartridges by the rocks in the arc. We've found thirty-caliber empty cartridges on every high rock we've visited by the fox paths."

"Let me say, Plack, what I started to tell ye," Op continued. "After Lutie told me about this man, I told her, back in the days when Grover Cleveland was President there ust to be Newsomes in Looten County. There was old John Newsome who ust to live at the mouth of Ironweed. He had a boy named Ted, who come back here from servin' in the Army after the First World War, and he was bushwhacked over a Dortch gal who ust to live right across the road over there in the double-log cabin. I ust to know Ted Newsome. And the way Lutie described 'im, it's the same Ted. He's buried in the Freewill Baptist Churchyard."

There was a roar of laughter among the fox hunters.

"Ye mean to tell us, Op, Ted Newsome's ghost is back here with an army rifle shootin' our foxes?" Plack Rivercomb said.

"Ye can laugh all ye want to," said the small man with the black mustache who was carrying the long rifle. "But there's been a lot of things seen on Laurel Ridge. I'm not surprised. I wouldn't walk this ridge alone at night fer anythin' on this earth!"

"Would a ghost leave man tracks on the fox paths?" Plack asked, turning in his saddle to look down at him.

"I don't know about who leaves man tracks on the fox paths," said the small man, looking up at Plack, "but I know ye won't get a hundred yards away from the rest of us hunters on a dark night. Ye said yerself ye saw twelve yoke of oxen a-pullin' a big-wheeled wagon loaded with charcoal one night."

34

"So, ye don't know the way Ted Newsome went when he left this cabin?" Hawgie Cawhorn turned to Lucretia.

"No, I don't, not exactly. It was just like Dad told you. He vanished in the twinkling of an eye. Disappeared like smoke." Lucretia looked slowly from one face to another until she had scanned the expression of every hunter.

"Hootbird said he saw a man a-layin' flat on his stummick on a big rock in the arc," Hawgie said. "A man dressed in khaki pants and shirt and brown shoes. Said he carried a rifle with a sling, but we didn't believe Hootbird. We thought Hootbird might be a-shootin' the foxes and a-pullin' our legs. But we went down to the rock. And we found ten thirty-caliber empty cartridges around that rock."

"Anybody who can kill a fox at night with a rifle is a sharpshooter with a hoot-owl eye," Penny Shelton said. "We've found seventeen dead foxes. If that good marksman keeps on a-shootin' our foxes, there won't be a long-winded red fox left on Laurel Ridge."

"Op, we believe somebody's a-killin' the foxes and eatin' 'em," Hawgie Cawhorn said. "We think he's some strange man that don't know any better."

"I can't believe a man would eat a fox," Op said, shaking his head sadly. **821393**

"Amongst the seventeen we found kilt, six were young foxes and they'd been skinned," Hawgie explained. "Two of the old ones had been skinned too. The other nine old, tough, long-winded foxes had been shot and left where they fell. We found fox bones around ash piles, too. Looks like somebody was atter somethin' to eat. Boy, I wouldn't want no part of fox meat!"

"I'd like to know why," Jimmy Torris said. "Everythin' a fox eats is clean. They eat birds, quail, pheasants, rabbits, squirrels, mice, and moles. Why wouldn't one be good to eat? It's just a

35

crazy notion people've got about foxes! I'd think a young fox would be mighty good . . ."

"I agree with ye, Jimmy," Plack interrupted. "I read in the papers about people eatin' crow, rattlesnake, and horse meat. I'd rather have me a piece of a young fox fried right nice and brown any time."

"If ye'd get hungry enough, Hawgie," said Turkey Maddox, "ye'd be glad to have a piece of fox. I believe somebody's a-killin' the foxes to eat. I believe he's some strange wild man here. He might be a criminal drifted in."

"Looks like a hungry man could find somethin' else to eat," Penny Shelton said. "There's plenty in these hills fer a man if he'll only hunt fer it."

"Boys, I've been a-scourin' this old ridge fer about fifty years, and April and May are lean, hungry months," Op told them. "All the wild game is a-havin' young and the birds are a-layin' eggs. And it's too early fer the nuts and the berries. Middle of May gets better—when the wild strawberries begin to ripen. But a man has to have more'n wild strawberries to fill his stummick. Ye might have somebody a-killin' yer foxes and a-eatin' 'em. It's a sight what a body will eat when he gets hungry enough. A man can find creek turtles, land turtles, and fish in March, April, and early May. I never liked a land turtle but I've had to eat a few of 'em in my time when the fish didn't bite. I don't believe one man has kilt all seventeen," Op finished. "Ye'll find more than one man a-killin' yer foxes!"

"Op, we're glad ye're on our side," Penny Shelton said. "Sheriff Ackerson will be, too. He knows which side of his bread has butter. He knows we've got the votes to turn him out."

"We're goin' to Pawpaw Gap, Op," Plack explained. "We'll ride the ridge and watch fer a man to run across the Laurel Ridge road. Six others are a-goin' to scatter and comb the hills on the Little White Oak side and six are a-goin' down under on the Sandy Valley side to comb the Artner farm. We're a-goin' to find out if anybody's a-hidin' in these woods!"

"We'll find the cliff he's a-sleepin' in," Penny Shelton said as they began moving on.

"If ye hear anythin' more, let us know," Hawgie Cawhorn called back. Hawgie walked on leading a hound that was limping on three legs and holding a fourth leg up against his lean, gaunt stomach.

"Ted Newsome's ghost." Turkey Maddox's laughter came on a gust of wind in the pine boughs over Laurel Ridge. "Maybe it's Ted Newsome's ghost a-killin' and eatin' our foxes," he said as he rode away.

Lucretia stood on the porch and watched the party of fox hunters walk and ride out Laurel Ridge road in the direction the fox had been killed. Then she grabbed the water buckets and started toward the spring.

7

"Op, how's the blind man?"

"Doshie, is that ye?"

Theopolis was leaning his big frame against the paling fence with a cane in his hand.

"Yes, it's me and Hoot," she said. "April's here and we've been out a-scourin' the earth fer somethin' green."

Doshie was a short and skinny woman supported by slightly bowed pipe-stem legs. She had a long thin nose, beady inquisitive eyes, and a half dozen bright red combs held up her mousy brown hair. Her fingernails were painted red, but the paint had chipped and anybody looking real close could tell that Doshie wasn't altogether clean.

"Find anythin'?" Op asked.

"Water cresses in Shinglemill and plenty of poke in Coonden," she said. "Wish ye could see what me and Hoot have picked. I guess ye could take us to a lot of green pickin' if ye could find yer way around. You allus knowed where to find the best patches."

"But I'm a-goin' to save 'em till I can see," Op said. "I'm not a-tellin' ye where to find anythin'."

"Op, ye might never see agin," Doshie said. "That was what I's a-tellin' Ben last night. That would be an awful thing fer ye, Op, to be led around the rest of yer life."

"But I'm a-goin' to see," Op told her. "In a couple of days I'll be seein' agin."

"That'll be so much better than yer putterin' around with a hickory stick or havin' somebody to lead ye," Doshie sighed.

"Mommie, don't talk like that to Op," Hootbird said.

"But Op's run over these paths like a wild colt fer the last fifty years," Doshie said. "I've run over 'em too and I'm a-puttin' myself in Op's place! What if I couldn't see, I've been a-thinkin'. What would I do? My little young'uns would get mighty hungry."

Op growled, "They're old enough to take keer of themselves. How old are ye, Hoot?"

"Old enough to vote and to sleep by myself," he replied.

"I know ye hear all the news, Doshie," Op said as he tapped his cane against the ground, "but I would like to know how ye heard about my eyes."

"I stopped to milk Mr. Isom's cow on my way from Honeywell the other evenin'," she explained. "Ye know he gives us milk when I milk the cows. And he come out to the stable and was a-tellin' me he saw ye pass a-headin' fer the Laurel Ridge

38

road with a young woman a-leadin' ye. Mr. Isom said the young lady was purty as a picture."

"Op, I've been a-wantin' to know who that woman is?" Hootbird said.

"I reckon she's my daughter, Hoot," Op retorted, after a pause.

"I didn't know ye had a daughter." Hootbird was surprised. "I thought ye just had Run-around Jack!"

"That's all ye know about it, Hoot," he answered sharply.

"Well, I'd like to meet yer daughter, Op," Doshie said. "Is she here?"

"She's in the cabin."

Doshie turned with her basket of water cress on her arm. She hurried through the open gate, skipped across the yard, and hopped upon the porch like a ground sparrow. She pecked nimbly on the door.

"I'm Doshie Hammertight"—she started introducing herself before Lutie even appeared. "I'm awfully glad to meet ye. I've known yer pappie, Op, since he's been on Laurel Ridge. But I didn't know he had a daughter. Thought he only had Run-around Jack. I'm awfully glad to meet ye, honey."

"I'm glad to know you," Lucretia said, facing little Doshie Hammertight, whose sallow cheeks were red with paint.

"I want ye to meet my son," Doshie said as she eyed the neat blue-and-white-striped dress Lucretia was wearing.

As Lucretia started across the yard, Doshie followed behind looking down at her leather sandals. There Hootbird stood, dressed like her father had described. He was wearing his broad-rimmed Texas hat, tight-fitting pants that encased his skinny legs and looked as if they would break when he bent his knees, flowered boots with a pair of shining spurs, and a black shirt with white trimmings. He smiled when Lucretia looked at him. He was holding a little peck-sized flour sack in his hand.

"Lucretia, this is my son, Hootbird."

"Gee, ye don't look a thing like Op." Hootbird's face spread in a silly grin.

"Can ye whistle, Hootbird?" Op changed the subject.

"Yeah, why?" Hootbird's smile showed two rows of dead-phlox-colored teeth.

"Somebody stood right out there on the ridge betwixt this cabin and the sty the other night and whistled," Op said. "We've never heard sicha purty whistlin'. I told Lutie it probably wasn't ye, Hootbird. It was too purty."

"I wish it had've been me if Lutie liked it," Hootbird said, wetting his dry lips with his tongue.

"Can ye play a geetar, Hootbird?" Op asked.

"I can play some and I'm larnin' fast," Hootbird replied. "Want me to come over some evenin' and play and sing fer ye?"

"Then it wasn't ye we heard," Op said. "I guess it must've been Ted Newsome."

"Who's Ted Newsome?" Hootbird asked.

"Ye wouldn't know 'im, Hoot," Op said. "He's been dead thirty years."

"I don't guess I would know 'im if he's been dead that long," Hootbird answered, looking strangely at Theopolis.

"But ye believe in sperets, don't ye, Hoot?" Op asked him.

"I believe in 'em, Op," Hootbird answered seriously, "but I don't believe one would be back here on Laurel Ridge, whistlin', singin', and playin' a geetar!"

"If it wasn't ye out there on the ridge the other night, it must've been Ted Newsome," Op said. "That's the way I got it figured out."

"Well, it wasn't me," Hootbird admitted regretfully. "I wish it had been me. Guess I'll haf to do more practicin'," he said, looking at Lucretia. "I don't think that was Ted Newsome's speret. I think he must've been a flesh-and-blood man."

40

"Might be that man ye saw a-layin' flat on his stummick on the big rock in the arc," Doshie said. "That strange man loose in these woods who's a-killin' all the foxes."

"Don't believe one man's a-killin' 'em all," Op interrupted. "Penny Shelton told me day before yesterday the hunters had found where seventeen foxes had been kilt. The hunters think somebody is a-killin' the foxes fer food."

"Yeah, they thought I's a-killin' their foxes," Hootbird broke in. "I told 'em and Poppie told 'em too, that I wasn't a-killin' their foxes, even though the foxes were a-killin' our chickens. They hinted around like I was a-killin' them fer us to eat. I'll go hungry before I'll eat a piece of fox. I told 'em so too!"

"Ben talked awful straight to 'em when they accused Hootbird," Doshie said. "Ben said: 'My boy's not a-killin' yer foxes. But why don't ye do somethin' about yer foxes a-killin' our chickens?' And old Plack Rivercomb, the old son of Satan, said to Ben: 'Foxes like chickens. And fox huntin' is the only sport left fer old men like me where we don't haf to pay any license to hunt.' 'And ye let other people feed yer foxes with their chickens,' Ben said right back to him. 'And ye hunt on other people's land.' 'This ain't yer land, Ben,' Plack said. 'This land is Snake Blue's. And Snake told us to hunt in here when we pleased.' Then old Plack started laughin' and Ben sidled up to his hoss. 'Come down outten that saddle, Plack,' he said, raisin' his long arms up, and Plack rode that hoss away with sparks a-flyin' from his hoofs. 'Don't ye ever accuse my boy,' Ben shouted as he rode away. And all that pack of hunters left in a hurry."

"That strange man's the one a-killin' the foxes," Hootbird said, "but I don't keer if he is. Maybe we can raise some chickens now."

"I don't think about the foxes," Doshie said, a mournful tone coming into her voice. "I don't worry about who's a-killin' 'em. I think about a-scourin' over the earth a-huntin' somethin' to eat. I think about my poor legs. My legs are a-goin' to wear out one of these days a-walkin' to that town and back the same day, a-doin' a powerful lot of scrubbin' and moppin' there, and milkin' cows on my way back and a-totin' a load big enough fer a plug mule."

"Ah, Mommie," Hootbird said, color coming to his face.

"But it's the truth, Hoot," Doshie said. "Ye know it's the truth. I give ye young'uns birth and I've about raised ye with my own hands and wits. Ben won't leave these hills. He works all the day and half the night but he's so slow. Op knows how slow Ben is! He can't get nothin' done."

Op opened his mouth to say something, but Doshie ran on like a leaky water faucet. "And now I'm a-thinkin' of Op and his bad eyes. Op can't scour the earth fer greens and berries in the spring and summer and gather nuts in the fall. He can't raise a garden like he's allus done. He can't hunt wild game on Laurel Ridge like he ust to." Then Doshie's beady little eyes sparkled with an idea. "I'd like to take Lutie to Honeywell with me some day to let 'er look around fer somethin' to do."

"But I need Lutie here," Op said quickly.

"I know ye need 'er now," Doshie said. "But there'll come the time when Laurel Ridge will be white with snow, and winter will be on ye."

"Mommie, hadn't we better be goin'?" Hootbird said.

Doshie walked away like a sparrow, calling back over her shoulder, "Ye folks come and see us."

"Doshie, we might come to see ye when two moons meet," Op said.

Hootbird didn't follow his mother. He lingered behind.

"Lutie, I wish I could whistle like that man on the ridge the other night," he said. "I've got somethin' here I'd like to give ye. I want ye to have this good, tender April poke!"

"Thank you, Hootbird," Lucretia said, taking the sack.

"I hope to be a-seein' ye agin," Hootbird said.

Lucretia watched Hootbird walk away, swinging his hands in the wind and swaggering a little.

"Lutie," Op said, "now I *know* Hoot'll be back a-tryin' to spark ye. That's the first time in my life I've ever known one of the Hammertights to give anythin' away."

8

Theopolis, wearing dark glasses, got off the Red Ribbon bus at Lancaster's Drugstore in Honeywell. Lucretia was not leading him now.

"This old town looks good," he said to her. "First time I've seen it real well in a long time."

Theopolis looked up Main Street, then he turned and looked back.

"I'm a new man," he said proudly. "My sight is better'n it's been fer years. How awful it was to be blind! Now I have a good eye! Think of it! Eighty per cent vision!"

"Hello, Op," said Marvin Lancaster, the Honeywell druggist. "Glad to see you back in Honeywell. We've missed your coming to town."

"I didn't know I was missed," Op said. "But I'm glad I can see agin. I'll be able to pick huckleberries fer ye come August."

Theopolis and Lucretia started walking toward Seaton Hollow.

"Lutie, when Doctor Turnbo took the bandages from my eyes, I've never been as happy in my whole life as I was then," Op said. "I've allus been a happy man too. I've been happy when I found a new patch of pawpaws in October ripened by the frost. When I found a new grove of 'simmon trees and looked up and saw that golden fruit betwixt me and the blue sky, I couldn't wait to climb the tree and shake the 'simmons down and hear 'em hit the leaf-kivvered ground like big, soft drops of rain! And old Jerry'd be down under a-fillin' his belly till his skin was tight as a banjer head."

Along the streets and up the back road that skirted Honeywell, people stopped Theopolis and Lucretia. These were Theopolis's friends, who for years had seen him bring sacks of roots to Honeywell to sell in their season. He had sold hundreds of gallons of wild strawberries, blackberries, and huckleberries to them. Now people hailed Theopolis to engage berries and nuts for the season.

Theopolis stopped to look at a dogwood that grew beside the narrow-gauged Seaton Hollow road. Its bushy top was covered with white blossoms that were filled with honeybees.

"Lutie, it's almost like seein' a dogwood in bloom fer the first time," he said. "Ye'll never know what it is to want to see somethin' when ye can't."

Theopolis started walking on at a faster pace.

"I want to get up on Laurel Ridge," he said. "I want to see Six Hickories and the arc."

"Dad, take it a little slower," Lucretia called. "I can't keep up with you."

Theopolis stopped to look at a whippoorwill flower growing beside a lichen-covered rock by Seaton Branch. A swarm of multicolored butterflies rose up, fluttering on their soft, transparent wings.

"It's good to see one of these agin," he said, plucking a blossom, holding it up, and examining it carefully. Op caressed the red blossom with his stubby fingers.

He sniffed the sulphur smell of ragweeds growing beside the old road as he climbed Seaton Hill. He could see even the sulphur dust from the ragweeds and the little fragments on his pants legs.

When he stopped again to let Lucretia rest, it was beside a clump of white violets that grew from a sterile bank where iron ore had been dug in the distant past and had left the earth upheaved.

When I first looked at Lutie, flashed through Op's mind, I thought I was a-lookin' at Beadie when I married 'er. She has the same color of eyes and hair and she's the size of her mother. But Beadie was never bossy, his mind rambled on. And why did Lutie stay out yander in Dayton so long? Why didn't she come back afore now? Beadie wouldn't a-done a thing like that.

When they had climbed uphill another fifty yards, along a path not often used since Op had been blind, he stopped at a cluster of sumac growing beside a rotted stump. Their leafy fronds were waving in the slow stir of a late-April wind. Op smoothed one with his big, rough hand.

"It's fine to see the shoe-makes agin," he said. "No good fer anythin' but to look at. I've heard to bile their antler seeds with mullein stalks was good fer the quinsy. But I've never had the quinsy. Thought if I ever did have, I'd try this remedy and see if the shoe-make was good fer anythin' 'cept to look at and to smell." He started climbing again. "Lord Jesus put everythin' here fer a purpose. Everythin' but crab grass that tries to take yer terbacker fields and cornfields and gardens. But the purpose of crab grass, I believe, is to make men and wimmen use a little elbow grease and backbone strength with a hoe."

Near the top of Seaton Hill he stopped again to show Lucretia a wild flower.

"Here's one of the purtiest flowers that grows," he said, "a blue trillium."

It was growing beside the old road where a little wet-weather

45

spring bubbled from beneath a rock. Theopolis broke a stem of trillium and gave it to Lucretia.

"It's beautiful," she said as she held it up and looked at it carefully. She watched her father too, marveling at his high spirits.

"It grows in coves and on the bluffs," he said as he hurried on.

"I've never seen anybody who can walk like you can," she said as she ran uphill, breathing hard, to catch him.

"And right up there is Six Hickories," Op shouted. "Here's where Laurel Ridge begins. And Laurel Ridge is my home. I'll soon be home! And I can see!"

There were only three giant hickories standing where the steep hill road joined the Laurel Ridge road. This place, Theopolis had been told, had been called Six Hickories for more than a century. Back in the days when all the timber had been sheared from Laurel Ridge, cut into cordwood and burned into charcoal for the seventeen furnaces in Looten County, the timber cutters had left six tall, straight hickories. In the more than a century that had passed, three of these trees had been struck by lightning. Only three remained, but the place was still called Six Hickories.

Op stood beneath one of the giant trees, breathed deeply, and looked down into the Sandy River Valley.

"I can see my river," he shouted. "Look at the sprays a-goin' up when it falls over the rocks!"

Lucretia's breaths were short and fast. After following Op up Seaton Hill, she was glad to watch the sprays flashing in the sunlight while she rested.

"Back home on Laurel Ridge!" Theopolis was almost weeping. "There's a white cloud floatin' around out there over the Sandy Valley just level with the ridge. Home agin! Home! Look at the arc down there! Look at the big rocks!"

Dwarfed saw briers, growing from the sterile Laurel Ridge

46

road that was shaded by interlacing branches of the tough-butted white oaks, pulled at his shoelaces and pants cuffs. One saw brier untied his shoelace, and he had to stop long enough to tie it.

"Tell me to slow down, Lutie, if I walk too fast fer ye," he told her. "But I'm back home. I might have only eighty per cent vision in one eye but it's as good as a thousand. I can see!"

Since the giant charcoal-wagon and ore-wagon wheels had long ceased to roll over this road, and the oxen's shod hoofs no longer pawed up the dirt, the tough-butted white oaks' brace roots crossed the road like knotty clumps of black snakes. Lucretia realized that Theopolis' eye-sight was better than she had expected, since he never caught the toe of his shoe in one of these brace roots while he was looking right and left trying to see everything.

"Old Op Akers is a-goin' home!" His words came as freely as a puff of wind among the oak leaves overhead.

9

Theopolis was taking long strides now where the ridge road ran parallel with Sandy River. He was walking under the tall yellow pines on either side of the road. And the dry pine needles whetted beneath the thick soles of his brogans. Lucretia walked until she fell behind, and then she'd run a few steps.

"First time I ever saw a bicycle in my life was on this ridge when Teddy Roosevelt was President," Op said. "And I come to this ridge to see the bicycle races along the straight part of this ridge where we're walkin' now. I'll never ferget that day. People a-hollerin' and yellin' fer this one and that one as they raced along."

"It's hard to believe," Lucretia panted. "This is such wild country now."

"I know it is, Lutie," he said, as his steps grew faster, "but I remember the days when young reckless men rode their hosses at full gallop around this ridge road and emptied their pistols at the lizards runnin' up the trees and at the snakes a-sunnin' on the rocks. They kilt lizards and snakes by the dozens. But the funniest thing I ever remember was a-comin' to a buttin' out here."

"What's a butting?" she asked.

"Minton Artner, a brother to Fidis, was to butt against a ram," Op began his story. "Some crowd of people here to watch it one Sunday afternoon. Minton was a short bullish man with shoulders broad as a corncrib door and had a head not much bigger than the ram's, on a short thick neck stuck in the middle of his shoulders. When he got down to run on his all fours and butt against Charlie Worthington's ram, a lot of people yelled fer Minton. But there were more people a-yellin' for the ram. Minton had fit too many men with his head. He'd butted them nearly to death. But when Minton and the ram clashed head on, he had found his match. Ye could hear their heads pop when they went head on a half mile away. A lot of people felt sorry fer Minton, since the blood ran from his nose, his eyes, and his ears. But Minton did somethin' that turned about everybody fer the ram."

Lucretia ran a few steps to overtake Op to hear the rest of his story.

"Old Minton squirmed around and got in line with a tree, and when the ram charged, he jumped outten the path and let it hit the tree. The ram broke his neck and Minton winned the buttin'. The people didn't like it when Minton outwitted the ram. They didn't think he butted fair."

Then Op stopped and looked back at Lucretia. "Ye sit down

48

on the sty and rest," he panted. "I would rather go on by my-self."

While Lucretia gladly sat down on the sty, Op hurried toward his cabin. He didn't stop to listen to the water pouring over the rocks at the Sandy Falls. Op stepped excitedly from the green tunnel into the clearing where he could see his squat cabin beneath the tall yellow pines. It had been months since he had seen the full outline. His heart beat faster as he increased his steps. Jerry ran to meet him and jumped up, licking his hands. He pushed open the door and stood still in amazement.

"Curtains! Rugs! B-gad, Jerry, everythin's moved. It'll never be the same!" He slumped into a chair, grumbling and shaking his head. "Where'll I spit my terbacker? Where'll I store my roots?"

10

Op walked to the window, pulled the white lace curtains apart and looked on Laurel Ridge road in the direction of the sty. This would be the direction Lucretia would come from Honeywell. He stood there with his face against the window-pane watching the road for her. It's time fer Lutie to be back, he thought as he looked across the Sandy River Valley at the big red wagon wheel of sun dropping behind the Allcorn Hills, dragging a patch of sky behind it.

He pulled his face back from the window and closed the curtains carefully just the way Lucretia had arranged them. He walked across the clean cabin floor where Lucretia had washed the old homemade rugs Beadie had sewed more than twenty years ago and arranged them like gray patches on a brown hound-dog's back. Op walked out onto the porch and looked on the ridge road again. The road was the same as it had always been, yellow hardpan clay with only saw briers and wild wood grass able to survive. The road ran straight to where timber grew on both sides. There it went into a tunnel covered by the interlacing branches of white oaks and yellow-pine boughs. He watched for Lucretia to come from this tunnel.

I'd like to know what's a-keepin' her, he thought as he walked back into the cabin to look at the bread. I didn't want her to go with that Doshie and Hootbird Hammertight, nohow.

When Op opened the oven door and looked at the corn pone, it had not begun to brown. He thought he needed to put more wood into the firebox. He opened the door, and the firebox was filled with wood and the fire was roaring.

Not anythin' ever ust to bother me, Theopolis thought, as he walked to the three-cornered cupboard to get dishes and silverware to set the table. I took my time and never looked fer anybody. Now, I have a woman in this cabin. I have a worried mind.

Lutie is a purty girl, he thought, comparing her to Beadie. She's too purty fer that Hootbird, whether she's my daughter or not. I hope she'll never give him the second look. Theopolis set a plate for himself and one for Lucretia. Then he stood looking at the big bowl filled with wild flowers in the center of the table. He was afraid he might upset this bouquet of redbud and dogwood blooms, mixed with whippoorwill flowers, blue and white violets, and trillium. Lutie has fixed this cabin until it's nice, in a way, he thought. But it's not as handy as it used to be when I did the work and Jerry and I lived here alone.

She's got me puzzled, he thought as he looked at the wild flowers. I owe 'er somethin' fer what she's done fer me. But it's none of my business if she does go to Honeywell with the ornery Hammertights. She's a woman old enough to know right from wrong. I've told 'er about the Hammertights. She doesn't haf to have old Doshie a-tryin' to find 'er work in a store or a restaurant or a house.

But she's not one of our people, he thought as he worked getting supper on the table, or she'd know how much Laurel Ridge provides, free. All ye have to do is watch the plants and the trees when they bear fruit in their seasons. She's been ust to buyin' from the stores. I know the places to find everythin'. I know where the berries grow and the trees that bear nuts. . . . Jerry lay sprawled on a gray rug watching Op. I'll have supper ready fer 'er if she does come back, he thought. She's done a lot fer me.

Then he wondered how she would like the bread he'd baked, potatoes he'd fried, and the poke greens he had picked and cooked. He'd searched until he found enough poke for a mess. And he knew how to cook poke better than Lutie. But the place was not the same. Dishes were neatly arranged in the cupboard. Cabin so clean and well arranged he was most afraid to sit down. This wasn't the way it had looked when he kept the place himself. Then he wasn't afraid of dropping a piece of bread, a spoonful of potatoes, or spilling soup beans on the floor and letting Jerry clean them up. Jerry's job had been to keep the scraps picked up, but now Op was careful about letting anything fall. Lutie's living in his cabin had made the difference. The change was hard on him but harder on old Jerry. He lay there on the rug looking up with his sad brown eyes from under little roofs of grizzly brows.

Supper was finished and Op had it on the table. And he'd not spilled a thing. The place was just as Lutie had left it. With the food on the table, he went to the window again. He pushed the curtains back in time to see Hootbird holding Lutie's hand, trying to pull her close to kiss her. That was where the tunnel of leaves began on the Laurel Ridge road. He stood there watching while Lutie pulled away and hurried toward the cabin alone.

He saw Hootbird standing there watching until Lutie was on the porch. Then Hootbird turned and walked back into the tunnel.

11

"Well, ye finally got here," Op said. "I wasn't shore ye'd come back. I was a-thinkin' that atter I got supper on the table, I'd put Jerry up in his chear like I did before you come. Give account of yerself, young woman!"

"Oh, I'm too tired," she sighed as she sat down. "I'm even too tired to eat."

Op pulled himself up a chair and sat down in front of Lucretia. He eyed her suspiciously.

"The vittals are awfully hot," he said. "While they cool, I want to know about yer trip to Honeywell."

"Dad, I've never walked so much in my life," Lucretia groaned. "This morning when we left here, Doshie took the lead around Laurel Ridge. I believe she can walk faster than you. She said she was in a hurry to get to her work. And when we got to Honeywell she didn't work at all. She just walked the streets all morning and we followed her."

"Didn't old Doshie work in the courthouse?"

"No. We went over there but they were holding court. Some trial over who owned a half an acre of land down in Big River Valley and there were three lawyers on each side and four surveyors and over fifty witnesses. The sheriff had a hard time keeping order. Courthouse was filled until there wasn't standing room. I stood until I thought my legs would go from under me. Finally Doshie left and Hoot and I followed her like two little dogs."

"What did Hootbird do?"

"He stayed beside me and wanted to hold my hand on the street. We must have walked up and down Main Street a hundred times from the Palace Theater to the courthouse. He wanted to go somewhere and make love to me. Said I was the prettiest girl he ever saw."

"I'm not surprised at that," Op replied, frowning.

"He told me he'd been practicing his whistling so he could perform for me." Lutie laughed. "But those flowered boots blistered his toes halfway down the ridge and then he had troubles."

"Did ye walk all day up and down the streets?" Op asked. "What did ye do about somethin' to eat?"

"Doshie said she had some housework to do for a Mrs. Shales."

"That's Blanche Shales," Op interrupted. "She's secretary for her brother, Odder Timmons, attorney, undertaker, and real-estate dealer."

"Doshie told us how well off for food Mrs. Shales was. Mrs. Shales had given Doshie the key and turned her loose in the house. The first thing Doshie did was go to the refrigerator and find enough for our lunch. She set the table for us and we ate about all the food there was in the house. Then we helped Doshie do a little work in the house, a very little, and then we left."

"That sounds like Doshie all right," Op said. "She loves to raid the pantries. I've picked up that much about 'er just a-talkin' to people on the streets. Men and wimmen I know in Honeywell ust to come up to me and say: 'Op, there's a woman by the name of Doshie Hammertight livin' out yer way. She wants to work in my home. What about 'er?' 'She never worked fer me,' I'd tell 'em. 'Ye'll have to try 'er to find out.' Next time I'd see the person that ast me about 'er and he wouldn't speak about it. No one she's ever worked fer will tell the next feller. He wants the next one to have the same experience he had with 'er. She never leaves much grub when she gets through a-feedin' Hoot and herself."

"Then in the afternoon," Lucretia continued, "we went to the picture show. Doshie pulled a roll of bills from her purse and paid our way. I wanted to pay my own but she wouldn't let me. When we went into the Palace Theater, Doshie sat on one side of Hootbird and I sat on the other. In a few minutes Doshie sort of disappeared and Hootbird wanted to put one arm around me and hold my hand. But his blisters were aching him so that he had to take his boots off to massage his feet. I was just as glad."

"That's Hootbird all right," Op said.

"When the show was over we came outside and Doshie was waiting by the ticket office."

" 'I didn't stay, Lutie, honey,' " she said. " 'I've seen that Western twice. I know it by heart. I come out to look the manager up to see if I couldn't make a bargain with 'im to sweep the theater for free tickets but he already has somebody.' "

"Didn't she try to find work fer ye?"

"She never said anything more about that," Lucretia replied. "When we left the theater, we went to a nice-looking home where some woman gave her a bundle of clothes. We went to another home and she picked up a bundle there. Then we went to two stores and picked up groceries. Hootbird carried the lighter load. Honest, Doshie carried a load too big for a mule. I offered to help but she wouldn't let me. And we never stopped walking. 'It's getting late,' Doshie kept saying. 'I've got to get home to Ben. He'll be uneasy about us a-walkin' this ridge at night with so many strange people a-hidin' on it.' "

"Didn't ye stop to rest on Seaton Hill?"

"Never stopped anyplace," Lucretia replied. "When we got to the path that turns from Laurel Ridge road, Doshie told

Hootbird to come around the ridge with me. I told him I could come alone. But he hid his sack of groceries back in a huckleberry patch. 'I wouldn't let you go around that dangerous ridge by yourself,' he said. Then he limped along with me to the cabin."

"Come on and eat a supper I've cooked." Op changed the subject. "I've been eatin' the grub ye've cooked, now try some of mine."

"Dad, if you hadn't cooked supper," Lucretia sighed as she went to the table, "we just wouldn't have eaten. I'm too tired to cook, but I'm hungry."

"Ye don't haf to find work in Honeywell," Op told her. "The earth will provide us everythin' to eat, and wood to burn. That is, if ye don't want a lot of fancy vittals."

"I don't want any kind of work in Honeywell," Lucretia said, dropping in her chair at the table. "I don't want that ten-mile walk ever again, much less every day. But you should have seen Doshie running along the ridge bent double like a hairpin under that load. She's not human!"

"Well now, I've said some mean things 'bout Doshie in my time, but I do believe she's human." Op scratched himself thoughtfully. "Nope, Doshie's no speret."

12

The sun had gone down on Laurel Ridge. The calico clouds were spread like thin sheets above the Sandy Valley. They were held up in space with props of bright evening wind. Theopolis and Lucretia sat on the porch and watched these clouds while a whippoorwill sang from the middle of Laurel Ridge less than a hundred yards away in the direction of Pawpaw Gap. On a finger ridge on the Sandy Valley side, in the direction of the sty, another whippoorwill sang. Lucretia and Theopolis sat watching the clouds and listening to the whippoorwills.

"A whippoorwill makes a nest on a leaf on the ground," Op explained to Lucretia. "The hen bird lays only a couple of eggs. I've never found three eggs in a nest in my life and I've found over a hundred in my time. I've seen their red eyes shinin' in the moonlight like wind-fanned embers. I've walked right up to 'em on their nests. They set on the eggs, hatch the young on the ground. The whippoorwill is a strange bird. They can sing as purty as any bird I've ever heard but they're too lazy to build a nest. They take life easier than any birds I know. Sorta like me, I guess."

"Their singing has such a lonesome sound," Lucretia said.

"I've often thought about how much smarter some birds are than others," Theopolis went on, talking as much to himself as to Lucretia. "I know every kind of bird that lives on Laurel Ridge. But I don't understand how the whippoorwill is able to keep his kind a-goin' with so many snakes crawlin' over the ground lookin' fer young birds. Foxes, possums, and terrapins like young birds too, but the whippoorwills keep a-comin' like sassafras sprouts."

Just then the whippoorwill stopped singing in the direction of the sty. Seconds later he flew about ten feet above the ground, fanning the bright wind in a hurried flight.

"Somethin' disturbed that whippoorwill," Op said.

"The other one's stopped singing too," Lucretia said as Op looked on the ridge in the direction of the sty.

"I see somebody a-comin' out of the tunnel," Op said.

Lucretia didn't answer. The whippoorwill that had flown past changed his course and was flying back with the second whippoorwill beside him. The two birds wheeled in their flight over toward the feathery clouds in the Sandy Valley. Op watched the pair get smaller until they disappeared. Then he peered at the man who was getting closer.

"Somebody is comin', Lutie," he said again, turning to her.

But Lucretia was looking in the other direction and there was a new light in her eyes. Op looked the way she was looking and saw another man coming. He was farther away than the man Op had seen first, but both were walking in the direction of the cabin.

"This place is a-gettin' mighty full-up with people," Theopolis muttered.

"Good evenin', Op," Hootbird said when he walked up to the gate, shouldering a guitar and a rifle. "Good evenin', Lutie."

"Hootbird, what are ye a-doin' with that rifle?" Op asked.

Lucretia didn't speak. Her eyes followed the other man as he left the ridge road and went down under among the cliffs on the Sandy Valley side. He, too, was carrying a rifle.

"Oh, good evening, Hootbird," Lucretia greeted him on second thought.

"What did ye see up that way, Lutie?" Hootbird asked curiously. His eyes traveled up and down Lucretia's yellow dress, making a slow trip of it.

"Oh, just a man," she replied. "I thought he was coming here but he didn't."

"Which way did he go?" Hootbird asked.

"Over the ridge and down among the cliffs," she replied.

"Op, ye asked me why I brought this rifle," Hootbird said. "What Lutie jist saw is the exact reason. It's dangerous on this ridge nowadays."

"Are ye comin' in, Hoot?" Op said, without enthusiasm.

Hootbird came through the gate and leaned his rifle against the porch.

"I keep this rifle near me," he said, "but it's an unhandy weapon. It's too long. I've got me a twenty-two pistol ordered that will shoot eleven times."

"Not anybody's a-goin' to bother ye, Hootbird," Op said. "Ye're the biggest coward that ever walked on Laurel Ridge."

"I ain't so shore about that," Hootbird said as he stood in front of the porch and looked up at Lucretia. "The other day when I was a-walkin' the ridge with my rifle, I looked down into the arc and a man was a-layin' sprawled on a big flat-topped rock. He was behind a yaller poplar that's grown up beside the rock. But I could see his legs behind the tree. He was dressed in brown and his heels were up, a-showin' his brown shoes. And I saw somethin' that seemed to be leanin' against the tree, shinin' like a bull black snake in the sun. When I looked closer, it was a rifle barrel, and the stranger had his sights leveled on me. My heart almost stopped beatin' and I began to back-back on legs a-tremblin' so they would hardly hold me up. I was afraid I was a goner. And when I backed to a tree, I jumped behind it and with the oak betwixt me and his rifle I made a beeline down under on the Little White Oak side."

"Did you say he was dressed in brown?" Lucretia asked.

"Yes, he was," Hootbird replied. "When I moved, the bright thing agin the tree moved. When I discovered it was a rifle with somethin' on the barrel that shined like a piece of silver in the sun, I was skeered stiff. I wouldn't walk on this ridge agin without a piece of hardware. We've got two pistols. Poppie carries the autermatic wherever he goes. And Mommie carries the little twenty-two in her bosom when she goes to town. She got the life skeered out'n her when she come from Honeywell the other night. She saw a strange man run across the road in front of her with a rifle in his hand out there at Six Hickories."

"I don't believe anybody would harm old Doshie," Op said. "That's another one of 'er big tales. To hear 'er tell it, there's allus a young, fine-lookin' man after 'er. Shucks, I don't believe it. There's not anybody after 'er, or ye either."

"I'm not takin' any chances," Hootbird said. "I come around here tonight to play my geetar and sing some to ye and Lutie. But when I think of the man that had his sights leveled on me at the arc, it gives me the weak trembles."

"But you're not too weak to play the guitar and sing, are you, Hootbird?" Lucretia asked.

"No, but I could've done a lot better," Hootbird apologized as he began to tune his guitar, "if ye hadn't told me ye saw a strange man. He might pop up along the road the way I go home. He might be a-waitin' behind a tree to bushwhack me."

Hootbird tightened one string. Then he plucked it and held one big ear close.

"When I go back tonight, I'm not a-goin' around Laurel Ridge," he said, plucking at another string. "I might not even take a path at all, not even a fox path. Think I'll go back through the brush."

"Ye'd better watch as ye go through the woods, Hoot," Op teased. "A big terrapin might get ye by the toe. If one does, he won't let loose till it thunders."

Hootbird ignored Op. "I'll sing 'The Little Rosewood Casket,'" he said. "It's awfully sad but Poppie and Mommie like it. I've been a-practicin' on it."

> *In a little rosewood casket,*
> *That's a-restin' on the stand,*
> *There's a package of old letters,*
> *Written by a lover's hand.*

Hootbird strummed the strings of his guitar to the lonesome tune. He sat on the edge of the porch looking up at Lucretia, then down at her toes in barefoot sandals. He almost forgot the words, looking at her red-painted toenails. The night wind in

the horsehairs on the cabin walls had begun to make strange
sounds too.

> Won't ye go and git them, Mother,
> And read them o'er to me;
> I've often tried to read them
> But fer tears I could not see.

"It's a sad song," Hootbird sighed after he'd finished. "It
brings tears to my eyes. Maybe I shouldn't a-played anythin' so
sad a-comin' out here to see ye, Lutie?"

"Ust to hear that song when I's a young buck a-kickin' up my
heels," Op said. "But that geetar of yers sounds like it's been
a-sittin' out in the rain, Hoot."

"Now here's another one that we like down home." Hootbird turned his back on Theopolis. "I thought ye might have
heard it. It's an old ballad." Hootbird sat a moment, remembering the words.

> Woke up this mornin'
> Before the break of day,
> Thought about my darlin'
> A thousand miles away. . . .
>
> Some says I won't
> And some say I will
> Go back to Lickin'
> To get my bottle fill'd. . . .
>
> Standin' in the depot,
> And I seen a train go by;
> I thought about my darlin'
> And hung my head and cried. . . .

> *I'm goin' back to Lickin',*
> *I'm goin' back today;*
> *I'm goin' back to Lickin'*
> *And there I'm goin' to stay.*

Hootbird patted his foot on the grass and strummed his guitar energetically, his arm moving like a brown piston through the evening dusk as his long fingers plucked the strings. When he finished the song, Hootbird looked up for approval.

"That's not too bad, Hoot," Op admitted. "I ain't heard 'Goin' Back to Lickin' ' fer forty years."

"I like it," Lucretia said very politely.

"I know the words and the tune to another song," Hootbird said as he began to strum again. " 'The Hoot Owl Song.' Mommie and Poppie like this one special."

> *Oh, when you hear that hoot owl callin'*
> *It's gonna turn cold, it's gonna turn cold;*
> *And when you see my teardrops fallin',*
> *I'm thinkin' of the days of old.*
> *I don't know why I love you, darlin'.*

Hootbird looked straight at Lucretia on the porch.

> *It's plain you never cared for me;*
> *But still my mind is on you, darlin'*
> *It makes no difference where I be.*
>
> *I'm goin' down to the deep blue river,*
> *Down where the cool sweet waters flow;*
> *Gonna lay me down and sleep forever,*
> *Down where the snow-white lilies blow.*

61

Oh, bury me beside the river
Where the nightingales sing sweet and low,
There let me rest in peace forever,
Down where the cool sweet waters flow.

Where the fog is on the deep blue river
And the mist is on the mountain high
And the nightingale sings in the twilight,
There let me slumber when I die. . . .

When you hear that hoot owl callin',
It's time to plant corn, it's time to plant corn;
And when you wake and hear sweet music,
It's the nightingale at the break of morn.

When Hootbird had finished, he wiped a tear from his eye.

"What's the matter, Hoot?" Op asked. "Ye didn't play and sing it purty enough to make yerself cry, did ye? I've heard rain crows a-tryin' to carry a tune that teched me more."

"I think it was real pretty, Hootbird," Lucretia told him. She thought Op was being unnecessarily mean.

"But I'm still not so good as that man ye heard on the ridge 'r ye would have said so," Hootbird said.

While Hootbird was singing "The Hoot Owl Song," the whippoorwill had come back to Laurel Ridge road near where the fox had been killed and started singing. Just beyond the sty on the Sandy Valley side of the ridge another whippoorwill burst into song. It was eleven o'clock and the winds had risen and strange sounds were coming from the cabin walls. Hootbird arose from the edge of the porch and got his rifle. He gripped the rifle at the trigger guard, holding it close to his side as if his life depended on his having this weapon.

"I must be a-goin' home," he said.

"Come back again when ye haven't got as long to stay," Theopolis said.

"Which way are you going, Hoot?" Lucretia asked.

"Down the fox path to Shinglemill," Hootbird replied. "Down Shinglemill to Little White Oak. Up Little White Oak to the Wince Leffard Gap."

"If there's any man about ye, ye'd walk out the ridge," Theopolis said. "Ye're a-goin' five miles outten yer way!"

"This ridge is dangerous!" Hootbird spoke heatedly. "When I go into the woods with my rifle, I believe strange eyes are a-watchin' me from behind every tree and cliff. Laurel Ridge is not the place it ust to be when we lived here in peace and went where we pleased without totin' a gun."

"I'd go home on the Laurel Ridge road," Op called, as Hootbird walked toward the gate. "Remember, I've seen snakes down on White Oak big enough to swaller ye!"

"Good night, honey," Hootbird said to Lucretia.

"If the old scratch gets ye tonight," Op said as he watched Hootbird disappear into the semidarkness, "he'll turn ye loose when daylight comes. Ye're jist like old Doshie." He reached into his back pocket and pulled out a big burley leaf. It was dried and cracked and crumbled where he'd been sitting on it. He wadded it into his mouth. "Boy's got all the guts of a grasshopper," he mumbled.

13

When Theopolis reached Six Hickories, he rolled the heavy sack from his shoulder to the ground. He took a red bandanna and wiped the sweat from his good eye. Sweat got in his eye again as he climbed the Seaton Hill with his load of supplies, but he put down his head and doggedly kept on going until he reached the top.

The cool breeze from the yellow poplar tops dried the wet-weather springs of sweat on his furrowed brow. He stood beside his sack, resting as he looked at the world down under in all directions but one. That direction was Laurel Ridge, which curved around the vast arc beneath him and then ran in a beeline toward the cabin.

While Theopolis stood resting at Six Hickories, he looked at the foundation stones where the church had once stood. A low cluster of sapless, shriveled, wild-rose vines grew from the hard, dry, sterile clay. There was one wild-rose blossom, a beautiful thing, pale pink in color, soft as satin with one layer of petals. Op wondered how a flower so beautiful as this could come from such worthless earth. This is the place where lumberjacks, ore diggers, and oxen and mule skinners ust to bring their famblies to church, he thought. Now the wild-rose vines, saw briers, and the wood grass have taken over. Maybe there's a black snake or a copperhead among the foundation rocks.

Suppos'n the ghosts of the speret world come back to this place, he thought. Maybe they come back here every Sunday night and have church, and when a big lumberjack gets under conviction and shows signs of repentance, the two strong moderators, who allus kept a watchful eye in the church during services, go back and get 'im and carry 'im to the altar a-kickin' and a-squealin'. That's the way they ust to do it. Then everybody watched 'im as he laid his sins upon the altar. They lissened to his confession, which was allus somethin' to hear when a lumberjack, ore digger, or a collier confessed.

He shouldered his sack again and was on his way around the arc with his load of supplies. His dogwoods and redbuds had shed their blossoms. He looked once across the Sandy Valley to see where the sun was. When he saw a red path of sky over

64

the Allcorn Hills that looked like a brush pile afire in the sky, he knew it was time for him to be getting back to the cabin.

It was never this way when I lived alone, he thought. I never heard singin', whistlin', and geetar playin' in the woods at night till Lutie came. I could spit my terbacker where I wanted and drop scraps fer old Jerry. I never had that Hootbird to sit on my porch and croak ballads fer me. I lissened to my own music. Laurel Ridge is not the same.

I'd a-never believed, if the cataract hadn't been taken from my eye, that I could beget a daughter as fair as Lutie. All the young men will be good to me now fer they'll be eye'n' Lutie. She's as purty as a speckled pup. But why did she leave Dayton and come to me? I can't understand her woman ways, he thought as he shifted the sack to his shoulder. But I do know a woman is an expensive thing, and he remembered the two lists Lutie had written down for him to get. He had to go to the Honeywell post office to post letters for her and to call for her mail. He had one list for the grocery store and one for the drugstore. Lutie had given him the money to pay for everything in the sack on his back. He'd never spent ten dollars at one time before. Lutie couldn't have too much left, and what would happen after she'd spent the last of her savings? Maybe Doshie Hammertight was right when she warned him about the winter days when the snow would be deep on Laurel Ridge. Out of the ten dollars she'd sent by him, he was taking back to her some pocket change. He pulled the bandanna from his pocket and wiped his face as he kept on walking with his load. He wanted to get home to Lutie.

Somebody might come from the woods. Hootbird might slip back there. She doesn't like his playin' and singin'. She's polite to him but she knows he can't stay on the tune. Hootbird is wild about Lutie! It's better never to leave her alone on Laurel Ridge. I ought to have brought her with me, only she didn't want to walk the ten miles. Hammertights are thin and hungry and they run the ridges like lean foxes. Begad, life is a-gettin' complicated.

Op had determined not to stop until he reached the cabin. Just before he reached the sty, he had to put his sack from his shoulder to the ground. He rested while the cool wind hit his face. Between puffs of wind when the rustling leaves were silent, he heard something in the direction of the cabin. He cupped his hand and held it behind his ear to catch the sound better. Guitar music and singing!

Hootbird's there again! He'll be a pest all spring and summer. He'll be a-hangin' 'round as long as Lutie is with me unless we run 'im off. The little coward! Afraid of his shadder at night. A-goin' around with a rifle! When I leave the cabin, he sneaks in!

Op walked faster. He passed the sty and reached the first grove of yellow pines on his left. He put the sack down again. He put his cupped hand behind his ear, turned it toward the cabin to listen. The singing and guitar playing had stopped. There was talking and laughing. It was Lutie's laughter all right. He had never heard her so happy! He could hear her words but he couldn't tell what she was saying. And he could hear a man's voice. It was Hootbird's too. He'd have to get closer to understand what they were a-sayin'. The sun was down behind the Allcorn Hills. The moon was in the sky. He was not home and somebody was at the cabin with Lutie.

Op went a few steps and stood there listening. Was the man's voice Hootbird's? He wasn't sure. He wasn't close enough and the wind was blowing from the Sandy side toward Little White Oak and it carried their words from him. He would have to get closer. If he would only start playing the guitar and singing again, he could tell. He took a few more steps toward the cabin. He didn't want to walk out of the tunnel where the moon's rays, shining down through the open spaces between the oak leaves and the pine needles, left little pencil-size lines of dim light against the semidarkness. If he walked out of this tunnel, they might see him.

"Honey, I'll have to leave you," said a voice. "I'll see you soon!"

"When?" This was Lutie's voice.

"Soon as I can," was the reply. "Soon as it's safe. Might be just any time."

It must be Hootbird all right, a-sneakin' around like a lizard. When Op reached the clearing near the cabin, he saw a man walking away from the gate in the direction of Pawpaw Gap. He carried a rifle on his shoulder, and a guitar in his hand. Op could see them in the moonlight. Lucretia was standing beside the gate watching him hurry along the ridge.

14

"Did ye take advantage of my bein' away to have yer company, Lutie?" Op asked as he laid the sack from his shoulder onto the porch.

"No, I didn't," she replied. "He just dropped in and I wouldn't tell him to leave just because you weren't here."

"I've warned ye about that Hootbird," Op said, pointing his finger at her.

"That wasn't Hootbird."

"Who was it then?" Theopolis mopped his brow.

"Ted Newsome."

"Oh, Ted Newsome!" The expression on Theopolis's face changed. "That's a lot different. I don't feel bad about ye a-seein' Ted! He's not a flesh-and-blood man!"

Lucretia said, "Why would a spirit fall in love with me?"

"That's not hard to understand, Lutie," Theopolis replied. "He remembers what happened to 'im onct over the Dortch gal. Lucinda Dortch put 'im where he is today. Now he yearns fer a happy love affair. He's not content in his long home in the Freewill Baptist Churchyard. And he wouldn't be afraid of Hootbird's rifle. Hootbird could shoot at 'im all he pleases and it would be like shootin' at the wind!"

"Dad, I don't want to fall in love with a spirit," Lucretia smiled. "And I'm afraid I am falling in love with Ted Newsome!"

"I think that's wonderful," Op said. "Better a speret than Hootbird Hammertight. I don't want Hoot to come around when I'm gone. Ye'll larn more about Hammertights atter ye've been here awhile!"

"Dad, do you really believe in spirits?"

"Believe in 'em?" Op said, looking strangely at her. "I hope to tell ye I believe in 'em. I know there's a world of 'em on Laurel Ridge. Too many people have seen 'em. Too many reliable people, includin' myself, have heard 'em. Ye believe me, don't ye?"

"Well, I'm not sure," she replied. "I never heard tell of so many spirits until I came to Laurel Ridge!"

"Laurel Ridge is a land of the sperets," Op explained. "So many people ust to live here. They died the natural deaths. But their sperets have come back. I believe everybody who ever lived on Laurel Ridge and who is now numbered with the blest are back here! The way ye described Ted Newsome to me, I know he's the Ted I ust to know. I just can't understand why he's a-goin' around with a rifle. That's the only thing that plagues me."

Op picked up the heavy sack and Lucretia opened the cabin door for him. Inside he drew up his favorite chair while Lucretia lit the lamp.

"Has Ted been here before when I've been away?" he asked, as Lucretia began unloading the sack.

"Yes, Dad, he was here one day when you went to cut wood," she confessed. "He brought me a bouquet of wild flowers for the table. You remember, you thought it was very pretty."

"Well, ain't it wonderful he's so thoughtful of ye?" Theopolis was pleased. His lips spread in a big smile.

"I think so, Dad." Lucretia took her cosmetics from the sack.

"Ted Newsome is a good speret, Lutie," Op said. "I want ye to bring 'im home while I'm here. I want to sit down and have a talk with 'im about the old times when he was a young flesh-and-blood man and I was a saplin' of a boy! I want to talk with 'im about the old people who ust to be around here then. You tell 'im not to go a-hidin' but to come while I'm here."

"I'll tell him, Dad," she said, "but I doubt if he will. He might not want to talk about the past. He might not want to re-member. You've already said he was bushwhacked over the Dortch girl. He might think Hootbird would bushwhack him over me!"

"Lutie, he can't be bushwhacked now," Op said in a serious tone. "Hootbird nor no bird can ever hurt Ted agin. He's paid the price of love onct and he'll never haf to pay agin. That's why he's enjoyin' himself now. He shorely didn't have much enjoy-ment before. Not when he was shot square betwixt the eyes! I want him to love ye and ye to love him. Anybody that would bring all these nice flowers and be so good to ye, it pays to be nice to 'im. And I don't want ye to get too close to that Hootbird Hammertight."

"Dad, I'm not interested in Hootbird." She laughed. "I'm not quite as nasty to Hoot as you are, that's all."

"But sometimes wimmen change their minds," Op said. "Beadie changed her mind when she married me. She'd told everybody she wouldn't have me on a Christmas tree, but I kept on until she changed 'er mind and then I married 'er jist as soon as she was in the notion. If I know anythin' about men, Hoot-bird'll keep after ye like a hound-dog."

Lutie took her cosmetics to the table and sat down. She opened little packages, Op watching every move she made.

"What's all that stuff?" he asked.

"Oh, just some lipstick, powder base, cold cream, and nail polish. This is wind-and-weather lotion." She opened a jar and started rubbing some cream on her face.

"What's the matter with yer face?" Op asked, alarmed. "Looks all right to me. Never saw Beadie do that to herself in all the time I knowed 'er."

"This is the way I clean my face of rouge and powder."

"What's wrong with soap and water?"

"Oh, Dad! That makes your skin rough and dry," Lucretia answered. "All girls my age use cosmetics like these. I need them on Laurel Ridge the same as I did in Dayton."

"What's that red stuff your're a-puttin' on yer fingers?" Op leaned forward, squinting.

"Why, it's nail polish, Dad. Surely you've seen nail polish before."

"Only from a distance," he admitted gruffly. "But the only reddenin' Beadie ever did was to bite 'er lips and pinch 'er cheeks. To bring out a little natural color, she usta say."

"Well, nowadays girls use rouge and lipstick to do that. You liked the color in Mother's cheeks and lips, didn't you?"

"Are ye a-fixin' up fer Ted, Lutie?"

Lucretia smiled and nodded, "Yes."

"That's the way I like to hear ye talk." Op was smiling. "Lutie, keep on a-seein' Ted. Let him fetch ye new bouquets. Ted lives on Laurel Ridge and probably knows where every patch of wild flowers grows. I'll bet he knows Laurel Ridge better'n I do."

He stopped suddenly, frowning. Then he smiled again. "Course he no longer has need of vittals. I don't haf to worry about his a-pickin' the berries and shootin' the game. Let 'im fetch ye flowers. And tell 'im when ye see 'im agin that I want 'im to come to this cabin when I'm here and sit down and talk with me."

"I'll tell him, Dad." Lucretia hid her smile.

"I feel much better, Lutie," Op told her. "I can go to bed and sleep without worry. I ust never to worry about anythin'. But a woman in the house and now I'm a-frettin' like a hen."

15

Over the Sandy Valley the white mists formed a cloud floor from Laurel Ridge to the Allcorn Hills. Down under, the Sandy River, the turnpike, and all the valley were hidden. And the sun shone brilliantly on this cloud floor. Op was standing in his front yard looking at this scene when Doshie and Hootbird walked up.

"It's a pretty mornin', Op," Doshie cackled at him. Doshie always reminded Op of a bow-legged underfed hen, a-pickin' and a-scratchin'.

"If the clouds would hold me up, I'd like to walk straight over to the Allcorn Hills," Op said. "I'd love to try cloud walkin'."

"Yep, the clouds are awful purty." Doshie smiled, and her long loose mouth looked a foot wide. "Hootbird just said it would be wonderful if the valleys in this county could be spanned by cloud bridges and people could walk across 'em from hilltop to hilltop. And Looten County could be a level county, part clouds and part land. Sure would save a lot of walkin' and the use of a body's legs."

"Looks like ye're a-goin' to pick some berries this mornin'," Op said suspiciously. "Where ye pickin'?"

Doshie was carrying a bucket in each hand, although Hootbird had come empty-handed.

"Hootbird found a patch of wild strawberries yesterday," Doshie said. "Thought maybe ye and Lutie would like to go with us and pick this mornin'. That trial about the half acre of ground is a-goin' on in Honeywell and I can't scrub the courthouse floors. So I thought we'd get out and pick somethin' from the floor of the earth. Thought maybe ye'd like to go since ye can see agin."

"Hoot, ye found my berries," Op said. "Ye found 'em in Shinglemill on the right-hand side of the little fork that branches off toward Coonden."

"How did ye know, Op?" Hootbird asked.

"I ought to know," Op told him. "I picked strawberries there this time in May before ye was born. Big clusters on the vines, red as blood and sweet as sugar, with terrapins a-crawlin' amongst 'em. Yes, I'd better go if I want to get any from that patch. But I know where there's more patches, Hoot!"

"The sun has pulled up the dew by this time of day," Doshie said, looking up at the sun, "and we thought ten o'clock would be a fittin' time to pick. The berries will be fresh, clean, and sweet atter they're washed by dew and dried by the sun."

"I'll go ask Lutie," Op told them. "Don't suppose she's never picked any kind of berries."

When the party started out Laurel Ridge, they paired off. Hootbird and Lucretia led the way. Doshie and Op walked behind.

"Hootbird, ye fergot somethin'," Op called to him.

"What did I ferget?" Hootbird said, stopping to look back.

"Ye don't have yer rifle."

"But I'm not alone this mornin'," Hootbird said. "I'm not afraid. That stranger in the woods would have enough respect fer ladies that he wouldn't shoot amongst 'em."

Hootbird turned and hurried on to catch Lucretia.

"He'd better have respect fer us, Op," Doshie whispered. "I've got somethin' here—" she patted her flat bosom—"that will make him respect us. Ye let anybody try to pull anythin' on us. I'll tell ye a body's patience can be tried jist so long. This ridge woman will jist take so much."

Theopolis let Doshie walk in front of him. He let Doshie lift a greenbrier from across the fox path so she could go on. Hootbird walked in front of Lucretia to practice his good manners, pushing the greenbriers aside with his body so Lucretia could pass unmolested. Op watched Doshie fighting the briers, a glint in his eye. She was wearing a red skirt and a purple blouse. It hurt Op's eyes to look at them worse than it did when he stared straight into the sun. On her fingers, as usual, were all kinds and descriptions of cheap rings. Most of them she had collected out of popcorn and crackerjack boxes.

Hootbird and Lucretia led the way, walking down the slope between the sumac clumps and the patches of wild-blackberry briers. They walked under the persimmons and pawpaws until they came to Shinglemill Hollow. Hootbird set his buckets down and lifted Lucretia across the Shinglemill Branch, though it was a narrow stream and she could have easily stepped over. Doshie looked at Op and smiled. Op saw where there was a tooth missing in front. Doshie hesitated at the bank, but Op stepped over and left her standing on the other side. When Doshie saw everybody walking on, she hopped across too and ran to catch up with the others.

16

"Look at the berries," Lucretia said, "and they're growing wild. Here for anybody to pick! It doesn't seem true! Not after you buy them at stores all your life for fifty cents a box!"

"They're here where I found 'em all right," Hootbird bragged.

"There are still pockets of the earth left as God made 'em," Op said. "Fruit, nuts, and wild game left as they must have been in the beginnin'. Laurel Ridge is one of these places."

They stood looking at the wild strawberries. Little plants with three leaves to the stem, tiny brown specks on the leaves, with a handful of clean red berries growing from a little leafless stem on each plant. And the berry plants were tied to one another by tiny runners. The steep bluff from the stream to the timber was covered with these plants.

In the middle of a slope on a little oak sprout, a catbird sat and quarreled with them.

"He thinks these berries belong to 'im," Op said. "We'll show 'im in a minute that ten fingers 'r worth more than one beak."

"Look at that old terrapin a-goin' up there," Hootbird said. He pointed to a terrapin that moved slowly on his outstretched scaly legs. His long black neck was thrust from his brown-and-black-checked shell and his nose was angled toward the sky. His little beady eyes glistened in the morning sun.

"He'll never go fast enough to wear his legs out," Doshie said.

"Wonder how he gets along with the catbird?" Op mused. "I'd like to know what they think of each other."

"This is the way to do it, Lutie," Hootbird showed her. "Pick four and five at the time. Put yer hand under 'em and lift 'em from the stem. Not one at the time."

"But I'm afraid of mashing them."

"Not with your purty soft white hands," he said. "Not when I don't mash 'em with my big hard ones. Use both hands at once, too."

Op and Doshie were picking, not far apart, each trying to out-pick the other. Op had often bragged that he was the best berry-picker on Laurel Ridge, and Doshie claimed she was the fastest woman berrypicker among the Looten County hills. This was the first time they had ever picked berries together. They listened, never looking up, for the sounds of the berries dropping into each other's buckets. Op trained his good eye on the berries, remembering where he saw the last plant and reaching down and getting the berries with both hands while he looked ahead for two more plants. Op had trained himself to do this. He could remember the spot he had last seen and put his hands on two different berry plants while he looked ahead for the next.

Hootbird picked beside Lucretia, dropping a handful of berries into her bucket now and then. Op listened to the words he murmured to her, but he couldn't tell what Hootbird was say-ing. Hootbird was as close to Lucretia as he could get, speaking softly.

While the berrypickers dropped strawberries into their buck-ets, a yellowhammer, with blotches of red on his head and body, zipped over their heads and alighted on a dead white oak. Only Lucretia and Hootbird took time to look up. They watched him bore into the sap rot of a dead white oak and take a worm from the tree. Then he climbed to the big hole a few feet above and dove in. Lucretia and Hootbird heard the crying of young birds inside the hole.

"Ain't fambly life wonderful?" Hootbird smiled like a half-moon, only sillier. Lucretia moved away.

"Jist be keerful about snakes," Doshie warned. "Look out fer the copperheads!" She spoke without raising her head.

"Snakes are like people," Op broke in. "If there was a snake

75

in this berry patch when we came here and started talkin', it's crawled away. A few of the old bull copperheads won't move fer nothin' nor nobody! They'll even fight a forest fire, a-strikin' and hittin' at the flames till they're burned to death, and their ashes leaves a little white strip on the dark-brown wood ashes."

Wild honeybees hummed slowly over the strawberry vines hunting for dogfennel, sheepshower, and the wild-rose blossoms. They bent the trillium, loaded with blossoms, near a rotting stump.

"Bucketful," Op shouted suddenly, rising to straighten his back.

"But my bucket is larger than yourn, Op," Doshie said.

"Same-size buckets," Op argued. "Let anybody look at 'em."

"Yourn is a two-gallon water bucket and mine is a two-gallon-and-a-half!"

"Jist to show ye, Doshie, I'll set my bucket beside yourn."

Hootbird and Lucretia stopped to watch the measurements of the buckets.

"See, the rims are even," Op said.

"But my bucket is bigger around," Doshie argued.

"We'll see about that," Op said. He broke a weed and measured the diameter of his bucket. Then he laid the weed across the top of Doshie's bucket. Its length was the exact diameter of her bucket.

"I knew ye's a-tryin' to beat me, Doshie," Op said. "Ye tried to slow me down by a-talkin' about snakes and ye kept on a-pickin'. But I fooled ye. I'm still the champion berrypicker."

"We've not got our five-quart buckets filled yet," Hootbird said.

"Ye're a-doin' more talkin' than pickin' up there," Op told him.

"But people are only young onct, Op," Doshie simpered, "and in the wild-strawberry patch there might be a lot of love a-goin' into their buckets with each strawberry. I like to see young people in love. When my girl Daisy meets a young man on the streets in Honeywell and he brings 'er home, I'm allus at their heels a-listenin'. And when he takes 'er to the house and kisses 'er good night, I pretend to be lookin' away but I watch from the corner of my eye. I love to watch young people kiss. Ben's awful slow about his kissin'."

"If old Ben kisses ye at all, Doshie, he's a-doin' all right." Op pretended he was joking. The very idea of anyone kissing Doshie made him weak in the knees. He glanced at Hootbird and Lucretia. Hoot's big Texas hat was leaning over Lutie, and he was pouring berries from his full bucket into hers. Op was wishing that the Lord had never invented strawberries.

Then a shot rang out that echoed and re-echoed across Shingle-mill Hollow.

17

"Spat"—the bullet hit the soft butternut tree above Hootbird's head, leaving a little light-colored hole where it entered the bark, and splinters where it came through on the other side. The shot was fired from the hilltop behind them, down into the little valley. When the shot rang out and the bullet hit the tree ten feet above Hootbird's head, he dropped his bucket of berries on the ground. They rolled down the steep slope like red marbles, lodging behind clumps of flowers and weeds.

Each one stood rigidly in his tracks. Even Hootbird stood for a moment, but not rigidly. He was trembling like a hickory leaf in the evening wind on Laurel Ridge. Then Hootbird moved off on wobbly legs, his face pale as a frosted beech leaf in October, his hands shaking like he had the palsy. He wobbled

77

around the steep slope toward Shinglemill Hollow until he came to the timber line and then he turned up the hill, clawing the ground with his fingers as he pulled himself up. He went up the slope on his all fours until he was fenced in again by the timber line, then he rose to his feet and started back on his wobbly legs toward Lucretia. He had staggered full circle, his eyes glazed.

"He's not hit," Op said. "Hoot's gun shy. He's skeered."

Doshie had not spoken, but she put her hand down in her bosom, pulled out her twenty-two automatic pistol, turned, and shot seven times in the direction from which the rifle shot had been fired. Each bullet spatted leaves and branches, and two bullets hit trees and sang into space.

"Hot lead is the only answer to this business," she said, blowing smoke from the barrel of her pistol.

"He didn't try to hit Hoot," Op said. "If a man can place a bullet like that in the center of a tree, he could've hit Hoot if he'd a-aimed at 'im."

"Then I'd like to know what he was a-tryin' to do?" Hootbird croaked with a trembling voice.

"He was a-tryin' to skeer ye," Op said.

"It's a poor way to skeer a person," Doshie retorted as she took cartridges from the little pocket on her skirt and reloaded.

Lucretia had not moved from her tracks. She had not spoken a word and she stood there still holding to her bucket of berries. She stared in the direction from which the shot had come.

"I believe it's somebody a-tryin' to take my son's life," Doshie said. "It's that strange man that's been seen on this ridge!"

"Maybe he's jealous of ye, Hootbird," Op cackled like a hen, "a-pickin' berries with Lutie."

Lucretia spoke to Op sharply. "Let's go home. I couldn't pick another berry here. I'm too nervous."

Op walked up the hill to the butternut tree. He looked up the

78

side where the bullet had gone in. Then he twisted his neck like a terrapin around on the other side and looked up.

"Ye'd better stay down here in the hollow, Op," Doshie warned. "Ye might get a bullet plumb through ye."

"That's a bullet hole all right," Op said, turning and coming down the hill. "It went clean through six inches of soft butternut wood. He's got a powerful rifle. Must be a Krag-Jörgensen."

"I'll never come back here agin," Hootbird said. He picked up his empty bucket with a shaking hand. "The catbirds can have these berries fer all I keer."

When Hootbird and Lucretia walked down the slope, he didn't walk close to her and he let Lucretia carry her own bucket of berries. His empty bucket jingled in the wind since he couldn't control his nervous hand.

"Everybody's skeered," Op said, "'ceptin' me. I've heard bullets fly through the brush in this ridge many a night as I walked along it. I've had to run backward and forward to dodge the bullets, but I wasn't skeered. That was when I was a young man and people still traveled this ridge."

"Were they trying to kill you, Dad?" Lucretia asked.

"No, jist a-shootin' fer the sport of it," he admitted, walking over the berry patch. "We ust to go huntin' with single-barrel shotguns on this ridge, and if the foxes had ketched all the rabbits and birds and we didn't have anythin' to shoot at, we got off a safe distance and shot at each other. It was a game we played. The man that had the most shot in him after we each had shot six times was Simeon Girty, the traitor. The man that had the least shots in 'im was Daniel Boone. I was Simeon Girty onct. And twice I was Daniel Boone."

"I don't believe that, Op," Doshie said, as the party continued down the little valley toward Shinglemill Branch.

"I don't keer what ye believe, Doshie," Op sputtered. "It's

the truth. I've got shot still in me to show. And I've got little white scars all over my shoulders and back and a lot below."

"I wouldn't play a crazy game like that," Hootbird said.

"If ye'd a-played it ye wouldn't be so gun shy," Op told him.

Hootbird didn't offer to lift Lucretia across the creek when they came to it. Each one stepped over it in single file. When they started up the hill toward the fox path, Hootbird walked close to his mother.

"Won't ye walk on the other side of Hoot?" Doshie asked Lucretia. "We're out in this open field and I wouldn't put anythin' past that criminal. He surely won't shoot a woman."

Lucretia calmly moved up beside Hootbird. Theopolis led the way up the hill, around the clusters of blackberry vines, over the saw briers, under the sumac fronds, the persimmon, and pawpaw boughs. "Hidin' behind wimminfolks!" he muttered. Then his tone changed, a note of admiration creeping in. "Ole Ted's got himself some rifle. Allus was a smart one!"

18

"Beadie, Beadie," Op screamed. "That's ye, Beadie! Ye've come back to me!"

Theopolis jumped from his bed onto the floor dragging the cover with him. He stood shaking in the darkness like a lean saw brier in a February wind.

"Where are ye, Beadie?" he asked.

The shooting of a rifle and the bullet's going harmlessly through a soft butternut tree had not bothered Op. But now his legs shook until he could hardly stand. He stretched his long arm and fingered for the side of the bed. He found it and sat down.

80

"Beadie," he wept. He could feel the warm tears flowing down his cheeks. "It's fer a purpose that ye've come. Tell me the reason! What is it? What have I done?"

There was not a sound in the cabin.

"Answer me, Beadie?"

Theopolis heard himself cry out. There was no other sound.

"I'm not dreamin'," he said. "I know I saw ye. I saw yer brown eyes and brown hair. Saw yer smile, Beadie, the way ye looked thirty years ago! Beadie!"

And they tell me people don't come back to earth from the speret world, he thought as he wiped tears from his stubbly bearded cheeks with his hand. They come back but they don't stay long enough.

"Beadie, come sit down on the bed beside me and talk," he said in a trembling voice. "I'm not afraid to talk to ye. I've got a lot of questions to ast. There's a lot of things I'd like to know. Come sit down beside me agin! I've been as good a man as I know how to be all the years since ye've been gone, Beadie! It's not been wimmen, Beadie. And I stopped a few years ago fermentin' the pawpaws and the 'simmons and a-layin' on the ridges on my back with my eyes upturned to the rain! A-lyin' dead to the world with the empty brandy jug beside me! Ye know that now, Beadie, because ye're amongst the blest. The crave of drink is no longer with me! I've repented a thousand times, Beadie, I didn't quit it while ye were with me on this earth! Hear me, Beadie! If ye don't sit down beside me and talk, I'll jist talk to ye.

"There's somebody here with me now, Beadie," Op continued. "She come to me in a time of need. And I know that ye know she's here. She lies in this room, Beadie! Is she our daughter?"

Theopolis sat in silence while a chill went over his body. His teeth chattered and he fought vainly to control his shaking.

His body trembled until he rattled the bed. Finally the chill began to leave him.

"Lutie, wake up," Op cried. "Beadie's appeared to me. She put 'er face down agin my face and my eyes were opened. I saw 'er, Lutie, plain as I ever saw 'er. Young and purty as she ust to be and she looked at me with her brown eyes without sayin' a word. She's come to me fer a purpose, Lutie! Maybe it's because of ye!"

Lucretia didn't answer Theopolis. He arose from the side of the bed, fumbled for the matchbox on the little table. With a shaking hand he struck a match and lit the lamp. He reached for his pants hanging over the foot of his bed. He slipped on his shoes but didn't lace them.

"Lutie, Beadie has appeared to me," he cried again.

Then Theopolis walked around behind the sheet partition and found Lucretia's bed was empty. He almost dropped the lamp he was holding in his hand.

"Lutie, Lutie, where are ye?" Op shouted as he stumbled to the cabin door. "Have ye left?"

He unlatched the door. The wind flicked the yellow lamp flame but the lamp globe would not let the wind blow it out. He held the lamp to one side as he looked down the road toward the sty. He heard voices.

Op turned quickly and looked in the other direction toward Pawpaw Gap. He saw the dim outline of a man disappearing in the semidarkness of Laurel Ridge. And Lucretia was walking quietly toward the cabin. When she came within the lamplight, she looked up at him. She was dressed in her best, but the lipstick was not all on her lips. Some of it had slipped down onto her chin and climbed up on one cheek.

19

"Lutie, where've ye been?" Op asked.

"In the yard most of the time," she replied. "Sitting on our bench watching the moon rise up and sink down!"

"Who was that man, Lutie, I saw a-walkin' over toward Paw-paw Gap?"

"Not Hootbird, Dad," she replied. "That was Ted Newsome!"

"Oh, it was Ted agin." Theopolis spoke in a softer tone. "Did ye tell 'im I wanted to have a long talk with 'im sometime about the past?"

"Yes, I told him," she said. "Ted said he'd try to drop in to talk with you sometime. But tonight he didn't want to disturb you."

"How did he wake you without wakin' me?" Op asked.

"Dad, it was a sound like the fanning of wings against my window when Ted came," Lucretia explained. "And I looked up and saw Ted's face against my windowpane. He beckoned to me and I got up and dressed quickly and went to him!"

"That's the way they come, all right." Op nodded vigorously. "I'd like to get next to 'im too, Lutie. He's a good speret."

"I think he is, Dad."

"But ye can't marry with a speret, remember. He'd never want to marry, anyway. Atter what he got betwixt his eyes, he'll want the enjoyment of a peaceful love affair right here on Laurel Ridge. He's come back to the scene of his mortal death to have his love affair. Maybe he's a-doin' this to spite Lucinda Dortch who two-timed 'im. That's why he's back here!"

Then Op stopped short, peering at the smudges on Lucretia's face. "He shore messed yer paint some and he didn't do it from no distance. Now I've heard tell of many people *a-seein'* sperets, and I've heard their voices myself, but I don't know a soul who's ever been kissed by one."

"Well, Dad—" Lucretia seemed embarrassed, and uncertain as to how to answer.

"But Ted's a speret all right if he waked ye with his wings fannin' against the winder," Op mused as he walked back onto the porch with Lutie following after. "He's probably dropped down from the thin air. If he's to sail over Hootbird on his wings spread like a big chicken hawk," Op said, "he'd skeer Hoot to death. We'd haf to make a coffin fer old Hoot. How I'd love to see him glide above Hoot, kickin' his feet in the air like he was a-swimmin' in the water! If I ever get close to Ted I'll put a few things into his mind!"

"Dad, Ted doesn't fly," Lucretia said. "He prefers to walk and talk like any other man."

"Lutie," Op stared hard at her in the yellow glow of lamplight, "I don't think ye believe in sperets! Be keerful about that. It's dangerous not to believe. Ye're sparkin' a speret and I'm glad, but ye'd better believe in 'im."

"I do believe in spirits, Dad," Lucretia told him. "I know since I've come to Laurel Ridge that they are here. I know they're real."

"Now ye're talkin' right, Lutie," Op said. "Ye should know it when ye've been beneath the moon a-spoonin' a speret. I've been right in this cabin with one, too. Beadie is disturbed about somethin'. Ted Newsome waked ye up and Beadie waked me. She's been here, Lutie, in this very room when it was dark. I never heard a sound of wings fannin' against the winderpanes either. When I opened my good eye, there stood Beadie right before me. Young and purty as the day I married 'er. I spoke to Beadie, loud enough fer ye and Ted to hear if ye were a-sittin' out there on the bench. I told 'er that I was a much better man than I was when she lived with me. I tried to get 'er to come back and

84

sit down and talk with me. She wouldn't do it. I was so upset I'm still a-shakin'. I'm not afeared of any animal or flesh-and-blood man that walks, Lutie. But when it comes to the sperets, I weaken. I'm humble, Lutie. It pays to be. Beadie was back here fer a purpose and if ye're our daughter it might be because of ye."

"Then, does Ted Newsome come to see me for a purpose?" she asked Op.

"Ye bet he does, Lutie," Op answered quickly. "Ted Newsome has a purpose."

"But what could it be, Dad?"

"I think to keep ye away from Hootbird Hammertight," Op replied. "I think old Hoot's intentions are evil. Ye're a purty gal, Lutie. No man will ever look at ye jist onct."

"Oh, Dad, you're wonderful," Lucretia said. "If you have the least suspicions about me, forget them. When Hootbird is with me, he stays in his place. And when Ted Newsome is with me, you know you don't have to worry. I can take care of myself."

Op held his big gnarled hand above the lamp globe and blew louder than the wheeze of a horse with the thumps. The tiny golden flame disappeared and left the room in darkness. "I'll allus be on Ted Newsome's side," he said.

20

"Hello! Is this where Theopolis Akers lives?"

Op lifted his hoe and turned to the direction of the sound.

"Yep, this is where he lives," he said. "Ye're a-talkin' to 'im now."

Op saw a man and woman standing by the garden gate. The man was slender and of medium height but stooped over. He was fanning his hot pale face and his thin blond hair with his hat. The woman beside him came almost to his shoulder. She was a plump, attractive, black-headed woman. And she was fanning too, with a little paper fan, the kind passed out by the funeral director, Oddis Timmons, in Honeywell. Op could see, between the palings, three suitcases on the ground beside them.

"Mr. Akers, it's some climb up this ridge," said the man, fanning his hot face with his crumpled straw hat. "We've been since early this morning coming from Honeywell."

"Do ye live in Honeywell?" Op asked as he walked toward the garden fence.

"No, we're from Dayton, Ohio," said the man. "This is my wife, Julia, and I'm Alfred Pruitt."

"What are ye a-doin' up here?" Theopolis asked. He walked over to the palings and eyed the strangers suspiciously. "How'd ye know about me? How'd ye know to come here?"

"Will and Corrinne Day are my uncle and aunt," said Alfred Pruitt. "My mother is Aunt Beadie's youngest sister. You're my uncle by marriage. Your daughter Lutie is my cousin."

"Shucks, I ain't so shore she's my daughter," Op said. "I've doubted it all the time."

"She's your daughter if you're Theopolis Akers," Pruitt said. "She's my first cousin and you're my uncle. Where is she?"

"She's in the cabin," Op said, looking strangely at the couple. "She's workin' the cabin instead of helpin' me hoe this patch of corn. I got it planted late on account of my eyes. I was blind as a bat when Lutie come down here!"

"Yes, we've heard all about that," Julia Pruitt said, smiling at Theopolis. "Lutie's been writing her uncle and aunt about you and Laurel Ridge. Aunt Corrinne read some of her letters to us. They were simply marvelous."

"And we decided Laurel Ridge was the place for us," Alf said.

"Say, what's all this about?" Op asked, his gnarled fingers

scratching in his long hair. "I do remember Beadie had a sister Alice. I'd fergot all about 'er! So ye're her son, are ye?"

When Lucretia heard Op talking she came out onto the porch. "Cousin Alf!" she cried. "And Cousin Julia! What are you doing on Laurel Ridge?"

"Your letters brought us here," the thin stooped man said emphatically. "We've come to stay! Laurel Ridge sounds like one of the safest places left in the United States! We've come to be with you and Uncle Theopolis!"

"Don't call me 'Uncle Theopolis,' " Op said quickly. "Call me 'Op' if ye gotta call me at all!"

"And you call me 'Alf' too," Pruitt said, friendly-like.

Lucretia hurried through the front-yard gate and ran down beside the garden palings. She shook her Cousin Alf's hand and hugged and kissed her Cousin Julia. Op stood on the other side looking over at the suitcases in disgust.

"It's wonderful to see you, Julia," Lucretia said, smiling. "You and Alf on Laurel Ridge! I can't believe it."

"I can't believe it either," Alf said, fanning again. "I never got as hot in my life as I did carrying two suitcases up that hill and out this ridge. I thought I'd faint, though I stopped and took a rest every few minutes. We've been since seven this morning getting out here."

Op shook his head sadly. "City folks fergit even how to walk."

"I thought I'd never make it, Lutie," Julia said. "But nothing would do Alf after Aunt Corrinne read your letters to us but to come to Laurel Ridge! 'That's the place for me,' Alf said to me one night last week. 'I'm going to that country. I'm going to spend the rest of my days there. I'm getting away from this dangerous spot.' So here we are. Alf got a leave of absence."

"And I think it's going to be a long leave of absence," Alf said proudly. "I spent ten years working up to my position there. It took me ten minutes after I heard your letters to decide to

87

leave it. I'd rather be a man without a job. I don't want to be blown up. I don't want to be consumed by fire!" His voice began to shake.

"Now, let's don't start all that again, Alf," Julia said.

"Yes, you tried to keep me from getting a leave of absence," he told her. "But I consider my life worth more than eight thousand a year. And what did we have after taxes? We don't have any dependents. We didn't have any way to cover up. We had to pay it all back to the government. And after we made payments on a home, bought a car and food and clothes, it was all we could do to live! And to live in that awful fear!" His voice kept rising like wind in the trees. "It was too much for me. It was getting on my nerves. I believe that Wright Airfield will be bombed one of these days! I've been reading in the papers about this atom bomb and those terrible explosions. I couldn't take it any longer. One of these days planes will cross the Atlantic and Pacific with atom bombs and wipe out our industrial cities and airfields. The only safe places in America will be the mountains and the rough spots where nobody lives. The safe places will be spots like Laurel Ridge!"

"What's all this ye're a-talkin' about?" Op said, staring at the intruders. "I never heard tell of the adam bumb!"

"Now, listen to that, Julia," Alf said, wetting his sun-and-wind-dried lips with his tongue. "This is just what I've been telling you. Lutie's own father doesn't know anything about the atom bomb! Look at the peace of mind he has. He's not a nervous wreck! He goes on about his daily living like people used to before science brought on this monster to destroy civilization!"

Alf couldn't hold his arms still while he talked. His lips twitched and he blinked his eyes rapidly.

"Dad doesn't read," Lutie explained. "And he's never had a

radio up here. That's the reason he's not up on all this atomic stuff."

"What does he do for music?" Julia asked Lucretia. "What did he do for the sound of a human voice before you came to live with him?"

"Make my own music," Op replied. "Look over there on the cabin walls. Talk to my dog, old Jerry, and he tries to talk back. Now and then I talk to one of the Hammertights. Guess I even talk to myself and then answer. But I like it."

Alf couldn't stop talking. "I rented our house and put our car in the garage. I would have sold both of them if Julia hadn't raised such a fuss."

"Hammertights are the only people who live near Laurel Ridge," Lucretia explained. "They live down under at Wince Leffard Gap."

"I guess we'll be getting acquainted with all these places with the quaint names." Julia smiled at Op.

"Maybe ye will, and maybe ye won't," Op told her. "The minute I saw yer suitcases there on the ground my mind started workin'. Our cabin ain't big enough . . ."

"Now don't get me wrong, Op," Alf interrupted. "I plan to build us a little one-room log house with my own hands! And if there is a big rock cliff close that's good and dry, I wouldn't mind living there till the cabin's finished. I want to live from the land like Lutie said you did. I want to rough it."

"Ever use an ax?" Op asked.

"No."

"Some cabin ye'll build without an ax!"

"I'll learn," Alf said, fanning nervously again. "But where'll we live until then?"

"I've got a smokehouse out there that might suit ye," Op said reluctantly, pointing to the squat little one-room log house.

"What I started to say, one house ain't big enough fer two famblies. I've allus had that smokehouse ready if my cabin burnt so I'd have someplace to go."

"That's wonderful, Op," Alf said. "But we don't want to impose on you. Are there any other houses on Laurel Ridge?"

"That cabin and smokehouse are the only two buildin's on Laurel Ridge," Op said.

"It looks like the smokehouse will have to suit us," Julia said. "It'll be quite a change after the home we built in Dayton."

"Then the smokehouse is where we'll live." Alf was enthusiastic. "Let's be on our way!"

"Not now. It's not ready," Op said. "I can't get outten keepin' ye in the cabin fer one night. We've jist got two beds. Maybe we can make out. Alf can sleep with me and Julia can sleep with Lutie."

"Thanks awfully, Op, you're a real brick." Alf pumped Theopolis's calloused hand and slapped him on the back. Then he picked up the three suitcases and staggered toward the cabin. Julia and Lutie followed, chattering like excited birds.

Op leaned against the fence and reached for his burley leaf. "A real brick, eh? I'll give ye five days on the Ridge. Gonna build himself a cabin without an ax!"

21

Op's mood brightened somewhat during the evening meal, and Lutie felt relieved. After they had finished, Op pushed his chair back from the table, put his hand in his pocket, and pulled out a long root. He held it to his mouth and bit off a big chew. Alf, who was sitting beside Op, looked on curiously.

"I don't mean to be too inquisitive," said Alf, "but I'd like to know what that is you're chewing!"

"That's my medicine," Op told him. "It's calmus root I find in the swamps along the Sandy River. Ever hear of calmus root?"

"Never did," Alf said. "Is it good for you?"

"I ust to see blind spots before my eyes," Op explained. "Ust to see little rings that looked like the sun and I'd break out in a sweat. And I wanted to run all the time like a wild turkey. But the calmus weed took away the spots before my eyes and it slowed me down. It made me feel like a new man!"

"How did you know about this weed?" Alf asked. "Did a doctor recommend it to you?"

"I never was to a doctor but twice in my life," Op told him. "Lutie took me twice to Doctor Turnbo fer my cataract. Calmus root was an old medicine in our fambly. Pap ust to chew it all the time. No doctor ever told him about it. Some Indian chief down in North Carolina told his father, my grandpa Powatan Akers, about it!" Op leaned forward excitedly. "And, Alf, there're roots, stems, and leaves that'll cure ye of all that nervousness! There's a weed a-growin' on Laurel Ridge fer every ailment of the body. The Old Master has a purpose fer every weed and flower He's created!"

Op ground the calmus weed slowly with his perfect teeth, and took tiny swallows. Alf took a pack of cigarettes from his shirt pocket and handed them across the table to Julia. She offered one to Op.

"Never smoked one in my life," he said. "I sometimes chaw a little light burley. But cigarettes is coffin nails. Allus believed it."

"Is that the only medicine you have to take, Op?" Alf pointed at the root.

"No, I've got a good supply of roots, stems, and leaves over

91

in the smokehouse," he said. "Ye'll see 'em tomorrow. I've got to lay in my medicine fer the winter same as I lay in a good pile of stovewood. After the plants die and the snows fall, a body can't find the roots. The only time my yarbs ever failed me was on my eyes. I hadn't found the right yarbs."

"No doctor bills to pay?" Alf said, blowing a cloud of sweet-smelling cigarette smoke across the table. "Some people left in the world still know how to live, Julia."

"Yes, but are you willing to try root remedies yourself?" she asked Alf.

"I'm ready to try anything," he said. "I've been to doctors and osteopaths, then psychiatrists, and even chiropractors! I've never been helped. I've still got this nervousness."

"Cousin Alf, what's the matter with you?" Lucretia asked.

"Oh, he's just nervous," Julia answered blowing a wisp of smoke from her full red lips. "Alf's had too much responsibility at Wright Airfield. He's over a crew of men and he worries trying to get things done."

"I worry about everything," Alf said. "When I park my car on a street in autumn and the leaves are falling, I get to thinking after I leave the car parked and locked: 'What if some irresponsible smart aleck comes along smoking a cigarette and throws it down with fire in the butt and it catches the leaves on fire? And the fire burns under my car and catches the gasoline and it explodes and blows my car up and sets a dozen houses on fire!' I have thoughts like these all the time. I don't know how many times I've gone back to my car and driven it away and parked it where there were no leaves!"

"That's easy," Op said. "Ye shouldn't own a car. Use yer legs!"

"And just recently, when there was a dark cloud in the sky, Alf got to unplugging all the light cords in the house before we went to bed," Julia said. "He was afraid lightning would strike the house and set it on fire and we wouldn't be able to phone the fire department."

"That's too bad," Op said, shaking his head sadly. "Ye need plenty of yarb medicine. There's a remedy fer ye."

"Will you be afraid of an oil lamp?" Lucretia asked.

Alf's attention was drawn to the oil lamp in the middle of the table. Since Theopolis always raised both windows in the cabin when Lucretia started cooking, the wind was bending the golden flame forward. But the flame clung tenaciously to the oil-soaked wick which fed it.

"You might lower the windows so there wouldn't be any danger of the wind blowing the flame into the oil," Alf warned. "I'm not too concerned about it but that's just a precautionary suggestion."

"I've had the wind to blow the lamp out many a time," Op said, "but never the fire into the oil. I've allus loved the fresh air on Laurel Ridge. Haf to haf it same as a fish hast to haf water. I don't like the smell of vittals. I'd rather haf the fresh wind. There will come a time, I'm allus a-thinkin', when I go to my long home in the Freewill Baptist Graveyard where I won't get all this good, fresh Laurel Ridge air."

"I think what started all of this for Alf was the discovery of the atomic bomb," Julia said. "He wasn't very nervous when I married him. When this bomb was used in the Second World War, Alf read the reports and couldn't sleep for days. Now, every time we have an atomic-bomb test, I have to hide the papers. He thinks we're going to be bombed. He thinks the world is going to pieces and . . ."

"It *is* going to pieces," Alf interrupted as he dubbed the end of his cigarette on his plate with nervous fingers. "The Bible says this world will be destroyed by fire! And what is the atomic bomb but fire? We don't have a monopoly on the atomic bomb and we don't have the fastest and best planes. If we figure on

93

bombing an enemy country, I figure they plan to bomb us too. And when we're bombed, the only safe places left in this world will be places like Laurel Ridge! Didn't I read in the papers with my own eyes about our large cities having a hundred thousand shrouds ready for our ashes? How can an undertaker put a shroud on a handful of wind-blown ashes? I'm not the only one worried. Others are thinking about it too!"

"When Alf started unplugging the light sockets every time there was a dark cloud in the sky, I agreed to leave Dayton with him," Julia said. "So here we are on Laurel Ridge! You don't have a radio up here and we won't get a newspaper!"

"I'm sure we've found the right place," Alf said, unconsciously lighting another cigarette with stiff white fingers. "When I heard this country had a million coffins stored for an atomic attack, I said to myself: 'Not one of these coffins is for Alfred Pruitt if he can do something about it!' When I read about a chain of air defenses to protect us from an atomic blitz, I couldn't sleep. Why are we building air-raid shelters? Why is our government building places underground to house our valuable documents? What about all those 'Shelter' signs?"

"Alf, ye talk like the end of time is near," Op told him. "It's skeery talk."

"These are scary times." Perspiration was running down Alf's forehead. "These might be the last days of what we call *civilization*. I hear we've got bombs a hundred times more powerful than the ones we dropped on Japan. Don't you believe our enemies have 'em too?" he asked, leaning forward toward Op. "And I've heard about a death dust that might even blow from Dayton to Laurel Ridge. It kills every living thing. And what about these flying saucers? And this new bomb we got that's a thousand times as powerful as the atomic bomb? I hear it's powerful enough to crack the face of the earth."

"I-gollies, I've never heard a thing about all these bombs,

saucers, and pizen dust," Op said. He looked suspiciously at Alf. Then he said, "But I'm not a-runnin' from nothin'."

Theopolis dug into his pocket for another chew of calmus root. Many times in the past he had had this same feeling— that the world was a-movin' too fast fer him. So he took a chew of root and thought about the things he understood.

22

While Lutie and Julia washed the dishes, Op and Alf sat on the bench under the tall pines. The bright moon was rising up over the green clouds of wind-fluttering leaves in Little White Oak Valley. A whippoorwill was singing down in Red Bird Hollow near the spring. And a cool early-June wind was blowing over Laurel Ridge.

"Now, this is the life." Alf exhaled two wisps of thin smoke from his nostrils and it was carried away by the night. "This is what I've looked forward to for a long, long time!"

Op chewed his calmus weed. A fox barked on Laurel Ridge near the sty.

"Op, have you ever been out of the state?" Alf asked.

"Nope, I've never been outten Looten County." Op's dark heavy eyebrows came down over his eyes in a frown. "In fact, I've never been over very much of this county. I've just walked to a few hills I could see from this ridge. I got curious about 'em and wanted to see what they were like. I looked these hills over and found the grass and the pine boughs were greener on Laurel Ridge. So Jerry and I walked back home."

Jerry had followed Op around the cabin. Now he was standing on his hind feet with his forefeet on Op's lap while Op stroked his head with a big hand.

"I've been in forty-four states," Alf told Theopolis. "I've seen a lot. But it hasn't done me much good."

"Ye've not been planted anyplace," Op said. "Ye're like our mistletoe and love vine. They don't grow from the ground and they're soft. I'm rooted right here as much as any oak on Laurel Ridge. And a Laurel Ridge oak has to be deep-rooted in the ground to stand these winds!"

"I just wonder why you've never left Looten County," Alf asked him.

"Alf, when I was a young man on Laurel Ridge, I ust to watch the spiders in the spring," Op said. "When I ust to go out bright and early on a warm spring mornin' a-huntin' fer wild strawberries, I'd come upon a whole city of spider webs in the woods. I'd stop and look 'em over and hunt fer a web that had the initials of my name. It's good luck to find one. There's more good luck in findin' yer initials in a spider web than there is in a four-leaf clover. Find yer initials in one on a spring mornin' and then make a wish and a body'll about get his wish."

"What did you wish for, Op?"

"Mostly to be left alone. 'Course if I was out a-huntin' wild strawberries I made a wish to find a patch red as a September sourwood leaf with berries. I wished fer a patch where I could sit down in the middle and pick enough berries to fill my stummick within my arm's reach. Yep, whenever I found a city of spiders where all the webs had different writin' in 'em, I'd look till I found the letters T.A."

"Sounds wonderful." Alf, leaning back against a pine tree, seemed to be relaxing for the first time.

"Now let me tell ye the nearest I ever come to leavin' Laurel Ridge," Op said. "One mornin' I was lookin' fer my initials among the spider webs; that was when I wanted to make a wish to find a bee tree. I'd found the bees a-waterin' down on

Little White Oak Branch but I couldn't course 'em only a short distance fer the bushy tops of the white oaks. So I found a neighborhood of spider webs and in one I found T.A., and I made my wish. But I saw somethin' else there that started me to thinkin'. I'd offen wondered if spiders were in other parts of the world like on Laurel Ridge. Since the sun was as hot as a brush-pile flame it soon dried the dew. And a warm wind was risin' and shakin' the webs like white clothes on a line. Then I saw somethin' I'd never seen before. Young spiders a-throwin' out ropes of silk and a-risin' up on the warm winds and ridin' away to other places beyond Laurel Ridge."

"When you talk about spiders I get the creeps," Alf broke in, sitting up straight. "I'm always thinking one is waiting someplace just to bite me. I've read so much about the black widow spiders and . . ."

"I'm a-tryin' to tell ye why I never left Laurel Ridge," Op said sharply. He turned and looked curiously at Alf. Then he continued: "I thought if spiders left that way, I had a good pair of young strong legs and I could leave, too. If spiders wanted to go beyond Laurel Ridge to find a new world and build their cities and beget their kind, I might leave, too."

"Op, what is so important about a spider, anyway?" Alf asked. "They catch flies and spin ugly webs. What else can these poisonous things do? Why are we talking about them?"

"Spiders were put here fer a purpose," Op said. "What would the mud daubers eat?"

"What's a mud dauber? Is it another poisonous pest put here to annoy people? What's it like?"

"Looks like a red wasper," Op said. "Ye'll find 'em in the smokehouse and . . ."

"Wait a minute, Op!" Alf interrupted. "Are these mud daubers dangerous?"

"Shucks, they don't sting, Alf. Ye'll find 'em under cliffs, in holler trees, houses, and about every place. They build a mud finger and the old she-dauber starts a-layin' eggs in it. The old he-dauber starts ketchin' spiders and a-puttin' 'em with the eggs. When they get enough spiders fer their young, they seal the end of the finger. When the eggs hatch, the young daubers have plenty of fresh spiders and they eat 'em and get so fat they bust the walls and fly away."

"But I've never read about mud daubers," Alf said. "I never knew they existed."

"Mud daubers and spiders make wonderful friends. They don't worry people. Instead of talkin' to a lot of folks I don't know, I watch the animals, insects, and birds on Laurel Ridge."

This was something Alf could agree with. "At least they don't have this know-how to invent ways of exterminating one another. The spiders spin their own ropes and fly on the wind. We spend millions for metal wings to carry our weapons of extermination! What fools we are! Tell me more about the spiders and ants, Op!"

"Well, there's a fambly I call sour ants," Op began. "They look a lot like these big sour gnats that're allus a-tryin' to get into a body's eyes. These sour ants are the only ones the Master gave wings. When I was a boy, I rooted over an old dead sourwood to get some peckerwood eggs. I didn't know ants could fly till a swarm left this sourwood and got betwixt me and the sun."

"Where did they go?" Alf asked.

"Flew till they lost their wings," Op replied. "That's the Master's plan fer scatterin' 'em over the land."

Alf interrupted with a trembling voice: "Are there any man-eating ants out here?"

"Ye do need yarb medicine," Op said, staring at the stranger beside him. "Shucks, I never heard tell of ants that big!"

"But I have," Alf said. "I've read about 'em."

"Must be a lot of funny things in books," Op sighed. "Good thing I can't read."

23

"I want you to get an ear and an eye full of this night, honey," Alf said to Julia as she and Lucretia came from the cabin. "This will be a little different from the honking of cars, the screaming of whistles, and the racket of a city all night long. In the morning I won't have the early paper thrown on my doorstep to read while I gulp coffee and eat a doughnut. I won't be disgusted with the new scare headlines and read where somebody's been hit over the head with a bottle in a tavern. Somebody murdered. Somebody robbed. Not even a radio to get a five-minute summary of the latest international atrocities. Not anything to scare the hell out of a man out here. Only the four of us on this whole ridge!"

"Only four flesh-and-blood people on Laurel Ridge," Theopolis corrected Alf.

"What do you mean, Op, by flesh-and-blood people?"

"Sperets, Alf. No one has ever left Laurel Ridge. A hundred years ago there was more than eighty shacks on the ridge. All the people that lived here then are dead and all that's numbered with the blest are back here!"

"Let's don't get off on the spirits, Dad," Lucretia said. "Cousin Alf and Julia won't believe in them."

"Ye've larned to believe it, ain't ye?" Op retorted. "Ye ought to believe it when ye're a-sparkin' a speret!"

"What's that?" Alf asked, his voice rising in surprise.

"Lutie's in love with a speret," Op told him.

"What a joke," Alf sputtered.

"That's not a joke either," Theopolis warned. "Be keerful how ye laugh about the sperets. They're allus a-listenin'. They're around us and over us every hour, night and day! Bad luck might come to ye, Alf. If ye and Julia laugh, it's an insult to the sperets. I had to warn Lutie about it."

"Who is the spirit, Lutie?" Julia asked. She looked at Theopolis as if at any minute he might climb straight into the air, hand over hand.

"Why don't ye answer, Lutie?" Op said. "Don't be ashamed. He's Ted Newsome."

"Who is this Ted Newsome?" Alf asked.

"He's a good speret," Op answered. Lucretia remained silent, looking off into space across the valley. "He's a good-lookin' speret, too. Lutie knows how to pick 'em."

"Have you seen him, Op?" Alf asked.

"I say I have," Theopolis answered quickly, "but only at a distance. I never got close. I've tried to. I've told Lutie to get 'im to come to the house so I can talk to 'im 'bout old times. I remember Ted back when I was a saplin' of a young man. Ted fit through the First World War, never got a scratch and come back here and was bushwhacked over Lucinda Dortch. Buried in the Freewill Baptist Churchyard, he is."

"Have you been seeing this Ted Newsome, Lutie?" Julia asked, staring hard at Lucretia.

"Yes," she admitted.

"And if he's not a speret, why won't he let me see 'im?" Op said. "Why does he come when I'm not here? The flowers on the table ye noticed tonight were picked by Ted Newsome's own hands. There's a feller here named Hootbird Hammertight and he's fallin' in love with 'er, too."

"Tell us about Ted Newsome, Lutie." Alf laughed. "And Hootbird Hammertight, too. What a name!"

"Hootbird lives down at Wince Leffard Gap, and Dad doesn't care for the Hammertights," she said. "He's warned me about Hootbird and prefers that I go with Ted Newsome." Lucretia turned away, frowning. It was obvious that she wanted a quick change of subject.

"Where does Ted Newsome live?" Alf persisted. "If the boys back in Dayton could only hear this one!"

Op cut in, annoyed. "He lives in his long home in the Free-will Baptist Graveyard. There's a stone out there a-showin' where he lives. And I wouldn't be a bit surprised if he ain't close here a-listenin' to us right now!"

"I once had an aunt who used to go to a medium," Alf mused. "She'd tell us about moving tables and hands in the air and the voices of the dead. But I never believed a word she said."

"That's dangerous talk, Alf," Op warned. "Fox hunters on this ridge have seen the old ore diggers back here a-diggin' ore. They've seen tall wagons a-goin' around this ridge loaded with charcoal and the drivers a-sittin' on the little seats a-crackin' their whips and yellin' at their teams. Ye don't know this coun-try! I've heard General Morgan and his men pass this cabin many a night when they spurred their hosses and yelled as they rode by. I've heard their hoofs beatin' against the ground like thunder and I've jumped up and run to the door!"

Jerry, who had been lying at Op's feet, climbed up into his lap. The wind was rising, and mournful sounds were coming from the horsehairs on the cabin walls.

"Onct when I'd been out on a long hunt, old Jerry and I got back to this cabin at about two in the mornin'," Op said. "That's just been two years this comin' November. The moon was down and the night was black as an old ground hearth where the col-liers ust to burn the cordwood into charcoal. I'd hold up my hand and couldn't see it before me. But I made it to the Laurel Ridge road from down under before the oil in my lantern was used up. And I felt my way with my feet along the ridge road to this cabin. When I got here I heard all sorts of noises in the cabin. I pressed my face against a winderpane and I saw white dishes all around my table. I could see the forks a-goin' up to their mouths and coming back to their plates. And I could hear their laughin' and talkin' same as I've heard all of ye here tonight. But I couldn't see a person around that table. They were men's voices around my table, jist like at one of the old boardin'-houses that ust to be on this ridge back in the ore-diggin' days. I knowed it was the ore diggers back fer a meal together like they ust to eat a hundred years ago on this ridge. But why do they haf to eat my grub? I thought. Why do they haf to use Beadie's dishes? So I went over and opened the door and rushed in. There was silence as I felt my way across the floor till I found a matchbox and lit the lamp. There was not a dish on the table. There was not a speret in the cabin. My grub hadn't been teched. I allus hated it that I broke up that party of men that had got together in my cabin!"

"Op, that's your imagination," Alf told him. "You must have dreamed it. I just can't believe that there are ghosts or that dead men return."

"Alf, ye're a-talkin' to the seventh son of the seventh son," Op retorted. "Some night over in that smokehouse, I'll haf to convince ye. Some sperets are seen. Some only knock. Atter the way ye talk, I doubt that a speret will show hisself to ye. But I'll raise the knockin' sperets fer ye. I'll raise old Red Jacket, the king of the knockin' sperets. When ye hear, I guess ye'll believe."

"I will when you convince me, Op," Alf said, stretching sleepily. "Now if I could only get into a tub and take a good hot bath, this evening would be perfect."

"But ye can't do that here unless we put a fire back in the stove and heat water in the teakettle and pour it into the wash-

102

tub," Op said. "We'd haf to carry more water from the spring, too."

"Why did you bring that up, Alf?" Julia asked. "Are you thinking of home?"

"No, no," he replied, frowning.

"Instead of carryin' the water up here, it's better to carry yerself to the water down in Red Bird Holler," Op told him. "That's where I go. The water's not exactly hot down there. It's shaded by the green leaves and the ferns, and the sun never shines on it. But atter a body takes a bath in that water, he feels like a new man. Think ye'd like fer me to take ye down there tonight?"

Alf shivered just thinking about it. "I'll wait for my hot bath, thank you. I'm ready to lie down for a night of good rest."

"Yep, ye've got to get into the smokehouse tomorrow," Op said. "What time have ye been gettin' up?"

"About seven-thirty," Julia said hopefully.

"Ye'll haf to be up by five in the mornin'," Op told them. "That's our gettin'-up time here."

24

"I feel like I've never gone to bed," Alf muttered as he followed Op across the garden. Op was swinging the lighted lantern as he stepped across the planted rows. The sky was full of stars and the wind cool. "I don't know when I've ever got out of bed this early before."

"It makes a body feel good to get up early," Op said briskly. "I've allus made it a practice to rise before the sun. I ust to rise at four."

Op pulled a little stick, which was fastened to the smokehouse with a string, from the staple. Then he pulled the hasp from over the staple and yanked on the door. It creaked on rusty hinges as it swung open.

"That's certainly a rustic door," Alf said as he stepped into the smokehouse.

In the yellow glow of lantern light, Alf looked about him at the little piles of roots lying in the cracks. He looked overhead at the bundles of stems tied to the rafters with hickory bark. There were joints of stovepipe tied with hickory bark. Over in one corner were the tools, axes, froes, handsaws, and mauls. In another corner squatted the body of a rusty stove. And across the far end of the smokehouse, opposite the door, was a three-fourths-size iron bed with springs attached.

"Say, that stove's not got any legs," Alf said, looking it over.

"That won't matter," Op told him.

"We can't let it set on the floor, can we?"

"Nope, we can't let it set belly-buster," he replied. "It might burn the smokehouse down. We can make it some legs!"

Alf was silent. He looked strangely at Theopolis.

"Ain't that a nice bed, Alf?" Op bragged, turning to the bed.

"It's not too bad," Alf said, shrugging his shoulders. "It's a little narrow. My wife and I are used to twin beds."

"I wouldn't have two beds in the house if I's young as ye, Alf." Op spoke to him in a somber tone. "What's the matter? Don't ye love yer wife?"

"C-certainly," he stammered. Op's words had taken him by surprise. "But a man can be in love with his wife and sleep in another bed."

"When Beadie and I kept house, we slept in a double bed," Op said. "There were cracks in our shack back in them days. I was a little keerless and Beadie complained about the wind a-blowin' in. But every time she complained about gettin' cold, I'd hug 'er close and put 'er feet with mine. Her head would

104

use my arm fer a piller and her cheek would touch mine and we'd get warm as young redbirds in a soft-lined nest in late May. Offen I'd dream of gatherin' peaches on a hot July day while the winter winds blowed through the cracks over Beadie and me. A man should sleep with his wife, Alf. It's good fer nervousness, too. This three-quarter bed will be the thing fer ye. Solve all yer problems."

"But we'll want these cracks closed for the winter," Alf told Theopolis. "This would be just a little too rough—on Julia, I mean."

"Ye'll be surprised what a woman can stand," Op answered. "They'll complain at first. But it will be the real test of love. If Julia loves ye she'll stay with ye, cracks or no cracks. If she won't stay with ye, then she don't love ye. Don't be afraid to try this test of love. I tried it in my young days with Beadie. She loved me then. Poor Beadie, long dead and gone, but she thinks of me. She still loves me, Alf. Jist the other night she appeared to me in the cabin!"

"What?" Alf was astonished.

"She was back to see me," Op said, his voice softening. "She looked into my face in the cabin. I saw her plain as I see ye now. It made my knees tremble when I got outten the bed. I thought it was a token of some kind, her a-comin' back to see me. I thought somethin' might be a-goin' to happen to Lutie! Thought somethin' might've happened to Jack!"

"I've heard Aunt Corrinne and Uncle Will talk about your son Jack," Alf said.

"Ye never heard 'em say anything good about Jack." Op's voice got angry. "I've stuck to that boy. I've raised 'im. And I worry about 'im."

"Where's Jack now?"

"Ye know as much about 'im as I do," Op said sadly. "Jack's been in as many states as ye have, Alf. He's been places I ain't seen and never will. He's like the spiders that the warm air lifts toward the sun on little silver ropes. He's somewhere on a farm, I'd think, a-drivin' two big hosses. I've been lookin' fer 'im since butterflies have come back!"

"Butterflies?"

"He's raised up with 'em," Op replied. "Little feller ust to hunt with me in winter. And he got acquainted with wild animals. And when I'd start to kill one, he'd cry. I'd haf to get away from Jack when I broke a possum's neck with my ax handle over it and my two feet down on the ax handle and a-pullin' on the possum's tail. Jack allus loved for the huntin' season to be over and spring to come so he could chase the butterflies. He's a big strong boy with the heart and mind of a child. He never had any young uns to play with 'im when he's little so he played with butterflies and wild animals, land turtles and even little harmless ground snakes."

"I never heard that about Jack," Alf said.

"Nope, ye heard he's simple-minded from Corrinne and Will," Op snapped. "Jack'll be roundin' in here one of these days soon, if he's still alive, with his butterfly net. He never kills 'em, allus turns 'em back on the wind."

Op walked over to the corner of the smokehouse and picked up an ax.

"We've got to get ye into yer new home, Alf," he said. "Now, as I whack the bark that's holdin' the stems to the rafters and let 'em fall, ye ketch 'em."

Op reached overhead with his ax and whacked the bark holding a bundle of stems. Alf stood under it with his hands far apart, and the stems bounced off his shoulder. Op went around the smokehouse, cutting them down. When he came to the stovepipe joints, he told Alf to stand aside. He swung the double-bitted ax overhead with one hand and cut the hickory bark that held them. The pipes came tumbling down with a clatter, and Alf jumped for the door.

Since daylight came to the ridgetop early, stars had now set for morn. Theopolis blew the light from his lantern and glanced at Alf. "Ye're so skeery I'm afeared ye might burn yerself up with a lamp. Ye can help take some of these things to my cabin now. I'll give ye a light load so ye won't break down."

25

Op and Alf carried the tools and bundles of stems from the smokehouse and put them under the cabin floor. Op laid his stems away carefully in the little dry pockets where the sills fit onto the sleepers. His short-handled tools he put here too, while the long-handled ones he left on the ground. He was even more careful with the roots he had gathered. He took them inside the cabin and put them in a dresser drawer.

"There's a lot of work a-gatherin' these yarbs," he said. "Here's enough medicine to cure all the ailin' people in Honeywell. I'm a-takin' keer of these yarbs and a-gatherin' more this summer. A body must have plenty of 'em when the deep snows fall on Laurel Ridge and the winds drift the snow. I've seen drifts up to my ears in the little hollers."

Op was taking a half dozen meat rinds from the warmer above his stove when Lutie and Julia staggered in under a load of mops, brooms, pails, and dust rags. Each had a bandanna tied over her hair, and on Julia's face there was a comical expression of unbelieving.

"I've never done much mopping," she said. "I have it done in Dayton."

"Ye'll do it yerself here, if it's to be done at all," Op said. "It won't hurt ye to use a little elbow grease."

The four of them walked toward the smokehouse in silence. Op watched Julia stepping to miss each little pebble and clod and frowned in disgust.

"So this is my new home!" Julia stood in amazement, peering into the smokehouse. She was trying to sound happy and excited but not quite making the grade.

"This is it all right," Alf told her heartily.

After staring in disbelief for another moment, Julia grabbed a broom and began sweeping the cabin floor feverishly. "From the looks of these cracks, our new home might be a little airish, even on warm nights." She laughed shakily.

"Sleep close together's what I told Alf," Op retorted.

Julia stopped sweeping. She looked strangely at Theopolis. "Even the stove's not got legs," she said, changing the subject.

"We'll fix that," Op said. "We'll make it some legs."

Then Op started applying one of the meat rinds to the stove. "A meat rind is a wonderful thing," he explained. "Each November, atter Fidis Artner butchers, I ketch 'im a mess of fish fer meat rinds enough to last me the season. Old Fidis ain't much of a fisherman and he loves fish. So I trade 'im fish fer meat rinds. I grease my bread pan with a meat rind. I grease my rifle barrel to keep it from rustin'. I use 'em on my stove in the cabin to make it purty and shiny. I use 'em to grease my boots so the water won't soak into the leather when I walk in the November rains and the deep snows in winter. There's not anythin' more valuable to me on this ridge than the meat rind. I even use 'em fer animal bait and fish bait. You'll haf to get ust to a meat rind, Julia, if ye stay here."

Julia looked at the greasy rind in Op's hand and changed the subject again. "Where did you buy this bed, Op?"

"Didn't buy it at all, but it's a dandy, ain't it?"

108

"Yes, it's—it's very good looking."

"Ye didn't come past the junk pile yesterday where Honeywell hauls its garbage, did ye? About a half mile this side the town beside the road and just above Sandy River? I come along there one day and found this bed, so I toted it up here to use in the smokehouse. Thought if ever my cabin burnt down I'd have myself another bed."

When Op finished greasing the small flat-topped stove, it looked like new. Then he used the meat rinds on the stovepipes to remove a few dots of rust. And while Lucretia wiped dust from the bed and Julia swept the floor, Op and Alf went outside the smokehouse and found four flat stones. Op placed the stones on the floor and he and Alf lifted the small stove upon them.

"Dad, where'll you put the stovepipe?" Lucretia asked. "There's not a flue in this smokehouse."

"I'll show ye," he said.

Op put his toes in the cracks between the logs and climbed carefully up to the top of the window. Holding on with one hand, he took his knife from his pocket, removed putty and tacks that held the pane in the sash. He lifted the pane from the sash and handed it down. Then he arranged the stovepipe, while Alf watched helplessly. He used the elbow and directed the pipe through the open hole where he had removed the pane.

"That's got it," he said. "Just as good as a flue."

"But how'll I raise the window?" Alf asked.

"Ye can raise the bottom sash up to the pipe, can't ye?" Op said. "If ye can't, have Julia to raise it fer ye. If she can't, call on me."

"We won't need to raise the window, honey," Julia smiled. "We'll get plenty of fresh air. Look at these cracks."

After Lucretia had mopped one corner of the smokehouse, Op and Alf heaved on the iron bed to set it in the corner.

"I don't see how you ever packed it from Honeywell," Alf grunted as he strained to lift one end.

"This ain't heavy," Op said. "When ye pack as much as I have, ye'll get ust to it. That's the only way ye can get anythin' up here. Remember that. Ye gotta be a good pack hoss, Alf!"

They worked until noon getting the cabin ready. Op had a spare bedtick filled with bright oak leaves he'd gathered in sunny October. "I don't think I raked up any snakes in these leaves," he said. "I'll loan ye this bed to sleep on, leaves and all." Then Op fetched Alf a large water bucket. Alf and Julia had brought a change of sheets and blankets, and such as drinking cups, towels, knives, forks, spoons, and dishes. As they unpacked, Theopolis's face grew longer and longer. They were really a-movin' in.

"Here, Alf," Op sighed finally, "if ye're bent on a-stayin', I want to loan ye this most useful tool on Laurel Ridge." He reached for a double-bitted ax. "It's the dullest one I got. Won't cut hot butter. There won't be any danger of ye a-knickin' yerself."

26

After lunch, Op and Alf, with axes across their shoulders, went out Laurel Ridge toward the sty. After they had walked a few hundred yards on the level ridge road, Op turned right into the deep green wood.

"Follow me, Alf," he said.

Op waded up to his knees into the deep pea vine that covered the dark loamy earth like a green plush carpet. Alf sniffled the fragrant smell of the pea vine as he followed Op's broken path deeper down the slope.

"What kind of ground is this?" Alf asked.

"Jist ground," Op said.

"Is this green stuff any good for anything?"

"Wonderful pickin' fer cattle."

"It's a shame to waste land like this," Alf said. "This ought to be cultivated. I'd sure love to own about two hundred acres."

"What would ye do with it?" Op asked curiously as he looked this way and that for a small dead tree. "Ye couldn't do anythin' with it, could ye?"

"I'd cut the trees, make meadows, grow corn and tobacco," he said.

"Then ye'd ruin it." Op was disgusted. "The loam on these slopes would all wash down into the valleys and soon the hills would turn yellow and be gully-streaked."

"But it doesn't produce like it is?"

"It *does* produce," Theopolis answered quickly. "Look at these trees. Look at these yarbs. Ginseng under my feet. Look at it. Takes good land to grow ginseng."

"Yes, but it doesn't produce anything that will make you money."

"It does if ye know the right roots to dig and where to find the nuts and the berries," Theopolis replied. "It produces all a body needs!"

"But wouldn't tobacco be more profitable?" Alf persisted. "Say you raised an acre of tobacco. Wouldn't that make you money?" In his mind, the green acres had become a long string of digits for adding and depositing in a bankbook.

"Calmus weed is better'n terbacker," Op told him. "Ye want to ruin this land, Alf?" Theopolis stopped in the green carpet of pea vine which was up to his thighs. Above the pea vine stood the tall yellow poplars, their first limbs twenty feet up and the wind rustling their soft soap-bellied leaves. "Did ye say ye'd clear this land and farm it if ye had it? What would ye do with these big poplars?"

"I'd sell 'em for timber!"

"I hope ye never buy any land near me," Op told him. "I hope Snake Blue keeps it as long as he lives and his son takes over and keeps it like old Snake has. Ye hunt a safe place in the world and first thing ye have in mind idears that would destroy it."

"But if you'd clear some land, you could raise cattle and hogs and be self-sufficient here when the rest of this country is destroyed by the bomb." Alf was getting excited by his vision. "I'd dam one of these little streams and have a small electric plant built so I could have refrigeration and lights and heat and everything."

"If ye know where to find the old pine stumps and dig 'em up and split 'em into kindlin' with an ax, ye'll have plenty of light," Op said. "Pine torches make wonderful lights and they're cheap. All a body has to do is dig their roots from the ground. And if he looks close and finds a pine log rich with resin, then he has somethin'. That's the kind of kindlin' I store fer winter. Ye can't beat rich pine." He looked around at the rich green carpet covering the land. "And, Alf, ye don't haf to raise corn and have cattle here. There's enough wild game to furnish a body meat. Enough nuts on these trees to take the place of corn. The kernels from the black walnut and butternut are sweeter'n the kernels from corn! Why work and dig and tear up somethin' God Almighty has made, when there's no use to it? This won't be my land any more when it's torn up and destroyed."

"But it's not your land now," Alf reminded him. "You told me it belonged to Snake Blue."

"He's got the deed on paper," Op said. "I've got the deed fer it in my heart. I own this land more'n anybody else." Op turned disgustedly and started breaking a path through the pea vine.

"But I'm thinking farther ahead," Alf said as he followed. "I know we're in for trouble in the future. Each family ought to establish itself on a little spot where it can be self-sufficient. That's more important than pea vine and tall trees when the atomic bombs rain down and destroy this earth with fire."

"I don't believe all that, Alf." Op shook his head and his long uncut hair waved in the breeze. "This earth won't be destroyed. Not by any kind o' bumbs. They might burn the cities and scorch the earth, but there'll be people left to start it all over agin. I don't think ye ought to worry like ye do about the adam bumbs. Shucks, I ain't a-worryin' about 'em. I never heard 'em mentioned before ye come out here!" He turned suddenly and bumped into Alf. "Now people in Honeywell have really got somethin' to worry 'em."

"What could possibly worry them more than atomic bombs?"

"All the bottoms are a-fallin' outten their wells," Op said. "Not a well in that town with a bottom in it. That town might sink. Shucks, I never did trust a valley!"

"What?" Alf peered at Theopolis. Perhaps the old man was kidding him like the boys back at the plant used to do. "Do you mean that—?"

"Are ye right with Him on High, Alf?" Op interrupted.

"Why, I think I am," Alf stammered.

"Then it's safe ye to go to Honeywell," Op said, looking up at the trees. "If a body is right, he don't think. He knows it. He'd better be numbered with the blest if he wants to live ferever and soar back over Laurel Ridge. There's a lot of people I want to hear my wings a-flutterin' against their winderpanes at night. A lot of people I want to float over like a big chicken hawk, pumpin' my wings jist a little and kickin' the bright air with my feet like I'm a-swimmin' up there above 'em. Yep, I want to skeer the mortal hell outten a few people. Old Doshie's one. I'll make 'er think 'er little short legs are a-ailin' 'er. When

I get through floatin' above 'er, a-fannin' the wind and kickin' the air, she'll take off faster'n she's ever run in 'er life. I'll dive at 'er all the way from Honeywell to Wince Leffard Gap. Make 'er even drap some of that good grub she's begged in Honeywell. I'll have old Hootbird a-runnin', too. I'll be better to Ben. I allus liked old slow Ben!"

"Are you sure, Op, the bottoms have dropped out of the wells in Honeywell?" Alf asked. "I'll have to be going back there for the rest of our supplies we sent by parcel post."

"Don't let it worry ye, Alf," Op said. "But I don't know of a well in the town with a bottom in it. All of 'em are tiled right down in the sand. They never could wall one up with rocks like I walled my spring so the good freestone water could ooze in from the old dirt. And a long time ago when Pap was a boy, there was a break clear out to Lonesome Hill—that's the Honeywell Graveyard. It went out from Big River in the shape of an oxbow and then went back to Big River. All of Honeywell was inside that break. It was so deep ye couldn't see the bottom. I've heard people could walk up and look down and sniff the brimstone."

"Did the people move?"

"How could they?" Op asked. "They'd a-had to've swum the river 'r built a bridge across the break. They stuck to that island and prayed. The strong men trembled and the wimmen with pride lowered their faces till the rain stopped fallin' into their nostrils."

"Then what happened?" Alf asked shakily. "I didn't see a break or any sign of one when Julia and I walked out here."

"That break closed up in a single night," Op said. "And fer a long time atter that, the merchants in that town started treatin' the country people right, they were that skeered. Yessir, the Old Master takes keer of his own. That town is jist a-sittin' there

114

on a ledge of ground with all the underpinnin' gone. The Master can spring the trap any time. He's warned 'em by lettin' the bottoms fall from their wells. It's a token."

Alf followed slowly in silence as Op crossed a deep ravine and climbed a steep bluff on the other side.

"I see good stovewood poles, Alf," Op said. "Dead dogwoods." Theopolis walked up to one and laid his hand on the naked, dry, seasoned body where the dead bark had fallen.

"Why have these dogwoods died?" Alf was glad for a new topic of conversation.

"It's Nature's way," Theopolis explained. "Diseases kill people and thin 'em out. Big trees grow up and smother the little uns. Trees thin themselves out. But nothin' can squeeze out the tough-butted white oaks. These tall poplars squeezed out the little dogwoods. All of 'em are dead around here. But they make wonderful stovewood. I'll let ye cut this tree, Alf. I want to see how well ye can use an ax."

"First, I'll get myself squared away," Alf explained. He backed away from the little tree like a crayfish backs in water. "Then, I'll let the tree have the works!"

Alf planted his feet firmly on the bluff as if he were about to begin cutting down one of the giant poplars, and then sighted down the ax as if he were looking down a rifle barrel and lining up sights. Then his thin body bent backward and he came down with a stiff-armed swing. The axhead struck the wind beyond the tree, the ax handle hit the tree and broke. The ax mowed a path through the pea vine and then sank into the soft loam.

"I missed the tree," Alfred said, surprised. "What do you think of that?"

"Not much." Op groveled down in the soft loam for his double-bitted ax. "That's the reason I gave ye a dull ax. I was

115

afraid ye might hurt yerself." Then Op turned to Alf who was holding the broken ax handle. "Alf, I heard ye say ye made eight thousand dollars a year in Dayton."

"I certainly did," he answered quickly. "Why?"

"I'm a-thinkin' of that big money," Op said, shaking his head. "Put ye on yer own and let ye scratch fer a livin', I believe ye'd starve to death." He came up with the axhead. "I'll chop down these dead dogwoods. Ye watch me. And this afternoon, I'll put a handle in yer ax and I'll larn ye how to chop wood on a block. Ye're a-livin' in my smokehouse, but I ain't a-goin' to chop yer stovewood. Ye'll haf to larn to work—'r starve."

27

The sun was still high above the Allcorn Hills. Laurel Ridge was a place, the fox hunters had often said, where the sun never set. But the day was done for Alf and Op. Op had shown Alf all afternoon how to stand near his chopblock and swing his ax. And when Alf had tired of swinging the ax, Op had chopped a few sticks of wood for his stove. Lucretia had helped Julia with the final cleaning up in the smokehouse, knowing how Op disliked visitors in his cabin. Sometimes Op's stubborn independence made Lucretia wonder about his attitude toward her. Would he prefer to be left alone again, now that he could see?

Julia, working hard with her hands for the first time in years, wondered about Ted Newsome, the "good speret." She and Lutie had returned from the cabin after lunch to find another bouquet of fresh wild flowers on the little table they had borrowed from Op. It had been a very long day for all of them and a very strange day for Alf and Julia. Back at the cabin, Alf com-

116

plained of being sticky and that he had to have a bath. Op led the way to the water.

"One of the things I miss here is my good hot bath," Alf said as he carried soap and a cloth in his hand and a towel across his shoulder. "I like a bathtub filled to the top with soapy water so hot it nearly burns me. I like to sit in it and soak myself and read the newspaper."

"Ye'll get a good deep hole of water down here, too." Op pointed down the path toward the spring. "More water down here than ye can get in a tub. I can take ye to holes under the tall poplars where the water's thigh deep, navel deep, or neck deep. Give ye yer choice. 'Course it's cool water, good cool water that fills up a bathtub made of dirt and ringed with ferns. Think if ye take a few baths down here, ye'll never want another man-made tub."

"I don't know about this cool water," Alf grumbled. "Now back home—"

Op interrupted him, looking down at Alf's shoes. "After this ye'd better have on boots like I got instead of them low-cuts. I've got a lot of snake teeth in these boots!"

"What kind of snake teeth?"

"Oh, copperhead, rattlesnake, water moccasin," Op answered. "A lot of copperhead and water-moccasin teeth but not many rattlesnake. The rattlesnakes allus give warnin' and I go some other way. I don't keer too much about goin' the same way with a rattlesnake."

"Did a snake ever bite you, Op?" Alf walked closer on Theopolis's heels.

"First time a snake ever bit me I was six-years old," Op said. "That was back in the days when I ust to spend my Sundays a-wadin' up and down the Little White Oak creek, carryin' a club about the size of a mattock handle, a-killin' water moccasins fer fun. I'd slip up on one and let 'im have it across the head. If he saw me first and fell offen a rock or overhangin' limb into a hole of water, I'd muddy the water. A water moccasin can't stand muddy water very long. After I muddied the water, I'd wade into a hole and stand with my club over my shoulder ready to strike. When the moccasin stuck his head up from the muddy water, he'd be a goner. I'd let 'im have it right on the bean and I can jist see that stuff spread over the water like the juice from a milkweed stem. It was a lot of fun. I wasn't old enough then to tote a pistol on Sundays and shoot at lizards a-runnin' up the scaly-barked oaks. That was the sport of the older fellers like Ted Newsome. I wasn't twelve yet. So I had to play along the creek and find my own way of havin' fun."

Op walked past the spring in Red Bird Hollow. The path narrowed beyond the spring and the long wild-blackberry and raspberry vines lapped over. They would soon cover what had once been a path. Op parted the wild-berry vines so Alf could follow.

"The first un that bit me," Op continued, "was a big, old, rusty-colored water moccasin, fat on creek minners, 'r heavy with young. It was a-sunnin' on the bank, and when I went up with my club ready to strike, the snake didn't get outten my way. It quiled, ready to strike. I stepped back and I said, 'Ye wouldn't fight me.' Then I stuck my big toe up to the snake and when it was ready to strike, I was too quick fer it. I'd jerk my toe back. So we played a little game fer a half hour or so. I'd stick my toe up and it would wiggle its big rusty-colored body back and get ready to swaller my toe and I'd disappint it. When I got my toe back, I'd do a powerful lot of laughin'. You know a water moccasin is the illest of all snakes. It's a lot of fun to tease one. So I kept on and if I hadn't a-got so tickled it wouldn't have bit me. I got to laughin' till I could hardly stand up and I didn't get my toe back in time. So it swallered my big toe and

118

sunk its fangs in and I took off a-screamin'. It stung like fire. I didn't even know whether one was pizen 'r not. I run all the way home and told Pa. 'Dadwrought it, Little Op,' he said, 'ye'll go out in the world a weaklin'. Can't ye take a water-moccasin bite? Ain't any more than a bumblebee sting.' Pap made me ashamed of myself and it quit hurtin'."

"But I thought water moccasins were deadly poisonous." Alf's voice had a little shake in it. He was walking so close to Op he was almost climbing his back.

"Nope, not the long, lazy kind we have around here, anyways. They just sting ye a little. Now with a copperhead, it's different."

"Did you ever have a copperhead bite you?"

"I shore did, Alf." They had reached a quiet pool of blue water. It was under the tall poplars and shaded by a fringe of ferns on each side that looked like long, green, feathery eyelashes around a big blue eye. Theopolis stopped beside the pool. "We're at the bathtub, Alf," he said. "There are other holes on down the creek but this is the best one. It's about navel deep on ye."

Op started unbuttoning his shirt. Then he threw his hat on the pea vines.

"About that copperhead that bit me," he talked on. "One evenin' late we young uns were a-sittin' in the front yard with Pap and Ma. We'd hoed a little corn that day and in the evenin' we were a-sittin' there takin' it easy a-lookin' up at the sky every now and then. We allus looked fer signs in the skies. And onct when I looked up, I saw a star leave the sky. It was a gollywhopper in size. I thought it was a-comin' smack down on us. There was a big gold streak right down through the blue evenin' air. And I jumped up and screamed. Pap and Ma saw it jist in time. It lit on the bluff in a locust patch across the creek from our shack. And when it hit, I started runnin' toward the very place a-keepin' my eye on the spot. I stuck up a stick on the very spot where it fell. When my brothers started claimin' part of what I was goin' to find, Pap said: 'Boys, I allus teached ye decency and order. And the finder here will be the keeper. The finder is Little Op.'

"So I went to bed that night dreamin' of the pot of gold I'd find where that star fell." Theopolis sat on the ground to unlace his brier-scratched boots. "I knowed the fallin' of that star was a token. It wouldn't 've come down there without a purpose. Gold in the ground not a-doin' anybody any good and we'd as well have it. I even dreamed about the money. Big, bright, shiny gold pieces in a pot, a two-gallon size, the kind Ma ust to cook green beans in with a big hunk of jowl pork. I dreamed I's right down to that pot, and it took Pap and Brother Beany to help me lift it from the ground. And when we raised the lid and saw the shinin' gold, that was too much fer me and I woke up and didn't get my hands on it. Thinks I, 'I'll have my hands on ye in the mornin'.'

"I's up bright and early, four in the mornin', when Pap got up first to fire the cookstove." Op talked on, undressing all the while. "And jist atter breakfast when the first light streaks popped over Cornpone Hill, I had my mattock across my shoulder and I took off up the hill past the well to the locust thicket. I found my stick and I started diggin'. I didn't see a movement of any kind around the place. I was a-diggin' fer who-laid-the-chunk and all bent over when I was hit from behind. I wheeled around, and somethin' long and almost the color of the gold I was a-diggin' to find swung around like a tail on a dumb brute. Soon as I got a glimpse, I let out a scream and Pap was on his way from the yard. He started runnin' toward me, but I'd pulled my pocketknife and reached around and got it right by the neck and choked him to pry his mouth open. He was a-tryin' to let loose because that's the way a copperhead bites. Lets loose and

120

lets ye have it agin and agin. I choked 'im good so he wouldn't leave a fang in my rind, and he let loose. I put the knife to his neck first thing I did. I knowed he'd never bite anybody else. By that time Pap was to me. And it's a rule around here when a body's bit by a copperhead, first person to 'im hast to cut a cross across the bite and suck the blood and spit it out. Pap was a-shavin' when he heard me first let out a scream and he fetched a long black-handled razor. 'Pull yer pants, Little Op,' he said to me. And that's what I done in a hurry. Pap laid a cross on my rind. 'What a copperhead, Little Op!' he said to me. 'It might be the last of ye. Biggest un I've ever seen yet. And powerful it must've been to strike uphill and jump that high to get ye.' Pap worked on all the pizen he could."

Op had removed his long white drawers and stood naked on the brink of the pool.

Is Op a varmint or a man? Alf wondered. He had taken a fleeting glance at Theopolis to see if he bathed often. But he couldn't see Op's skin. He was wooly from his neck to his toes except for the tops of his feet. His back was covered and his shoulders too. A streak up his back along his backbone was visible, for the long hair parted in different directions like a part on a man's head. A picture of Op ought to be on every bottle of he-man skin bracer, Alf thought. How could a snake bite him? Op leaped into the water with a washcloth and a bar of soap in his hand. He kept right on telling Alf about his copperhead bite.

"Now there're remedies we ust to have fer a copperhead bite," he said as he began laying down the wool on his body with water and soap. "I said to Pap: 'Don't give me the black-powder cure! I don't want it, Pap.' If Pap had a-given me the black-powder cure, I'd a-had to've turned my naked starn end to 'im and let 'im a-shot me seven times with cartridges without bullets. I'd seen Pap do it once to old Ike Strickland when he's bitten on the foot by a copperhead. Every time Pap burnt his foot with black powder, Ike'd let out a wild scream and kick like a mule until Pap would haf to place his foot back just right on the ground and let 'im have it agin. I didn't want to be burnt no seven times and Pap a-standin' right up close with his thirty-eight special. So said I, 'Pap, I want the black-cat cure.' "

Alf stood naked in the slow-moving wind with his teeth chattering. He looked at the pool and Op looked up at him with his good eye. There he stood, a lean, hairless man, his skin pink and his bones protruding against the skin like the ribs of a willow basket. Op stopped talking and watched while Alf took hold of his nose with his thumb and index finger on one hand and with the other held his cloth and bar of soap. He closed his eyes, shuddered all over, and made a wild leap into the pool, hitting it belly buster and splashing water in all directions. He let out a scream. Wonder if he goes into his bathtub that way, Op thought. Alf finally got his feet on the bottom and straightened himself up.

"That's the only way I could do it, Op," he said, his teeth rattling like pebbles washing over rock cliffs in a spring rain. "Go on with your story."

" 'Shoot the cat,' Pap yelled to Brother Beany," Op said. " 'Do it in a hurry!' And not much sooner said than done, I heard the shotgun go off. 'Shoot that old black minarky rooster too,' Pap screamed, as the old black tomcat lay on the yard a-kickin'. 'K-boom,' I heard another shot down by the stable. 'Now fetch 'em to me in a hurry,' Pap said. 'Fetch 'em while they're still a-kickin'.' "

Alf said shakily, "I'd rather die of the bite, I think."

"I walked like a string-haltered hoss down the bluff from the locust thicket," Op said. "Pap fetched the mattock down to the yard and he give it to Brother Adger. 'Start diggin',' he told 'im. 'Right out there in the garden where the ground is soft.

Dig in a hurry.' Brother Adger knowed exactly what to do. He knowed how deep to dig, fer he'd done it before. 'Take off yer pants agin,' Pap said to me. 'We've got to work fast, boy.' Ma come with a sheet and Pap split that old black tomcat right down the stummick and slapped his warm entrails and blood right on the bite. While Ma, who was a-sheddin' tears, held the tomcat on, Pap split the rooster and laid it on over that cat. He tied the chicken and cat around me with strings. Then they put the white sheet around the whole thing. But the sheet wasn't white very long. It soon turned red. 'That'll fetch the pizen if anythin' will,' Pap said. 'Come sit down in this hole.' "

Op noticed that Alf looked even whiter than before, but he went right on.

"Brother Beany had dug a hole big enough in the soft garden dirt to bury me in. I got down in that hole and Brother Beany started shovelin' the dirt around me till I was buried well above my navel. And all that day, old friends, a-hearin' about the token I'd seen that baited me on fer gold and the kind of gold I'd discovered, come to see me. I guess that's one of the reasons I never had a hankerin' fer gold in my lifetime. That teached me a lesson. When I think of the people who come to see me! They looked so tall a-standin' up there a-lookin' down, I felt awful small. I had to haf my dinner carried to me in the garden. I felt like half a man."

"Didn't it make you sick?" Alf splashed in the cold water, trying to keep his circulation going.

"When the sun got up high over the garden in the afternoon and shined down on me half buried alive there, my head dropped over to one side and then the other like a sunflower head wilted in the sun. My neck would hardly hold my head up. But atter twelve hours I's all right. Never got real sick. That black-powder cure would have burnt me till I couldn't have sat down fer a month. Black powder is shore a rough cure, Alf. I've seen both of 'em used many a time among the old people. Both good remedies but I'd rather have the copperhead bite than the black-powder cure. I'd take the black-cat cure every time."

"Are there many copperheads around here?"

"Woods are full of 'em." Op lifted a leg from the water and soaped it down to his foot. "One night I's out to Six Hickories a-possum huntin' with old Jerry and I carried a blanket with me and laid down on it at about three in the mornin' and looked up at the stars and was a-thinkin' about who all was up in that land beyond the blue and I begin to feel somethin' wiggle under me. I couldn't see too well then. That was when I was losing my sight. But I jumped up when Jerry got back from a long hunt. I raised the blanket and old Jerry grabbed somethin' and begin to shake it apart. One of the biggest copperheads ever kilt on Laurel Ridge. Longer than a fence post and big around as my forearm. He was an old residenter that had crawled from the Artner rocks down under. Jerry spiled his a-tryin' to get me."

Alf pulled himself up by the ferns until he could hold onto a poplar root. Then he clawed his way to the top of the bank. He turned his back to Op and rubbed his body with a towel to an early-turning sassafras-leaf pinkness. Op played in the cool water, enjoying every minute like a native speckled-bellied water dog. When he was ready to come out of his earthen bathtub, Op laid his hand upon the high bank and with the strength of his one arm leaped up like a fish out of water onto the bank in a squatting position. Then he rose and shook himself like a wet, heavy-feathered rooster.

"You'll feel like a new man now, Alf. Cold water will soothe yer nerves and make ye want to sleep. Hot water will keep ye awake all night. I never tried hot water but onct in my life. That done me."

"I never had a bath like this one," Alf said. "I'll remember it as long as I live."

124

Op was back in his clothes already and lacing his second boot. "You've got me scared to death of copperheads." Alf was jittery again. "I'll be afraid to walk back up this path."

"Ye walk in front," Op said, rising up. "I'll walk behind."

"What! You send me in front and you wear your boots!" Alf was irritated.

"The man that walks in front stirs the snake and gets 'im ready to bite," Op explained. "Ye walk in front and if there's a copperhead, he'll get ready and when he strikes, he'll hit one of my boots. I'll be over 'im about the time he's quiled and ready!"

"That s-sounds logical, Op."

"A lot of people don't know about snakes. Like birds. I've kilt many a black snake when he was a-charmin' a bird so he could climb up and swaller it. Bird jist sat there bound by the charm and couldn't flutter a wing."

Walking up Red Bird Hollow, Alf was in front and Theopolis followed. Alf pulled back the wild-berry vines and hurried along. "At least the bomb would finish one instantly. But to be bitten by a snake might mean a slow, painful death."

"I don't want to be burnt up," Op chuckled. "I'll take the snakebite. A feller has a chance. Fer instance, onct when I was a-walkin' from Honeywell, jist along about where the dump pile is beside the Sandy, Sallie Artner come along there a-drivin' one of old Fidis's gray hosses hitched to the buggy. I looked up and I could tell somethin' was the matter with 'er. She was as white as a milkweed furze. When she didn't speak to me, as friendly a gal as she was, I knowed somethin' was the matter. I ran over and held the hoss, put my foot on the buggy stirrup, and went up into that buggy jist in time. Sallie was about to breathe her last. A big cow snake had planted itself in the buggy when it was in the barn entry. A snake's got a lot of sense. It planted itself there to get Sallie. It had crawled up under 'er dress 'n' wrapped itself around three 'r four times 'n' was a-squeezin' 'er to death. I tore part of 'er dress off to get to the snake, cut it in two in nine places to get it off. Figured she'd rather be embarrassed than dead. Saved 'er life. She'd tell ye if she's here now, but she lives in Baltimore."

Alf let out a long sigh when he reached the broad worn path at the spring. He increased his pace as he climbed the hill with Op still behind him.

"But the bigger a snake the more harmless he is." Op talked on as Alf continued climbing, getting his breath like a tired horse. "Right betwixt the spring and where we took a bath, I onct laid down across a log to drink from a purty little spring where the water biled up from the ground. I was jist beginnin' to drink when the log started movin'. I guess that was the biggest snake ever seen in these parts. He made a path up the hill through the pea vine, like where a hoss had pulled a small log. And I followed 'im from behind. I didn't get too close afeared he'd turn and swaller me whole. He went down among the Artner rocks and went back in his den, a big cliff over there. That's one reason I thought it might be better fer ye and Julia to live in my smokehouse instead of on Artner cliff. I've never heard of anybody ever a-killin' that big snake. Boy, there're some gollywhoppin' snakes on Laurel Ridge!"

Alf reached the cabin out of breath. Op walked up beside him and stood listening to Alf breathe. "Anythin' else I can do fer ye tonight, Alf?" Op asked.

"Yes, Op, just wait here and see that I get to the smokehouse safely." He started across the garden path in a wobbly trot.

28

"Yep, now's the time, Alf," Op said proudly. "The turtle season is on. I'm hungry fer turtle meat!"

The two men were barefooted and their pants were rolled above their knees. Alf's feet were tender and he looked down at the path and chose the smooth places to step. He walked as if he were stepping on eggs.

"Ouch, I stepped on a rock," he fretted, holding up his white, tender foot.

"Put yer feet down and get ust to it," Op growled. "Grit yer teeth together and tell yerself it don't hurt to step on a little rock barefooted."

"But I'd be lying to myself. It does hurt."

"The water will be soft," Op said, "when we get into the creek. There will be soft mud on the bottom and it will be like a-walkin' on cool winter moss."

Theopolis carried his hunting knife in a sheath on his hip. That was all he took with him for hunting turtles. When the two men walked from the well-worn path that led to the spring onto the narrow path down to the hole where they bathed, Op stopped beside a little hickory. He took the knife from the sheath, reached high above his head and peeled down a strip of hickory bark to the ground. Then he peeled another strip down the same width and length and then a third and fourth.

"What are you peeling that tree for, Op?"

"Look on now and larn later." The man was always askin' questions. He never jist watched and larned for himself.

Op used his knife and peeled away the coarse bark, exposing the long thongs of inner hickory bark which was both durable and pliable. He wound these around his elbow and between his thumb and forefinger into a little bundle.

"That's neat work," Alf told him.

"I ought to be able to do it neatly," he said. "I've peeled enough hickory bark in my day to bottom chairs and use fer ropes. I've tried about everythin'. But a body can't get anythin' to tie with he can trust like hickory bark."

Then Op said: "Here's where the creek really begins, where I jump in. Carry the bark."

He jumped into the deep hole where the water came up to his navel. Alf fidgeted nervously along the edge of the bank while Op waded around in the pool and fingered under the bank with his bare hands. Where the water had splashed against the dirt walls it had left overhanging turf matted with the roots of ferns and wild snowballs. Op circled the pool, putting his hand back into every crevice.

"You mean you catch turtles with your hands?" Alf said. "And there's a possibility of finding one where we've been bathing?"

"Yep," Op replied as he fingered under the turf. "We might find one here."

"Won't a turtle bite?"

"Yep, they'll bite all right."

"Ever have one bite you?"

"Nope, never have." He fingered another spot. "Never want one to bite me either. A turtle is like an old stud terrapin. When one grabs a body it won't let loose till it thunders. If it don't thunder, he'll let go when the sun does down."

"Aren't you afraid one will grab you by the hand?"

"Nope," Op grunted. "When I want turtle meat I go ketch me a mess of turtles. A body hast to eat. And up here if a body don't go atter his grub, he won't eat. That's the way it's allus been with me. It's a lot of fun to ketch turtles but I don't do it exactly fer fun. I do it to eat."

Op jumped up from the hole and onto the bank, the cold blue water streaming from his clothes. "No turtle in there."

"I should hope not," Alf sounded relieved. "Not after jumping in there naked and taking a bath."

"Now a turtle won't come out jist to bite ye, Alf," Op grumbled. "Ye've got to do somethin' to a turtle! Don't be so skeery."

Below the bathing hole, the stream was shallow. It trickled over the rocks leaving little clear pools, fringed by the ferns here and there, and then it flowed away again, tumbling and splashing over the rocks. Op waded into each still pool and fingered around the brink into each little crevice, between the rocks and under the ferns.

"Aren't you afraid you'll put your hand in on a water moccasin?" Alf asked him.

"Not at all," he replied. "Water moccasins stretch out on rocks and dead logs in spots of sun this time of day and year. When one hides in a hole, he goes back into one too small fer a turtle. Turtles and water moccasins won't have anythin' to do with each other. What could a water moccasin get outta bitin' a turtle's hard shell? But I think if a turtle was a-mind to, he could clamp down with his iron jaws on a water moccasin's thin body and cut it smack in two. See, Alf, wild things in nature get along better'n most human folks. They know their enemies and keep outten their way. And they know their friends a lot better'n we do. The turtle can't eat the water moccasin and the water moccasin can't eat the turtle. So they're not atter one another and they make purty good neighbors. Now the water moccasins do swaller the little minners—I-gollies, there's one now!"

Alf looked up in time to see what appeared to be a thick piece of rope drop from a sunlit poplar branch into the water below.

"I'd never put my big toe up to a thing like that," Alf said, remembering Op's story. He looked down at his own white toes apprehensively.

"We'll get 'im." Op found a club a little longer than a baseball bat and not as large around. He stirred the sand in the bottom of the pool and made the water muddy.

"You mean *you'll* get him," Alf said, backing away.

"Be real quiet," Op whispered. "He'll stick his head up from the muddy water and I'll let 'im have this club right over the bean!"

Op and Alf stood quietly above the muddied water. When there were some little bubbles, Op trained his eye on the spot. The thick, hard, iron-rimmed mouth rose first and then the lidless eyes came above the surface just as Op came down with his club. There was splashing and writhing and a cream-colored substance spread over the surface of the muddy water. Op lifted the dying snake from the pool with his club. He tossed it writhing upon the bank and finished killing it with a few more strokes of his club.

"See, it didn't try to bite us," Op said. "It tried to hide. But I kill every kind of a snake. I can't say I like a-one. I've never larned why the Master put the water moccasin here unless it's to thin out the minners."

Then they started down the stream.

"I'm not surprised we didn't get a turtle in Red Bird Crick," Op said. "When we git down here where it empties into Little White Oak, then we're a-gettin' into the turtle country. Turtles love sand and more sunshine than a body will find up here under these tall poplars!"

Op fingered around in the pools where the two streams joined.

"I found one," he said. "The shell feels like a rock, only it's smoother. Come outten there!"

The undercurrent of water had washed away the land and left a little room where it was dark and cool. Op pulled the turtle from his resting place.

"Ye're too small, ye little devil," he said, holding it up for Alf to see.

The turtle wasn't as large as a saucer. His four legs stuck out from under his shell, clawing against the wind. His head was out too, moving this way and that on his long, scaly, black neck. "Ye grow up and I'll be back in a couple of years and get ye," Op laughed, throwing the kicking turtle into the stream.

"I wouldn't want to handle a little turtle, let alone a big one," Alf muttered. He watched the turtle swim over the water and crawl up the other side of the creek bank and hide under the overlapping turf.

"Ye won't be afraid atter ye handle one," Op told him.

They started down the stream again, Alf lifting his cold blue feet quickly from the water whenever he stepped on the little sharp upturned slate rocks. His teeth rattled from the cold water. They came to a bed of sand, and a cloud of butterflies flew up, frightened.

"Jack would like to see these," Op said, smiling and nodding at the multicolored fluttering wings. "He'd love to be here with his net now!"

The butterflies had been drinking warm water from the sand where the sunlight filtered through the sycamore and willow leaves.

"There's a good place fer a turtle," Op said, looking the place over carefully. He got down on his knees in the water. He put his hands back in a hole under the roots of a water birch. He reached back to his elbow. Then he pulled and grunted and finally fell backward in the water.

"He was pullin' one way and I was pullin' another," Op grunted, holding on to a turtle large as a four-gallon crock. "He's a big booger and he's heavy."

The turtle was snapping at the wind. His head was thrust out on his scaly neck which was larger around than a hoe handle. His legs were pulling and his toes were scratching the air. Op held grimly to the turtle while he lay in the hole of water on his back with his head sticking up.

"Help me, Alf. I can't get up with this load!"

"How can I help you?" Alf said sharply. "I'm afraid of that thing!"

"Take this turtle," Op commanded. "Take 'im before he takes me."

"I can't do it! I won't touch it."

"Take a thong of the hickory bark then, and tie a loop in it," Op instructed Alf as he lay there in the water. "Put the loop over the turtle's head. Ye can do that, can't ye?"

"Yes, I guess so," Alf admitted as he took a thong from the bundle. He tied a loop in the bark and ran the end of the thong through the loop. Then he dropped it over the turtle's head.

"Now pull on the thong," Op said. "Don't be afraid of chokin' it. Ye can't choke a turtle. And one's head is jist enough bigger'n the neck to make the loop hold good."

Alf pulled on the pliable, strong hickory bark and it tightened around the turtle's neck.

"Hold 'im now, Alf," Op shouted. "I'm lettin' 'im loose."

"I'll try." Alf braced his white feet against the bank.

Op turned the turtle loose on the sand, and Alf held to the hickory thong. Op got up, and the muddy water streamed from his clothes.

"Take it, Op," Alf grunted, as the big turtle dug his feet into the sand and started pulling away.

"Lift 'im up and get his feet offen the ground. Ye can tote 'im then."

"It's a heavy thing," Alf said as he lifted the turtle by the neck. "He'll weigh thirty pounds!"

Alf followed Op down the stream, swaying to and fro under the weight of the turtle.

"Is this a mock turtle, Op?" Alf asked.

"I don't know what ye're a-talkin' about, Alf!"

"You know, Op, the kind in mock turtle soup!"

"Mock turtle soup?" Op retorted, training his good eye on Alf. "Shucks, I never heard of a mock turtle in my life."

"Op, you've never been anyplace but around here," Alf said. "I used to have mock turtle soup for my lunch sometimes at Wright Airfield."

"We're not a-ketchin' 'em fer soup, I can tell ye that. We're atter turtles fer meat and eggs. Lutie knows how to cook 'em. I've larned her. But I never heard tell of mock turtle soup! Say," Op said, looking straight at Alf, "jist what is a mock turtle? We've only got hard-shell and soft-shell turtles around here."

"I don't know the different breeds," Alf said irritably as he held the big turtle's open jaws as far away as he could. "I'm afraid it's going to bite me."

"That's an old stud turtle," Op said. "That's what makes 'im so mean."

"How do you know he's a stud?"

"By his shell," Op replied. "The stud has a harder-lookin' shell and it has more color in it! Now let's look around here close and we'll find his mate! The old she-turtle is allus close to the stud. Turtles are never nervous."

"Look up there on the bank," Alf said. "Look!"

"That's 'er," Op shouted with joy. "She's started to lay 'er eggs in the sand, I-gollies."

When the turtle saw Alf and Op, she started back for the water. But Op ran up the bank to meet her, reached down, and picked her up.

"We've got turtle aplenty now," Op said. "And we'll have anywhere from a dozen to two dozen turtle eggs too. The eggs are wonderful but not any better'n turtle meat. Yessir! A body can taste seven different kinds of wild meat in a turtle. Pheasant, quail, rabbit, possum, coon, chicken hawk, and squirrel. All in turtle meat!"

"I don't believe I can carry this turtle all the way to the ridge," Alf sighed. At that moment he was more interested in the weight than the taste.

"Well, I'm not a-goin' to carry both turtles and let ye carry jist yerself. That load'll warm ye up!"

As Alf walked up the stream with his turtle, the sun filtered through the leafy treetops enough to warm his legs. His teeth stopped rattling and sweat broke out on his face. When he and Op reached the cabin, it was late afternoon. Op took the turtles directly to the chopblock where he laid their necks over the block and cut their heads off with his double-bitted ax.

Lucretia had a tub of hot water ready, and Op dropped the turtles in.

"A few minutes," he said, "and we'll pull the shells offen 'em and cut 'em up like ye cut a chicken. I'll show ye some of the purtiest, whitest, cleanest meat ye ever saw in yer life!"

"Look at this, Julia"— Alf turned to his wife. He had never left the wood block. He held the ax handle up to the turtle's mouth and it snapped at it although the body and head were severed. "Ever see anything like this?"

"I never did," Julia said, shuddering. "How can its jaws work when it no longer has a body?"

"It'll keep on a-doin' that till the sun goes down," Op said.

"Op picked up these turtles with his hands," Alf told Lucretia and Julia. "He reaches back under the creek banks and gets them. I wouldn't put my hand in one of those holes for all the tea in China."

Op looked up sharply from the tub of water. "What's tea an' China got to do with huntin' turtles?"

"Nothing." Alf laughed briefly. "Absolutely nothing." He walked toward the cabin on his sore bare feet. He looked bent over, as if he thought he was still carrying the turtle.

29

"Watch old Paul, won't ye!" Op said, smiling. "Birds have more sense than a lot of people. They can find enough to eat on the land. But I like to feed 'em so they will nest close to my cabin."

The rooster redbird ran a sparrow from the feedbox Op had nailed on the side of a yellow pine. Here he put the corn-bread crumbs from his table. "There's not another bird like old Paul. Sparrows can whop all the other birds around here but the red-birds! And old Paul is the daddy of all the rooster redbirds. Maybe they have respect fer their Pap."

Theopolis trained his good eye on the bird as he picked up crumb after crumb.

"Looks like he'd soon get his craw filled," Alf said. "I've never seen anything that small eat so much. Where does he put it?"

"He's not fillin' his craw," Op explained. "He'll carry his big bill full of crumbs to a half-grown redbird. Then the old hen bird will fly in and get a load as soon as he leaves. The redbirds take keer of their young long atter they're out of the nest. They're good parents. Now watch old Paul when he leaves with the crumbs. See where he goes!"

The redbird circled around the cabin to a little dogwood which was in plain view from where they were sitting on the porch. Perched upon a limb was a half-grown bird with red tips on his wing feathers. When the father redbird fluttered in the air in front of the young bird, he opened his bill and the father bird unloaded the crumbs into the young bird's mouth. While he was feeding this young one, the gray-feathered mother bird came to the feedbox and chased away a sparrow that had flown in.

"Before any of ye come around here," Op said, "they ust to fly down and light on my shoulder and eat bread from my hand. Since ye've come to Laurel Ridge to live, they shy away from me. They don't trust strangers any more'n I do."

"I never had time before to sit and watch the birds," Julia mused. "I used to go to movies or read magazines. There was always something to do in Dayton."

"I never sent fer ye, Julia," Op said, "but if ye stay up here very long and keep yer eyes open ye'll see a lot of things. This is a good world up here, fer birds and men both."

"I've been wondering if it is." Alf shook his head. "The night after you killed the water moccasin and told me about the snakes, I couldn't go to sleep. I could see them. They crawled in all directions and they were after me, too."

"When ye do a little more choppin', ye'll get so it won't be no trouble to sleep," Op said. "When ye use the hoe a little more in the garden and tater patch, ye'll be so tired at night ye could sleep a-standin' up. In a month or so ye'll larn to use them tools aright. Now, ye use yer arms like a woman!"

"That's what I want to do," Alf said, reaching for the old dream again. "I want to be able to make a living from this earth with my own hands. I want to live by the sweat of my brow and not by the Almighty Dollar like I did in Dayton." He stood up, taking a deep breath of the clean mountain air. Op was wonder-

136

ing if Alf was about to make a speech, when there was a noise by the gate.

"What's that ye're a-sayin'?" It was Doshie Hammertight's shrill voice. "What's all that talk about the Almighty Dollar? That's somethin' I'm a-interested in."

"Doshie, that's ye all right," Op said, turning toward the gate. "It's yer nature to slip up on people to hear what they're a-sayin'. What do ye want, ye old puff of wind?"

"Ye'd better be a-thinkin' about things closer to home than the Almighty Dollar," Doshie warned him. She opened the gate, and Hootbird, dressed in his cowboy clothes and a new dark shirt with white flowers around the collar, followed. He was carrying his rifle, and big Ben Hammertight, swinging his long gorilla arms and spitting bright sluices of amber spittle, came behind him. Ben was almost as broad as the space between the gateposts.

"What's the matter now, Doshie?" Op asked. "Did Hoot spy on Alf and Julia a-passin' on the ridge the other day? Ye come to check up and see who they are?"

"That's only part of it," she replied curtly.

"Hiya, honey," Hootbird said, smiling at Lucretia.

"Hi, Hoot," she said, then introduced her two cousins. Alf and Julia stared from one Hammertight to the next, unbelieving. Hootbird swaggered over and sat on the porch near Lucretia's chair. He let his fancy boots dangle down and leaned his rifle against the cabin.

"Honey, ye look awful purty with yer hair tied back in a ribbon," he said. Lutie smiled at him briefly.

"Mr. Pruitt, are ye and yer wife a-livin' here in the cabin with Op and Lutie?" Doshie asked.

"No, Mrs. Hammertight," Alf replied, "we're roughing it out there in Op's smokehouse."

"I told ye, Mommie, I saw a stovepipe stuck from the smokehouse winder and smoke a-comin' from it!"

"You must have been around pretty close, Hoot." Lucretia looked sharply at the moon face under the Texas hat.

"I'm allus closer than ye think, honey. Specially to ye!" Hootbird's smile broadened. Jerry came up and whiffed Ben's pants legs and walked away quickly.

"Op, that's perfectly good bread ye're a-feedin' the birds," Doshie said.

"Of course it is," he replied. "I want my birds to have as good a bread as I have."

"There's many a little hungry young un in this world, Op," she said.

"I s'pect there is, Doshie," he agreed. "But *ye* ain't a-feedin' 'em. And what I do with my birds is my own business, ain't it?"

"When I think about the loads I pack to my little young uns out that long ridge from Honeywell," she complained, "and the big loads I tote up that hill! It hurts me to see bread wasted up here on Laurel Ridge on the birds."

"If old Op wants to feed the birds, let 'im do it," Ben said. He spoke slowly, as if each word pained him a little. Then he let fly from his mouth a big sluice of amber spittle he'd collected while sitting there listening. "Doshie, we didn't come to talk about birds."

"Nope, we've come to talk about the strange man on this ridge," Doshie said. "The wild man! Any man that would kill and eat foxes must be wild!"

"What's this about a wild man?" Alf asked, turning to Julia. "We never heard anything about this!"

"Ain't Op and Lutie told ye about 'im?" Doshie said eagerly. She had a story to tell and she was near bursting with it. "There's a wild man on this ridge. Ain't been a week ago when I went to the Freewill Baptist Church by myself. As I was a-comin' home, that wild man jumped from the bushes and grabbed me. He

138

was as strong as an ox and shook me like a dog shakes a rabbit. I thought I's a goner."

"I don't believe it," Op said. "Why would he grab ye? He might grab Lutie or Julia. But only old Ben would grab ye!"

"There must be *somebody* loose around here. Hoot found three more dead foxes in the woods," Ben said slowly. "Found a big fine-lookin' red fox with his hindquarter taken off. The rest of his body and hide was left. Hoot found him at the arc. And down below the arc where the foxes den he found two pelts with the whole heads a-hangin' on. Somebody had cut their skinned bodies loose at the neck!"

"I didn't know there was anything like this going on," Alf said. He turned toward Lucretia. "Lutie, you said in your letters to Uncle Will and Aunt Corrinne it was the prettiest place you'd ever seen. You said Laurel Ridge was a paradise. But you never mentioned wild men and dead foxes! I came down here to find a safe place away from the atom bomb! The way you talk, I've come to the wrong place!"

If that man ain't afeared of one thing, Op thought, he's afeared of another. Snakes, turtles, cold water, bumbs, dead foxes. . . . B-gad!

"If ye come to find a safe place, Mister, ye'd better be a-travelin' on," Doshie chattered at him. "This ridge ust to be one and we were happy down at Wince Leffard Gap. Only old Op was up here on the ridge. Op and the fox hunters saw a few ghosts of the ore diggers and lumberjacks who ust to work here long ago. And maybe Ted Newsome's speret is disturbed and on the loose agin. But a ghost won't kill a fox. Why would he eat a fox when the Good Book tells us a speret don't need no nourishment? These are flesh-and-blood people loose on this ridge!"

"Yeah, an' I've seen one," Hootbird added. "A man with a rifle that took a bead on me and I backed behind a tree."

"Why don't you report this to the sheriff?" Alf asked Hootbird.

"Don't ye think I haven't," Doshie replied quickly. "I've told Sheriff Bill Ackerson every day I've been in Honeywell since Hoot first saw the wild man! And I've told all his deputies. Since they won't do anythin', I've told Jake Ratcliffe, Justice of Peace of our district. Jake said he'd wait a while longer and if Bill didn't do somethin', he'd deputize some men and come out here and clean up this ridge and make it a fitten place to live!"

"And the other night when I was out a-walkin' the ridge, I heard the music of a geetar and singin'," Hootbird took up the story, looking at Lutie. "And it was a man's voice I heard and after the song I heard a woman laughin'. Her voice sounded like yer voice, Lutie, but I couldn't believe it was ye. Since the wind was a-blowin' the sound the wrong way, I couldn't tell. I was afraid to get too close!"

"When did you hear music and singin' at night, Hoot?" Op asked.

"Night before last."

"I was right here with you, wasn't I, Dad?" Lucretia said quickly.

"Pay no attention to Hoot," Op told her.

"I know Lutie was here until nine o'clock," Julia said. "Alf and I didn't leave the cabin until nine."

"It was about two in the mornin' when I heard 'em," Hootbird said. "Right about the time in the mornin' when the wind is blowin' strongest on Laurel Ridge."

"Hoot, ye're too big a coward to be out at two in the mornin'," Op told him. "Why do ye go around totin' that rifle all the time?"

"Ye'd carry a rifle too if ye'd been shot at." Hootbird lowered his voice confidentially. "I believe that strange man is atter me."

Doshie just had to open her mouth and words poured out.

1140

"Ye've forgotten, Op, that somebody shot through a butternut tree above Hoot's head down at the wild-strawberry patch that day when he's a-puttin' a handful of strawberries in Lutie's basket. Ye were right down there and saw it all. That's why Hoot carries a rifle. That's why I carry a piece of hardware right here in my bosom. And that's why Ben has a bright piece of hardware on him right now. If there is somebody atter us, we ain't jist a-goin' to stand still and take it!"

"Did somebody shoot into a tree when you were picking berries?" Alf asked, turning to Lucretia.

"Yes," she admitted. "But we think it was somebody in the woods squirrel-hunting, who did it for fun."

"I don't call that fun," Ben said slowly. "A bullet that will go clean through a thick tree will go through my son Hoot."

"I've had four boy babies to come stillborn," Doshie said. "Hoot's my only livin' son and I don't want 'im kilt on Laurel Ridge. Hoot's dear to me. He's my young un."

"And we came down here to get away from our worries, Alf," Julia said, laughing. "Sounds like it would be much safer back in Dayton, wouldn't it, darling?"

"We've come around here to warn all of ye," Doshie said. "It's not a laughin' matter and ye'll see."

"If I thought there was a dangerous character on this ridge, I wouldn't be runnin' to the Law about it," Op said. "I'd take my old rifle and go find 'im. Doshie, ye've wasted a lot of yer talk fer nothin'. Ye're a-stirrin' the pot until it's a-goin' to bile over one of these days!"

"I've come to warn ye, Op," she said, "and ye don't even appreciate it!"

"Ye've come to see who's out here," Op told her. "To snoop and stick yer nose in things. I know ye, Doshie!"

"Come on, Hoot," Doshie said. "Come on, Ben. We'll haf to be a-goin'. Op can't say he's not been warned. It's been nice to meet ye, Mr. and Mrs. Pruitt. Come down to Wince Leffard Gap and see us sometime."

"Op, I've sat so long I can hardly move," Ben grunted, getting slowly to his feet. He moved across the yard like an amiable gorilla. Hootbird tipped his ten-gallon hat to the ladies, reached for his rifle, aimed a silly smile at Lutie, and followed his folks.

30

"Come outten there!" Theopolis and Lucretia heard a man shout. "We've got ye surrounded! Come outten with yer hands up, too!"

Op jumped up from the breakfast table. He opened the cabin door and walked out onto the porch with his hands up. Lucretia followed her father, hands above her head.

"Who is it, Dad?" she whispered.

"I don't know who it could be," he replied in a hoarse whisper. "We ain't done anythin'!"

Op looked in his front yard and beyond the paling fence to Laurel Ridge road. He trained his good eye up and down the road as far as he could see. There wasn't a person.

"I don't see anybody," he said. "But I heard a voice, didn't you?"

"I certainly did!"

"Well—I've been tellin' ye fer a long time, Lutie, and now ye know it fer yerself," he said, dropping his hands to his side. "Sperets travel this ridge road. It might've been one of Morgan's men. Or maybe Ted Newsome. I'm a-believin' it's a troubled speret!"

"I expect it is, Dad." Lucretia couldn't control a slight giggle.

"Come outten there!" It was the same voice. "Get outten that bed! Come outten there before we bust the door down and come in and get ye! Come out in the name of the Law and be recognized!"

Op jumped down from the porch and started toward the smokehouse. "Sounds like Sheriff Bill Ackerson," he said, trotting toward the garden gate. "He's over at the smokehouse! He's atter them people! I've allus been suspicious of 'em!"

"They're all right, Dad." Lucretia ran beside him. "Alf and Julia are fine people. They're not running from anything!"

"He's a-runnin' from an adam bumb, he told me hisself," Op panted. "Allus a-talkin' about his bein' nervous. Why's a young man like him nervous? I'm a-thinkin' he's done somethin' to make him nervous. He can't use the ax and mattock any better'n a twelve-year-old girl. He's a quair one. It's hard to tell what he's done. We'll soon see! There's Sheriff Bill all right!"

Op stopped at the garden gate. Sheriff Bill Ackerson, a man with a big belly and thin legs, was standing in front of the smokehouse door.

"Who ye atter, Bill?" Op went through the garden gate with Lucretia beside him.

"We're not atter ye, Op," he replied. "But we want to know somethin' about these strangers ye got a-hangin' around here."

"They're my cousins," Lucretia said. "And they're all right!"

"What do you want?" Alf's voice came shakily from the smokehouse. He had partly opened the door and stuck his pale face up to the crack. His blond hair was as disheveled as a last-year's redbird nest. His lips trembled like sweet-corn blades in the morning wind. "Can't you let a p-person sleep?"

"Now, stranger, don't get funny with me," Sheriff Bill Ackerson said. "I've got my men with me and we'll take ye in a minute. We've not come fer trouble, but we don't want no foolishness! Come on outten there 'r open up and let us in!"

Two men came around one side of the smokehouse and one from the other.

"It looks bad to me," Op whispered to Lucretia. "He's brought all his deputies. He means business."

"Alf, watch how you talk." Julia's calm voice came from inside the cabin. "He might arrest us."

"I'd like to know what for," Alf said, closing the door in Sheriff Bill Ackerson's face.

"Lady, ye certainly will be arrested," Sheriff Ackerson shouted.

"Give us time to get dressed and we'll be out." Julia spoke politely.

Sheriff Ackerson scratched his head as if perplexed. "That seems reasonable. But don't be too long about it. We've got other things to do. More troublesome spots in Looten County than any place I know. And Laurel Ridge is worst of all!"

"What's this all about, Bill?"

"When ye lived alone here, Op," Sheriff Ackerson told him, "we never heard of Laurel Ridge. Never any trouble here. But now there's more'n we can handle. We've got a lot of things to get straight!"

"They've not done anything, Sheriff," Lucretia said.

"Ye stay outten this, Miss," Sheriff Ackerson warned her. "Ye wait until we're through questionin' them! Then we'll listen to yer story. I never seen ye before either!"

Sheriff Ackerson was a big man in a dark unpressed suit. Around his waist was a broad leather belt with a bright buckle and attached to this belt were two tan leather holsters with pistol handles showing under the flaps. On the front of his coat was a big silver badge with the word Sheriff engraved in dark letters. His clean-shaven face was flushed red. In the corner of his mouth he chewed a little sassafras twig as he looked at Lucretia with a pair of steady blue eyes.

144

"Never be too shore of strangers, Miss," he said to Lucretia. "It jist don't pay."

"I'm Op's daughter."

"We'll talk about that in a few minutes," Sheriff Ackerson said, chewing faster on the twig.

Theopolis knew each of Sheriff Ackerson's deputies and spoke to them by name. There was Sop Johnson, a big man with a sun-tanned, scarred face. Willie Onilee was a short, heavy man with thick, broad shoulders. He was wearing brier-scratched boots and carrying a rifle. Then there was Othie Yarberry, six feet four and broad shouldered. Othie had never been beyond the third grade in school but he had the makings of a good deputy.

"Sheriff, ye reckon I'd better keep the winder covered?" Othie said.

"No, stay here," Sheriff Ackerson said. "He's not a-goin' to try to get away."

"They've not even had breakfast yet," Op said. "I looked at the stovepipe as I crossed the garden and there wasn't any smoke a-comin' out. Ye got here before they even had their coffee!"

"That's the way to get 'em," Sheriff Ackerson boasted. "Mornin's the best time. That's part of our strategy."

"Ye must've left Honeywell early," Op said.

"Two o'clock this mornin'. An' jist to find out about these strangers."

The door started to open and Sheriff Bill Ackerson turned to watch. When Alf walked out with his skinny hands above his head, Op saw that he was shaking even more than he did in the cold water when he took his first bath in Red Bird Hollow. Julia followed behind him. She didn't even have her hands up.

"Good morning, Sheriff," she said, smiling. "Good morning,

gentlemen," she spoke to the deputies. "Have you come to get us? If you have, I welcome you!"

Then she let out a little chuckle. Alf was shaking so he couldn't speak.

"There's a lot of trouble on Laurel Ridge," Sheriff Ackerson began, as his deputies watched and listened. "I've never had so many reports. And all sorts of stories are floatin' around over Honeywell. I've come here to check up on all this talk. I want to know jist who ye are and what ye're doin' here."

"Since my husband, who is a little nervous, can't speak for himself," Julia explained, "I'll speak for him. He got a leave of absence from Wright Airfield in Dayton and he's come here to spend a little time for his health!"

"Put yer hands down," Sheriff Ackerson said to Alf. "Ye're not a-goin' to be as dangerous as I thought ye might be."

Alf dropped his hands.

"What's this all about?" he stammered. "When we moved in the city, the police never investigated us."

"Darling, somebody's reported us," Julia told him.

"That somebody is old long-tongued Doshie Hammertight," Op said. "All she does is keep the path hot between Wince Leffard Gap and Honeywell. Doshie packs a bigger load of lies to Honeywell than the grub she fetches back."

"We're glad to get this information," Sheriff Ackerson said. "People are not allus a-packin' loads of lies when they haf to tote firearms to defend themselves. It's our duty to make Looten County a fitten place to live. We know our own people. We want to know who the strangers are a-lurkin' on this ridge!"

"We are strangers here," Julia admitted, "but that's no crime, is it? And I wouldn't say that we were 'lurking,' exactly."

"But I've ketched many a guilty man by noticin' he was nervous," Sheriff Ackerson said, looking at Alf. "Ye're the nervousest yet!"

146

"But that's what I'm here for," Alf said, "because I'm nervous. I'm afraid the whole world will be blown up in fire and smoke. I've come to a place where I won't see many people, where I can dig in the garden with a hoe, where I can . . ."

"But yer wife said ye worked at Wright Airfield," Sheriff Ackerson interrupted. "What did ye do?"

"I was a foreman there," he replied. "I was a boss and I own my own home and had a good position. They paid me eight thousand a year!"

"What are ye a-doin' here then?" Bill Ackerson asked. "Have ye lost yer mind?"

"Man, ye're crazy to leave that," Othie Yarberry said. "I'll take yer job and give ye mine!"

"Now, just a minute." Alf raised his hand for silence. He seemed more composed. "You people living in Honeywell and in Looten County don't realize the danger this country is in. If you had seen what I have seen and read as much as I've read about this atomic bomb, and if you lived in a place where the enemy will strike first, then you might be nervous too!"

Willie Onilee let out a little chuckle. He put his finger above his head and circled it a few times. Then he pointed to Alf.

"Nope, young Alf's not off in the head," Op said. "I don't believe that. He's a nervous man all right. But eight thousand dollars is a lot of money to pay a man who can't even chop wood. That's more money than I ever made in my lifetime. I'd haf to pick a lot of berries and sell a lot of hides and nuts to make that much!"

"That's big money," Willie said, shaking his head sadly as he looked Alf over.

"Now, just what do you want with me, Sheriff?" Alf asked. He had stopped shaking. "I've not had my breakfast, so let's come to the point! I was checked by the FBI before I got the position at Wright Airfield where I've worked for the last ten years. I can go back to my position any time I want to."

"I want to know if ye're the man that's been shootin' foxes on this ridge?" Sheriff Ackerson asked.

"They were killed before Alf came here," Lucretia interrupted.

"I never shot a fox in my life," Alf said. "In fact, I've never killed anything!"

"One of the fox hunters comes to my office every day beggin' me to do somethin' about this knockin' the red foxes off," Sheriff Ackerson complained. "And the fox hunters have a big vote. None of our people will eat a fox, so that's why we know he's a stranger. But ye don't meet the description of the man! They say he's about six feet tall, has hair the color of frosted crab grass, and carries an army rifle!"

"That describes Ted Newsome," Op said. Lucretia frowned, staring at her father.

"Who's Ted Newsome?" Sheriff Ackerson asked.

"He's a speret," Op replied. "He's been dead thirty years!"

Willie Onilee grunted in big huffs like a horse getting his breath when he has the whinnies. Sop Johnson slapped his thighs with his big hands.

"A speret is a-killin' the foxes, boys," Sop said. "We've come here armed to ketch a speret!"

"Ye can all laugh that wants to," Op said heatedly. "But it's not a laughin' matter!"

"I've heard everybody in Honeywell was a-livin' on borrowed time with all the underpinnin' gone from under the town and the bottoms a-droppin' outten the wells," Sheriff Ackerson said, "but I never heard of a speret a-killin' foxes! I'll tell the boys, when they come to my office, who is really a-killin' the foxes! A speret! That'll satisfy 'em!"

"Sheriff, I warn ye," Theopolis spoke in a serious tone, "it's dangerous to laugh at the sperets!"

148

"How do ye know about this speret, Op?" Othie Yarberry asked.

"He comes to see Lutie," Op said. "She's a-sparkin' with Ted Newsome!"

"Oh, Dad, don't talk such nonsense." Lucretia turned her head away in disgust.

"Now, jist a minute," Sheriff Ackerson said, holding his laughter. "We're a-gettin' some place. Who is this Ted Newsome? And where does he live?"

"He's Ted Newsome is all I know," Lucretia said. "And I don't know where he lives."

"Then he must be a speret," Othie added gleefully. "We're not gettin' no place, but let's go on!"

"Is she yer gal, Op?" Sop Johnson asked.

"She says so," Op replied. "Ted Newsome even picks bouquets of wild flowers fer Lutie to put on our table!"

"Sparkin' a speret," Willie said, nudging Sheriff Ackerson with his elbow. His wide grin showed two semicircles of big horse teeth.

"We'll tell the fox hunters to come and get Ted Newsome," Othie said. "I'd like to see Penny Shelton after a speret. Or Turkey Maddox or old Plack Rivercomb."

"I think yer a-tellin' the truth," Sheriff Ackerson said, turning back toward Alf. "I don't believe ye could hit a fox with an army rifle. Ye don't look like this wild man that's been reported to us!"

"Oh, how I wish Alf were a wild man," Julia said, laughing. "It would be wonderful to live in a wild country, in a smokehouse with a wild man!"

"But what ye said about this atom bomb," Sheriff Ackerson said, "it's enough to start a man's mind to thinkin'. I've never given much thought to bombs. I've had so much trouble of my own a-tryin' to keep peace and order in Looten County."

"I figure our enemies might have more than we've got." Alf

149

was off on his favorite subject. "Faster planes and more power-ful bombs and these circular things people call 'flying saucers.' It's something to think about! I know, where there's so much smoke there's bound to be some fire. I think the safest spots in this country are places like Laurel Ridge."

"I'm not so shore about that," Willie said slyly. "Not with Ted Newsome, the speret, in love with Op's gal and a-shootin' all the red foxes! Wait'll Doshie Hammertight comes back to our office and I tell 'er shootin' at a speret won't do 'er any good!"

"Op, ye say this man is akin to ye?" Sheriff Ackerson said.

"Nope, I never said he was," Op answered. "He's no blood akin to me. He said his mother was my wife Beadie's youngest sister who left this country with Will and Corrinne Day. They went to Ohio to get rich and I guess they have. They've never been back. I never want to see any of 'em agin atter the way they've talked about me."

"They're akin to me," Lucretia said. "Alf is my first cousin and that's his wife, Julia."

"And about ye, Miss?" Sheriff Ackerson said. "Are ye Op's gal?"

"That's right," she said. "The Red Cross got in touch with me when he was going blind. I came back here and took him to the doctor and had a cataract removed from one eye so he could see."

"Is that right, Op?" Sheriff Ackerson asked dubiously.

"That's right, Sheriff," Op admitted.

"I jist wanted to get straight," Sheriff Ackerson said, "who this purty young woman is livin' in yer cabin with ye!"

"Ye don't haf to worry about me, Sheriff," Op chuckled. "If she wasn't my gal she wouldn't be in my cabin. I like to live by myself. I've got my own idears about wimmen. I had one, Beadie, and she was enough. When I'm numbered with the blest, Beadie's all I want to be a-flyin' around over Laurel Ridge

150

with. It would look mighty strange to see one man a-flyin' with two sperets. I never want that. I look ahead, Sheriff!"

"Let's be on our way, boys." Sheriff Ackerson was already waddling away from the smokehouse. "We can't do much with these sperets. We've got some real people to look atter!"

"Well," Julia said as she turned toward the smokehouse door, "first time we've ever been checked by a Kentucky sheriff before breakfast."

31

"The first nest of young redbirds have gone!" Theopolis announced as he bent over a hill of sugar corn in the long garden row. "Now, Dollie is a-settin' on four eggs behind the cabin in a bushy-topped persimmon. 'Pears like in the last ten years Dollie and old Paul have kept gettin' a little closer to the cabin. I've tolled 'em in from the woods. Found 'em a-nestin' down in Shinglemill Holler and there I started feedin' 'em bread crumbs on top a stump."

Op crumpled a dry clod of dirt in his big hand and spread it around the corn. Then he fondled the stalks of young green corn as if they were living things that could feel the caress of his calloused hand. He pulled a little sprig of crab grass from beside the corn that was too close to cut with his hoe.

Lucretia was hoeing the row of corn next to Theopolis, and Julia was hoeing the third row behind Theopolis and Lucretia. And far behind Julia was Alf, doing the best he could to keep up with his wife. Alf didn't have the breath to spend talking because he was panting as he worked.

The good morning wind came from above the floor of clouds over the Sandy Valley and swept over Laurel Ridge. Laurel

Ridge was like a long green island on this late-June morning. It was surrounded by clouds. And when the morning sun slanted its rays down onto the great uneven floors of rolling white clouds on either side of the green ridge, this was something for Alf and Julia to see. They stopped, leaned on their hoe handles, and looked.

"I'll tell ye, Lutie," Op said, "many things've happened around here since Dollie laid 'er first eggs in the nest down there in the persimmon bush. I've got my sight back, a lot of foxes have been kilt, sperets have returned. There've been warnin's. I wonder what'll happen to us by the time Dollie and old Paul hatch the eggs down in the persimmon bush."

"It would be nice to know, Dad." Lucretia stared at the ground thoughtfully.

"That's what everybody would like to know." Alf looked up from his hoeing. "We'd all love to read our future. And we'd like to read the fate of the world. But maybe," he said, as he began to hoe again, "it's better for all of us that we don't. It's too bad people with so much intelligence in this world can't get along. We've got enough sense to blow each other up but not enough sense to get along as friendly neighbors."

"Here we go agin," Op whispered to Lucretia. "Let's don't get Alf started on that adam bumb. He'll worry himself to death!"

"You worry him too, Dad," Lucretia whispered. "You worry Cousin Alf about the spirits. You know he doesn't believe in them, so why talk about them?"

"But he'll believe in 'em one of these days," Op said in a low tone. The four long-handled gooseneck hoes made little ringing sounds against the dry garden earth. "I'm a-goin' to show Alf somethin' about the sperets. We're a-comin' to a showdown."

"Now, if people could only get along," Alf continued, digging crazily into the Laurel Ridge earth with his hoe, "it would be a better world. And we wouldn't have all these fears about going up in flame and smoke. The cemeteries would become obsolete. Undertakers, cemetery sextons, and tombstone salesmen would all have to go out of business!"

"They're already outten business around here," Op said. "They've never been in business. Well, they're jist now a-gettin' a little trade," he admitted as he leaned on his hoe handle. "But around here we've allus made our own coffins. The men gather and make the coffin, and the wimmen line it with silks and satins while other men go to the Freewill Baptist Graveyard and dig the grave. When a body dies around here, in a short time he's laid to rest. That is, if it's in the summertime. In the winter, if the ground is frozen purty hard, a body is held over a little longer in a cold room. Sometimes there's an awful lot of ice and deep snow up here on this ridge and around the Freewill Baptist Graveyard."

"I realize more every day we're living in a different world here." Julia spoke for the first time. She wiped her face with a kerchief. "If anybody had ever told me I'd be above the clouds hoeing corn, I would have laughed. But here I am. I'm getting my vitamins from the sun, wind, and dirt, I suppose!"

"A-gettin' yer what?" Op asked, turning around and looking at Julia.

"My vitamins," she repeated.

"What's that?" Op asked.

"Medicine, something to give more strength to the body," she explained. "There's a vitamin for every deficiency in the body."

"And there's a root, a stem, or a blossom fer every ailment," Op said as he turned around and began hoeing in his corn row. "Nothin' can take the place of yarbs!"

Op stepped over into Lucretia's row and hoed a few hills of corn because she was getting behind.

153

"If all the world was like Laurel Ridge," Alf said, stopping to clean dirt from his fingernails, "it would be a perfect mixture of good and bad. The air up here is fresh and good to breathe—but it's awfully chilly at night when it blows through the smokehouse cracks! There are vitamins in the sunshine—but the sun is hot on my poor back working in the garden. And the clouds . . ."

"The ground hogs are a-makin' their coffee," Op interrupted. "When ye see clouds a-hangin' over the valleys, the ground hogs're at work. That's the steam from their coffee bilers, the old people allus told me."

"Tell me, Op," Alf said. "How do the ground hogs make coffee?" He turned and winked at Julia. "Do ground hogs drink coffee, too?"

"Nope, but they're a-makin' it fer Red Jacket and his angels. Red Jacket's another speret on the ridge—"

Theopolis stopped talking to look back at Alf to see what was wrong. He had dropped his hoe and was making funny noises. He was swinging at the wind with his fists.

"What's the matter, Alf?" Julia asked. "I don't see anything! What are you fighting?"

"Damn bee stung me on the lip," he shouted irritably. "I'll kill it if I can!"

"Why don't ye feed yer friends, Alf?" Op interrupted.

"Feed them what?" Alf was still swinging with his fists.

"Sweat," Op said. "That's the little sweat bee the good Lord put here to make people work. Ye're a-starvin' it to death. That's what Pap ust to tell us. Work enough to sweat so we wouldn't starve the sweat bees and then they wouldn't sting us. He'd say: 'Sweat bees're put here fer a purpose. That's to sting lazy people and make 'em work.'"

Alf picked up his hoe. He mumbled, giving Theopolis a hard look: "The Lord didn't put any bee on my lip to sting it!"
154

"The sweat bee's a good timepiece too," Op said. "Nine, twelve, and three are his mealtimes and he looks to a body fer some sweat."

Julia laughed. "That was one thing you were saying just yesterday, that you missed up here, Alf—your electric clock. Now you don't need it. Whenever you get stung by a bee, you'll know what time it is."

Alf wasn't enjoying the joke. He fingered his swollen lip tenderly. "It's all right for Op not to have a clock. He measures time by what President was in office and by the nesting seasons of the birds. But I prefer my electric clock, thank you, to a bee sting every three hours. Besides, you've got to remember that I was an executive once and executives don't sweat."

"Anybody who don't sweat ain't human," Op said, rising up from pulling weeds from around his corn. "But there are other ways of tellin' time too. When a man lives without a clock, he gets so he can tell time to the minute by the insects and birds. Snails start a-crawlin' at six in the mornin'. The doodlebugs start work at seven. The rain crows croak at ten. Chicken hawks stir at noon to find a mess of young birds. Hoot owls hoot at about two. And at three the grasshoppers chew and spit their terbacker juice. At four the woodpeckers drill in the dead trees. At five the crows fly home. At six the white moths begin to fly."

"That kind of time is all right for you, Op," Alf said. "You never have to be anyplace promptly anyway. You'd lose your job if you worked at Wright Airfield."

"At night it's harder to tell time," Op talked on, paying Alf no heed. "But if a man has looked long enough at the night skies searchin' fer signs, he larns to tell time by the stars. Then, there're the katydids, nightjars, whippoorwills, moths, and foxes. But why worry about the time? I never did."

Op and Lucretia had reached the end of the garden with their sweet-corn rows. Op stood for a minute and wiped the sweat.

"Lutie, we'd better help Julia and Alf," Op said. "They're behind."

"Yes, I've about ruined my hands," Alf grumbled, stopping to examine the blisters. "I can't keep this wonderful garden dirt from getting under my fingernails either." He peeled dead skin from his hand. "And that reminds me of another job. We've got to fix that wonderful hole in the smokehouse roof before your wonderful mountain rain soaks our wonderful mattresses made of last-year's leaves."

His sarcasm was lost on Op, who was thinking about a hole in another roof. "A hole in the roof is what almost ruint Pap onct." Op, resting on his hoe handle, took one of his deep story-telling breaths. "Brother Adger, years dead and gone to his long home, was about thirty-five then and full of his devilment. Old Brother Ike Strickland was a-preachin' at the Freewill Baptist Church and he had a big revival a-goin' hot and heavy. Brother Adger had been a-goin' night atter night, jist like everybody else around here, to that month-old revival. One night Brother Adger wore a long, white nightshirt, stiff with starch and with a big pair of sleeves. And he wore low-cut shoes without socks. Brother Adger never kept his hair cut very short and in them days he let his beard grow. He had a sandy-colored beard.

"He slipped in at the door right when old Addie Smallwood rose up from his seat to testify. 'Oh, Lord,' Brother Smallwood said, 'come down from yer Heaven and be with us tonight. Come down through the roof'—and at about that time a lot of Amens went up from all over the house fer I was right there and heard 'em—'and right down through the ceilin'. We don't mind, Lord. We'll repair the roof.' And, about that time, Brother Adger, who was a-standin' in the back of the church house beside the door, unnoticed by anyone, said: 'Wouldn't it be better to walk in at the door, Brother Smallwood?'

"Brother Smallwood turned around and give one look and

fell to his knees. He crouched there on his knees and shook till he had to hold to his seat to steady himself. 'No need to tear up the roof and ceilin' and have a lot of extra work to repair 'em when there's a door to this church house,' Brother Adger said. 'I don't approve of a lot of extra work fer nothin'.' At that, Boadie Sloas, a terrible sinner but under conviction, went out the winder headfirst, with Jim Pennix, Hester Cremeans, and Jimmy Overton a-followin'. Young Shannon Burton took out a whole sash and cut his hand on the glass but he run into the dark woods and never stopped till he got home. He didn't even know he was cut till he got home and passed out. Wimmen run out the door screamin'. Little young uns woke up from their sleep and ran atter their mothers.

"But Brother Sweeter Barnhill, Sister Shug Meadows, Ossie and Tillie Redfern, Bill and Drusie Flannigan come with their arms lifted and fell at Brother Adger's feet. If Brother Adger hadn't had a birthmark on his cheek, a little gray scaly stripe where he was marked by a lizard, I don't know what might've happened. I think he might've come back agin and taken the church over and converted everybody. But Sweeter Barnhill looked up into Brother Adger's face and saw the mark. And he let out a wild whoop and jumped up, but Brother Adger, bein' much younger, was too fast fer Sweeter. He got out before the others knowed what it was all about. And he took to the dark woods and circled home."

There he goes again, Alf thought. I've heard so many of his weird tales they're beginning to get under my skin. I wake up in the middle of the night in the smokehouse thinking about his foolish "sperets." Then a twig scrapes against the windowpane and I sit up in bed shaking and swallowing.

"Well, Sweeter went to Honeywell and swore out a warrant fer Brother Adger fer disturbin' public worship"—Op had his second wind—"and it nearly broke Pap up. Pap had to stop workin' in his crop and he rode a mule day and night a-seein' people he knowed. The trial lasted two weeks and everybody come and it was like a Labor Day or Fourth of July celebration in Honeywell. It cost Pap his mule team, two yoke of oxen, and three milk cows before he got Adger outten that scrape. That ruint Brother Adger and that's why he left this country and went West. He went to Oklahomie and died and is buried there. But he planted our seed there with five sons afore he died. Ye'll find the Akers in Oklahomie! And all of this happened over a hole in the roof. Only reason poor old Brother Adger would give fer a-doin' that was: 'I wanted to see whether they really did want the Lord, Our Saviour, to visit 'em or not.' He said that in the trial. He was as white as a sheet all a-durin' that trial. Brother Adger was skeered to death. He was glad to take off fer a new country when it was all over. Yep, it ruint 'im around here."

Op had hoed Julia's row back to where she stood leaning on her hoe handle, listening to him. Then he stepped over into the row where Lucretia and Alf were hoeing. He started hoeing in the middle. "Atter we finish this row," he said, "we'll eat some dinner. No ust a-tryin' to do too much this mornin'." He bent to his hoeing and then straightened up abruptly. "Now what set me a-tellin' about Brother Adger? Haven't told that story in ten years."

"The hole in the smokehouse roof." Alf grimaced. "I made the mistake of mentioning it."

32

"Where are we now, Op?" Alf asked. He had to stop for he was panting for breath and bent over double on the hill. "And how much farther do we go?"

"Don't worry, Alf," Op told him. "It'll be much easier walkin' from here on! This is the last big hill. We'll be walkin' on the level and down a big hill the rest of the way. Ye're on Remines Ridge now. See, we left Laurel Ridge and crossed Pawpaw Gap. And the long hill up from Pawpaw Gap that we've jist climb is Pawpaw Hill. No more'n five miles now to Cedar Riffles!"

Op started walking on slowly and Alf followed, carrying a coffee sack on his back. He had in the coffee sack a bundle of pine kindling that was rich with resin. Op had split the kindling and had chosen certain sticks for this special occasion. He carried a hunting knife in a sheath on his belt and a cedar bow in one hand. In another sheath made of hickory thongs that rested on his shoulder he carrried a little bundle of arrows. The arrows were made of straight sourwood limbs Op had selected from the sourwood trees on Laurel Ridge. He had pointed the ends of these sourwoods with horseshoe nails, knocked the heads from the nails, and filed the blunt ends to pin-point sharpness. Then he had filed a little hook on the nail so that the arrow would hold.

"We'll take it easier until ye get yer second wind," Op said, as Alf trotted to catch up. "There's a place out here we want to stop fer a few minutes. I want to show ye somethin'."

They had walked approximately two hundred yards farther when Op left the road and turned right into a churchyard. There was a small, unpainted, weather-beaten church house with two windows on each side sitting under a grove of giant oaks. Around the church house on all sides except the front was a cemetery with white and gray markers. In the barren clay, there were rows of brown field stones with names and dates of the deceased crudely chiseled on them. Many of the letters and initials of the names were chiseled backward.

"It's down here," Op said, walking through the yuccas, white with bloom, and the little sand briers with reddish-brown leaves. The seeds from the wild grass caught under Op's boot strings. "Here's Ted's long home," Op said, stopping and looking over the long grave where time had leveled the once heaped-up mound. "It's here that he comes and goes and never leaves a trace."

"Private Ted R. Newsome." Alf read aloud the inscription on the government-bought stone. "Born June 7th, 1888. Died August 8th, 1919. Co. C. 40 Kentucky Infantry."

"Now come over here," Op spoke in a serious tone, "and I'll show ye what caused his speret to be troubled. She's not too fur away from 'im."

Alf grinned as he followed Op across the row of graves.

"Here she is," Op said, pointing to a large twin tombstone. "I don't think she goes and comes when she pleases. I think she's a-stayin' right down there!"

Alf read aloud for Theopolis the name, dates, and epitaph on the stone: "Lucinda Dortch Simpson, Born April 16th, 1892. Died August 20th, 1947. Gone but not forgotten."

"That's the truth," Op said. "She's gone but not forgotten. She's a-causin' Ted's speret to be troubled, probably ever since they laid 'er here."

Then Alf read a name and date on the other half of the stone: "Jacob Leroy Simpson, Born June 17, 1894 . . . . Died.—"

"He's not dead yet," Op said. "He's married agin. And it's a good thing if he wants a speret with 'im in another world.

Lucinda's speret would sure go with Ted's. A lot of the old people believed Jake bushwhacked Ted."

Op turned and walked away, his face somber. Alf followed him back across the barren yellow-clay yard to the wagon road. He wanted to laugh at old Op's incessant talk of spirits but somehow the bare, neglected graveyard drove all the laughter out of him.

33

Shadows of dusk had filled the Little Sandy River Valley. The wind moaned through the tops of the tall cedars growing on Sandy's banks. High on the bank, Theopolis pulled his hunting knife from his sheath and cut a long willow pole. Then he reached a hickory thong from his hip pocket. He took the pine kindling from the sack and tied it tightly around the pole with the thong. Finally, Op fingered down deep into his hip pocket and brought out a ground-hog string for his bow.

"It takes a long time to make a good bow," he said. "I make 'em in winter a-sittin' around my stove when I've not got much to do. I take my time and make 'em good. And I try to make every arrow count. I got the cedar fer my bows here at Cedar Riffles. Best cedar in Looten County grows here."

Theopolis looped one end of his ground-hog–hide bowstring over the bow and then pulled with all his might to bend the bow so he could loop the other.

Below them a bullfrog made the sound of slow beats on a big bass drum. Alf stood watching Theopolis, shifting his weight from one foot to the other and shivering in the wind.

"It's a-gettin' about time fer the frogs to open up," Op said.

"In a few minutes when the frogs and all the night insects open up, ye won't be able to hear the wind in the cedars!"

Op took an arrow from the sheath behind his shoulder.

"Let's get our boots off now," he said. "Hear that water a-splashin' down there!"

"You mean I've got to wade in that river?"

"Yep, when the big red hosses're a-playin'," Op said, "ye gotta wade. I'm hungry fer a good mess of fish!"

"Any swirl holes down there to suck a man under?" Alf peered uncertainly downstream. "Why do you want me in that river?"

"Ye wade along and hold that torch jist right and give me the light and I'll show ye!"

"But I've never handled a torch before."

"Ye'll never larn any younger," Op said. He pulled off his other sock.

The moon had come up over Remines Ridge flooding the bank with light. The two men sat under a cedar high up on the river bank. Below, along the riffles, the shores of the Sandy were lined with water birch, ironweed, sycamores, and willows. The treetops leaned over the water and formed a canopy of green that cut away most of the moonlight from the river. The silver could filter through the leaves in only a few places and leave its bright reflections on the water that poured over the riffles. Now Alf heard the roar of frogs and the singing of night insects that Op had predicted. The splashing of the water below sounded far away.

"This is a new life all right," Alf said, just to hear the sound of his own voice. "I've sure never seen fish caught with a bow and arrow."

"It's a lot better'n trappin' 'em," Op said. "A man matches his brains with the fish's this way. Now, when I was nearly blind I made nets and set 'em in the deep holes down by Artner's.

I had to have my fresh fish and turtles! I've had 'em all my life. But now that I kin see agin, I give the fish a chance."

Op struck a match to the pine kindling and the little flame took hold. It leaped into a bigger flame.

"Now hold the pole like this, Alf," Op showed him. "Tip the kindlin' up so the flame won't burn all the way down and burn the thong."

"I see what you mean," Alf said.

"Let's go!" Op's old voice was eager like a boy's. He picked up the empty coffee sack and lapped it over the thong tied around his waist.

They walked down to the water by a little path that had been made by other fishermen. They stood for a minute among the frog and insect sounds and the roar of water pouring over the rocks.

"I saw something jump up there," Alf shouted. "Look out there by that sycamore!"

"Don't yell!" Op said sharply. "Give me light!"

The two men waded into the river above their knees.

"Ow! It's cold," Alf whispered, "and the rocks are sharp and slippery."

Op trained his eye in this direction and that. With his right thumb and index finger he gripped the arrow against his bow-string. With his left hand he held tight to his bow. Once he threw up his bow but he didn't shoot.

"I saw 'im," Op whispered. "The red hosses are a-havin' fun here tonight. It must be a holiday fer the fish. They're a-havin' some kind of a big doin's."

It happened so suddenly Alf only heard the swish in the air and the arrow's "plump" into the water. Then there was a splash as Op waded out and reached down under the surface, lifting a fish with an arrow sticking through it.

"I hit 'im jist right," Op said proudly. "Not too hard, just hard enough. B-gad, an arrow stops one, but there's the danger of a-shootin' right through 'em."

"What kind of fish is it?"

"A red hoss."

"How much will it weigh?" Alf's teeth were chattering but he was determined to show a polite interest in Op's little fish.

"About four pounds," Op said. "But I'm atter a twenty-pounder here tonight. We ought to get one! This night is jist right!"

Op pulled the arrow on through the fish. He held the fish while Alf took the sack from behind the thong. Then Op dropped the fish into the sack.

"Let's tie the sack in the edge of the riffle," Op said. "Keep 'im fresh that way."

They waded over near the bank where Op tied the end of the sack to a bent-over sycamore.

"That fish will die," Op said. "And we've got seven miles or more to tote 'im home before we clean 'im."

Alf floundered in the water but he managed to stay on his feet as they waded upstream. "You don't have to remind me of that seven-mile walk home," he muttered.

Like his father before him, Theopolis Akers had used a bow and arrow and had come to Cedar Riffles at night and killed fish since he was big enough to remember. He'd fished with nets, throw lines, and poles, but on the riffles he had never used a gig like many of the fishermen he had known. He used his bow and arrow for the simple reason that he loved this kind of fishing best of all. When Alf returned to him with the light, they started across the river. There was a swish and another *plump* into the water. The fish started over the riffles with an arrow in its back. Alf reached down and got the arrow. He lifted the fish from the water.

"It's different from the other one!"

"It's about a two-pound white sucker," Op said, examining the fish. "Take it to the sack!"

Theopolis put the arrow back into the shaft. By eleven o'clock they had caught nine fish. Theopolis had missed only twice.

"We've got plenty of fish," Alf said, when he put the last fish in the sack. "Who's going to carry all that load back seven miles?"

"But we don't have a big un," Op grumbled. "We'll be a-carryin' home more fish than we have now!"

"These are all good-sized," Alf said. "They'll be mighty heavy by the time we get up on the ridge!"

"But there are some big red hosses here on this riffle tonight," Op told him. "They're playin' all around us. I saw a thirty-pound fish jump up into a strip of moonlight a while ago!"

"Not that big, Op," Alf chided. "That sounds like one of your big snakes."

Theopolis wheeled in the water. There was a swish and a plop.

"I never saw it," Alf said.

"Hold that light, Alf!" Theopolis was excited. He drew another bow from the sheath and shot again. "Take my bow! Hurry!"

Alf grabbed Op's bow, and Op went down into the water.

"I got 'im," he said. "He's a gollywhopper! Wait till I get my hand into his mouth! I'm afraid of pullin' the arrow from his back!"

Alf moved the light this way and that as he followed Op down the riffles. Op rolled over in the water as he wrestled with the fish.

"Ye ain't a-gettin' away," Op shouted. "Clamp down on me, dad-durned ye. I got yer mouth now."

Op's body lodged against a rock in the swift water. But he kept his head above and held to the fish.

"Oh, there goes the light," Alf yelled. "I couldn't hold it with one hand!"

Alf fell headfirst into the water.

"Save that bow," Op shouted. "Throw it out on the bank. I'll hold the fish till ye can hep me!"

Alf rose from the water, shaking with chills. With Op's bow out on the bank, he waded down the dark stream.

"Where are you, Op?"

"Right here."

"I can't see you!"

"Come to the sound," Theopolis shouted. "Hurry!"

Alf stumbled against Op, who was lodged behind the rock, and pitched over on his head into the riffles. When he arose from the water, there was a note of awe in his shaking voice. "I hit the fish, Op. I felt him, he's huge."

"Get two arrows from my sheath and sink 'em in!"

"What about the knife, Op?"

"Do as I tell ye! Hurry! Get arrows!"

Alf got arrows from the sheath which was under water. Then he waded down two steps and felt the cold and slimy back of the fish. He pushed an arrow as far as he could into the fish. And then he sank the second one.

"I did it, Op," he shouted with excitement.

"I felt the pressure let up," Op said, "I know ye have. Now get the fish by the tail. Get down in the water if it's shaller there. Hold its tail with one arm agin yer side and hold to an arrow with yer other hand."

"Got the arrow, Op," Alf shouted. "Got my arm around his tail!"

"We got 'im now," Op said. "The arrows are a-workin' on 'im. They're a-weakenin' 'im. Wait till I tie 'im with this hickory."

Theopolis pulled the thongs from his water-soaked pocket.

He put one into the fish's mouth and threaded it through his gills. Then he freed his hand from its mouth and held to the thong. "We've got 'im now, Alf," Op shouted above the roar of the water. "Come and hold 'im by this thong till I run another one through his gills."

Op pulled by one thong and Alf pulled by the other. They heaved the fish from the river and upon the bank where there was a patch of moonlight.

"Four arrows in 'im," Op said. "I hit 'im both times a while ago. But how could I miss a fish this big!"

"This is like a dream," Alf said excitedly. "I'll never forget this fish! How big is he, Op? About ninety pounds?"

"Not that big, Alf. He's about forty pounds!"

"He's bigger than that!"

"He jist seems that way atter ye wrestled with 'im in the riffles. A forty-pound fish can give a man a lot of trouble on the riffles! I thought there was a big red hoss there. I saw 'im under the water several times when ye got the light right."

Op and Alf were still panting as they looked on the big gray fish lying there subdued and gasping on dry land. Op said, "We'll have fresh fish aplenty now."

"It must be midnight," Alf remembered, his excitement dying. "I'm exhausted. I'd love to be in my little bed in the smokehouse."

"Ferget about yer little bed," Op told him. "We got the big fish, ain't we? What if we don't get home till daylight?"

"But I'm tired and wet." Alf thought of the seven-mile walk ahead of him and his face grew long and mournful.

"Ye'll get warm a-totin' that sack full of fish home! Ye'd better fetch it from the river."

While Alf went down to the dark river to find the sack, Op went for his bow. He counted and arranged his arrows in the sheath. Then he removed the ground-hog string and let his bow go straight again. He tied together the two thongs that went through the fish's mouth and doubled the ends to make himself a good handhold.

"Now carry my bow and the sack, Alf," Op told him. "Let's be on our way!"

Alf watched Op swing the big fish high upon his back. Its tail was almost touching the ground. Op held the thongs over his right shoulder, gripping them with both hands.

"I ketched a seventy-seven pound fish onct," Op said as they trudged up the bank toward the cedars. Alf was following Op, staring at the big gray fish that shone white in the moonlight. "I know it was that big 'cause we carried it to Honeywell and weighed it. I thought it would weigh a hundred pounds. I was younger then than ye are now and hadn't ketched too many fish." Op caught a half breath. "That was the biggest fish I ever ketched."

"Shoot it with a bow and arrow?" Alf grunted.

"Nope. I was down there a-fishin' in the hole at the end of the riffles. I had a line baited and the pole set in the bank. And I had another pole in my hand. I'd jist baited my hook with a little minner."

Theopolis paused to get more wind. Alf gladly stopped behind him, taking the sack of fish from his shoulder with a slight groan.

"I had a feelin' there was a big fish in that hole," Op said. "And jist as I's a-gettin' ready to drop the minner into the water on my hook, I saw a turtle about the size of an alarm clock come swimmin' across the river. He swum right up below me, and a big red hoss reached up and swallered him. My heart nearly pounded itself from my body when I saw that fish. My ribs were all that kept my heart inside. I held the little minner down jist above the water and that red hoss raised up to get 'im and I dropped the minner into his mouth. He started pullin' and I
168

knew my line would break. But I had my hand down his mouth and behind his gill. I had my feet behind a stump and I pulled with all the power in me and pulled 'im onto the sand. There I had 'im. He cut my hand awful. It bled but I didn't keer. I wrestled with that fish there on the sand till I weakened 'im and hollered to Brother Adger who was fishin' further down Sandy to come a-runnin'. He found me a-layin' beside the fish with one hand in his mouth and one arm around him, both of us a-kickin' and a-floppin'. Brother Adger tied him good and tight to a tree with two 'r three strands of trot-line through his gills. He couldn't get back to water and he soon lost his power. He put a fence rail through his gills and carried 'im to Honeywell. His tail drug the ground and he weighed seventy-seven pounds. And when we cleaned 'im we found a sixteen-pound pike inside 'im he'd swallered."

Theopolis started up the hill again. With a sigh, Alf shouldered his heavy sack of fish and followed Op up the path. For once he wished Op's story had been longer.

34

"Well, sir, I was down in Sulphur Spring Holler about a chew of calmus weed away from Ben Hammertight's when it happened," Op said. He stood under the oak's shade in the corner of the garden filing a hoe. "I'd found one of the best patches of ginseng around a little moss-kivvered rock I'd ever found in my life. Ginseng was a-sellin' fer eighteen dollars a pound then. There I was among the five-prong stems of ginseng, but somethin' told me that a pair of eyes was on me. I'd put a lot of ginseng roots into my poke when I raised up to look around. There was a big half-rotted log down the hill below the rock and

I saw a pair of little black beady eyes a-lookin' straight at me. The afternoon sunrays slanted down through an open space in the treetops, right onto that pair of eyes that had no lids. When it couldn't bat its eyes and looked right at me in the sunrays, I knowed he was a snake. So I called Jerry from the woods and he came runnin'."

Op pulled a calmus root from his hip pocket and bit off a chew of the tough, shriveled weed. His three listeners—Alf, Julia, and Lutie—sat under the oak tree enjoying its shade.

"I took my little mattock and I went down to take a look at the snake that was watchin' me," he continued. "Its head was on the log and it stretched down among the pea vines and wild oats twelve or fifteen feet. When Jerry ran up and took a look at the snake, he didn't do a thing. He trembled as much as I did. It was too much of a snake fer old Jerry. He backed off growling and I backed away too. 'Ye slipped up here and planned to swaller me,' I said to the snake. 'I'll give ye some trouble fer that.' I got hot as a mule under the collar. So I found a big dead pole, all I could handle, and I come down on his head with that. The snake started crawlin' up the hill and I followed, battin' 'im over the head. Jerry barked and growled and ran along beside me. Old Jerry has kilt many a snake—copperhead and rattler—but he was afeared of that one. He nipped at its body about ten feet back from its head while I worked on its head with my stick. I beat it enough to give it a headache, but over the ridge it went toward the Artner rock cliffs!"

"Yep, snakes can get close enough to swaller ye, Op, but ye allus see 'em in time," said a man on the other side of the garden fence. "But strangers can live in yer smokehouse and yer cabin and ye don't do anythin' about it."

Theopolis, Lucretia, Julia, and Alf turned around to look.

"Snake, where did ye come from?" Op was surprised. "I never saw ye a-standin' there."

"I've stood here long enough to hear that snake story for the hundredth time," Snake Blue said. "And ye've told it the same way every time so it must be the truth. . . ."

"It is the truth," Op interrupted.

"I've come out here to see who these strangers are," Snake Blue said bluntly. "I want to know who ye're a-harborin' on my premises. I've still got a deed for this land, remember. Look in deed book 90 on page 386 and ye'll see who the rightful owner is. Go to the Honeywell Courthouse and, if ye can't read, have J. L. to read it fer ye. I jist want it understood who owns this land before I start cleanin' house here."

Snake Blue was a little red-faced man, and he talked faster than an early-July wind blowing among the blackberry briers. He leaned his shotgun against the garden palings and wiped sweat from his turkey-red face while he talked.

"There's a-goin' to be one of the best hangin's around here there's ever been in the history of Looten County." Snake's words just poured out of his mouth. "And long, long time ago we ust to hang 'em here. Eleven was hung at one time on the Looten County Courthouse Square. That was before my day, Op. But the people are riled about Laurel Ridge. I've jist been to Ben Hammertight's place and talked to Ben. He totes a pistol while he works. Doshie carries one to Honeywell and Hootbird is skeered to death. Was shot at agin the other day when he was squirrel-huntin'. So I thought I'd better take my gun out and have a look around my property. I found old Plack Rivercomb a-sittin' down there on a big moss-kivvered rock with a Winchester across his lap. 'A-huntin' squirrels, Plack?' I said. 'I'm a-huntin' a big squirrel, Snake,' he said. 'I'm a-huntin' the squirrel that's a-killin' our foxes. If I take 'im alive, he'll swing to a limb over Laurel Ridge. We'll have an old-time hangin', Snake.' And then I found Penny Shelton down in Shinglemill Holler with a high-powered rifle he's bought himself jist fer the purpose of findin' this fox killer. Penny's a-wonderin' about these people ye're a-harborin' around here, Op. I am too. Now let's come to an understandin'. Let's have a showdown right here!" He finished his speech by waving vaguely in the direction of Alf, Julia, and Lutie, huddled together under the oak tree.

"Come on through the garden gate, Snake, and meet these people," Op said. "Right now."

Snake left his shotgun leaning against the palings. He walked through the gate.

"This is Lutie, Snake."

"Who's Lutie?"

"She says she's my daughter."

"Sounds suspicious to me."

"But ye know Beadie and I had a daughter?"

"I'm one of the few around here who does know it," Snake Blue said, looking Lutie over. "I remember the stormy night when yer gal baby was born. I ought to remember. My wife Sal came over that night to deliver her. But some people come here from Ohio and took that baby away from ye, Op. 'Cause you laid out drunk about every night. I'd haf to have proof she's yer gal."

"But I *am* Op's daughter," Lucretia repeated. "Why else would I come back to his cabin?"

Snake looked into her pretty face and decided he didn't want to argue the point. "Who are these other people?"

"Julia and Alfred Pruitt," Op said. "They say they're Lutie's cousins. No blood kin to me, though."

"Are ye the man who's a-doin' all this shootin' around here?" Snake asked Alf, looking him in the eye. "Did ye jump from the brush and grab Doshie Hammertight when she was comin' from church the other night?"

"I never killed a fox in my life," Alf said, the muscles in his

172

face twitching. "And I never grabbed Doshie Hammertight. Good Lord, no!"

"Old Doshie, that awful bag of hot air," Op sighed. "Still a-spreadin' lies."

"Young man, where are ye from?" Snake asked. "I want to know more about ye."

"I'm from Dayton, Ohio," Alf stammered.

"Did ye have a job in Dayton?" Snake asked.

"I worked at the Wright Airfield."

"Then what in hell are ye a-doin' out here on my ridge?" Snake asked. "This looks suspicious to me. Three strangers out here. And ye, Op, a-harborin' 'em!"

"Mr. Blue,"—Alf had found a subject close to his heart— "since the world has gone mad and the atomic bomb has been discovered, I don't believe industrial cities like Dayton, Ohio, are safe. In fact, I don't believe the world is safe. That's why I'm here."

"The world not safe?" Snake Blue peered closely at Alf. "That's hard to understand, stranger." Snake Blue wiped more perspiration from his face. "They say the world was destroyed by water onct, but that was in the Bible."

"That's what the atomic bomb'll do"—Alf's voice rose—"only with fire, not water. And one bomb will be enough for a big city and all the people in it will go up in flame!"

Snake Blue looked Alf over from head to toe, as if looking for a third leg or a single eye in the middle of the forehead.

"That's crazy talk," he said. "Mr. Pruitt, ye are a very nervous man. We don't have many nervous people around here. Ye need good nerves and a steady eye when ye sight over a gun barrel. Around here when a man is nervous and he talks like ye're a-talkin', we think he's a-runnin' from some foul deed. We know this country's a-goin' to stand. Ye stick around here with us awhile and ye won't have any doubts. Ye need some hard work 'r somethin' if yer nerves are bad. Ye need to dig in the dirt and chop stovewood."

"That's what I've told 'im, Snake," Op said; "and that's what he's a-doin' and he's much better'n he was the day he come here. Atter he takes medicine from the wild roots he'll be a different man too. Alf's not a-runnin' from a foul deed, Snake! I'm shore of that. Alf needs help. He's a weaklin', runt of the litter, or somethin'. About next spring, I figure he'll be able to build his own cabin on the ridge and make his own way. I don't dislike Alf and Julia exactly, but to have them in my smokehouse is too close."

"Op, I don't mind yer squattin' up here twenty years and not a-payin' rent. But," Snake warned, "to harbor strangers who kill foxes and shoot at people is somethin' I won't allow. I know somebody's a-doin' it. Where there's smoke, there's fire. Where there's strangers"—he pointed at Alf—"there's trouble." Then he scratched his turkey-red neck. "But I'll admit that ye don't look like no killer."

"I think it's Ted Newsome a-doin' it all, Snake," Op told him.

"Ted Newsome's been dead thirty years, Op!" Snake Blue looked strangely at Theopolis. "Ye mean the Ted Newsome we ust to know, don't ye?"

"Yes, I do," Op said. "He's been back here! And he says his name is Ted Newsome. His description fits that of the Ted we ust to know—six foot, blond, with pearly-white teeth and a square-set jaw."

"Who's seen Ted Newsome around here?" Snake Blue asked, serious now.

"Lutie's seen 'im," Op said. "He's a-sparkin' with Lutie. He's picked 'er wild flowers and drops in here to see 'er."

"What!" Snake Blue turned toward Lucretia. "When does this man come? Where does he live?"

"Ye know where he lives!" Op looked strangely at Snake. "He lives in his long home ye and I hepped dig thirty years ago. He lives where we laid 'im. The old temple of flesh lives there but the speret roams!"

"Ye and yer sperets, Op," Snake said. "Ye tell me about this man, Lutie?"

"He's a spirit all right." Lutie looked very earnest when she said it. "I can be working at the cabin and he'll come in with a bouquet of flowers. I never see him coming. I just look around and he's standing there. He goes just like he comes! He disappears like smoke on a high wind."

"No question in my mind ye're Op's daughter," Snake Blue said, shaking his head sadly. "I thought I was goin' to get somewhere. But like old Op, ye see strange things in the clouds and ye hear tokens in the wind. Watch poor old Ted that he don't kill the foxes. And"—Snake slapped Op on the shoulder— "don't let that speret Ted Newsome marry Lutie. What a combination that would be! Everybody'd come fer miles to see that couple. Then ye'd never be able to live in peace on Laurel Ridge!"

"I'd rather she'd marry a speret, Snake, as that Hootbird." Op's voice shook with anger. "He's the little sneak that's a-startin' a lot of these wild tales about Laurel Ridge. Better check 'im. He might be the one a-killin' the foxes and sayin' it's a wild man he's seen. I wouldn't put nothin' past 'im."

"But he's not as dangerous as his long-tongued mother," Lutie said, following Snake toward the fence.

Snake went through the garden gate without answering and got his gun. He went over the ridge line toward Shinglemill Hollow. Alf turned to Julia, a bewildered expression on his face. "Does—does he still think I killed the foxes?"

"No, darling," Julia answered absently; "he just thinks you're a little teched in the head." Then she added, in a voice too low for Op and Lutie to hear: "But did you hear Lutie calling this Ted Newsome fellow a spirit? There's something funny there. I know Lutie better than that. She doesn't believe in spirits!"

35

Theopolis wandered back to the tree, his lips moving in a mutter. "First the fox hunters, then old Doshie, atter her comes Sheriff Ackerson, and now Snake Blue. They ain't *all* crazy. Maybe one 'r two, but not all of 'em."

"Surely you don't believe this nonsense about a wild man, Dad." Lutie was openly disturbed. Julia watched her closely.

"Wal, if there *is* a wild man on this ridge, we should be the ones to find 'im. Atter all, we live up here." Op began filing his hoe again. "We'll finish this patch of corn and I'll go see Ben this afternoon. I know Ben will be willin'. Doshie and Hootbird've got 'im worked up in a sweat. And I'll want 'im with me. And I'll want ye too, Alf."

"Want me!" Alf was surprised. "You don't want me? I won't be any good!"

"It'll make a man of ye," Op said, as his file screaked across the hoe and Julia put her hands over her ears. "Ye might be a good un in the time of trouble. If it's a close call, ye might make the difference. Course I don't think we'll find a real man. And ye can't shoot the speret of Ted Newsome!"

"But I never carried a gun in my life," Alf said. "I don't even know how to use one."

"I don't have anythin' but a rifle and a good huntin' knife," Op said. "I'll let ye carry the knife. Ye could use a knife in close quarters, couldn't ye, if we do happen to find a wild man?"

"O Lord, no!" Alf's eyes grew wide at the very idea.

"But ye've got good eyes, ain't ye?" Op said. "Ye can see a man hidin' behind a tree or lurkin' at a far piece? Ye've got better eyes than I've got!"

"My eyes are good enough," he replied, "but I won't carry any knife!"

"I'll need ye anyway," Op told him. He laid Julia's hoe down and picked up Lucretia's. "Old Ben is awful slow. And my eye is none too good fer long range."

"Dad, I wouldn't go out hunting for a man," Lucretia said, frowning. "That's Sheriff Ackerson's job, him and all his fancy deputies."

"Old barrel-bellied Sheriff Ackerson," Op sighed. "Too much weight on his brier-stem legs and not enough Laurel Ridge air in his lungs. He can't do nothin'. He's just got a big name. I can do more'n Sheriff Ackerson and all his deputies put together!"

"Anyway, leave Alf here, Dad."

"Let Alf go along," Julia said heartily. "It may be good for Alf's nerves."

"What do you want to do, Julia? Get me killed so you can get a pension?" Alf said.

"But, Dad, you've got only one eye." Lucretia was grasping at straws.

"I don't know how to hunt a man." Alf still wasn't enthusiastic. "I came here for my health. I didn't come here to use a gun, or slice somebody with a knife." He shuddered at the idea.

"That's just it," Op told him. "When ye get in close quarters, ye don't have time to think. Ye jist act! It'll be better fer ye than a yarb tonic."

"You won't find anyone, Alf," Julia laughed. "Go with him; the walk will do you good."

"I'll go along and watch for you, Op," Alf said weakly. "But I'm a pacifist. I'll run."

"Ye won't run if ye know somebody is a-goin' to kill ye," Op said. "That life of yourn is the dearest thing ye have. Wait till ye're put to the test. Ye live in a little world in the head, Alf! Yer skull bone's a prison wall around yer speret. I ain't killed nobody in my life. I never want to. But if somebody's out to get me, my mind got made up long time ago: they's gonna have a tussle. I've thought this thing out when I hunted in the woods at night with old Jerry."

Julia spoke softly: "Don't worry so, Alf. It will do you good."

"I said I'd go." Alf was disgusted. "But I'm not carrying any knife—and that's final!"

"Then we'll hoe out the rest of the corn and I'll go see Ben," Op told them. "If there *is* a man loose in the woods, first day-light'll be the time. He'll be out lookin' fer himself a young fox. That's when all the animals and birds stir. They're up from their beds a-huntin' breakfast. I'll meat-rind my old rifle tonight. It's been a long time since I've had it down from the joist."

36

"Ben, this is shore the time to find strange men," Op whispered hoarsely. "Only Laurel Ridge is above the cloud floor."

"If one's a-loafin' on the ridge, we can find 'im this mornin'," Ben answered in a slow whisper. "Doshie says—"

"Never mind what old Doshie says. Jist keep yer eyes open."

Op was carrying an octagon-sided, heavy-barreled twenty-two–caliber rifle. He held the barrel with his left hand, and his right hand covered the trigger guard. Ben carried his twenty-two automatic in his right hand with his big index finger through the trigger guard. His arms were so long his hands brushed his knees as he walked. Alf was unarmed.

The three men were walking slowly, cautiously, toward the

arc. On their left, over the deep Sandy Valley, was a sea of muslin clouds. The Sandy River and the turnpike were hidden below. In the distance, across this sea of clouds, were the Allcorn Hills, jutting up like a long chain of green islands. Near the Laurel Ridge road, yellow poplars and pines lifted their misty tops above the sea of white muslin. And Little White Oak Valley on their right was completely lost beneath the fluffy mass.

"It's a good time to slip right up on a man and have the gun on 'im before he knows it," Op whispered. "A body can walk on the damp ground and his brogans won't make a whettin' sound. And a man can't see him through the clouds this mornin'."

"I'm a-doin' it fer Doshie," Ben whispered. "Op, she's been talkin' about this fer days. She's worried about Hoot."

"Yep, I'm a-worryin' about Hoot, too," Op answered. He thought to himself: "I'm a-worryin' about havin' him fer a son-in-law."

When they reached the flat rock about equidistant from the arc, Op stopped.

"Ye go with me, Ben," he whispered. "We'll go down among the big rocks and do some huntin'. Ye stay here, Alf, and watch this ridge road. If ye see a man, hide behind this rock and watch which way he goes. If he's the speret of Ted Newsome, jist walk up and shake his hand."

Alf mumbled, "I don't know. I don't know what's going on." Then he walked up on the little bank beside the flat rock where he would have a good view of Laurel Ridge toward the cabin and toward Six Hickories. Op and Ben started down the steep slope, soon disappearing from Alf's view into the cloud.

"It's better to stay together," Op whispered. "If we part, one of us might stumble onto the other. I might shoot ye. Ye might shoot me."

179

"Jist be keerful with that piece of hardware," Ben muttered. "If it wasn't fer Doshie's a-talkin' so much . . ."

They were within four feet of the first big rock before they saw it jutting up. They looked up its steep sides but couldn't see the top for layers of cloud mist that swam in the slow-moving morning wind.

"He could be a-layin' up there," Ben said softly in Op's ear. "He could shoot straight down at us. We couldn't see the gun barrel in the cloud."

Op whispered, "It'll look like a bull black snake in the snow."

They walked around the rock, looking up. Then they walked to another large flat-topped rock, scaled up the side, and looked on top. They went from rock to rock, looking around and on top. On the big rock by the yellow poplar, Ben picked up a handful of thirty-caliber empty cartridges. His fire-shovel hand trembled so that he could hardly show them to Op.

"We've looked about every place down here," Ben whispered. "We can't find anybody. Let's get outten this cloud."

"I hate to leave a place till I'm through lookin'," Op whispered. "But we know somebody's been here. This is a hangout."

"It's strange to be a-huntin' fer people," Ben whispered. "It makes me nervous. Like Alf."

"Jist remember it's fer Doshie then," Op hissed.

"I'm remembrin'." Ben shook his big head and disturbed the mist. "But that won't help us when we run plumb against this wild man in the fog."

The two men walked up the steep slope, not more than two steps apart. When they came up through the cloud to the ridge, they were three hundred yards beyond the rock where Alf was waiting. The sun was shining over the sea of clouds, and mist was rising toward the sun.

"Look at Alf," Ben whispered hoarsely. "He wants us!"

Alf was motioning wildly with his hand. Op and Ben ran toward him. Drops of water ran down Op's rifle barrel and dripped to the ground.

"I was sitting right here," Alf jabbered excitedly, "and I saw three men come up out of the cloud. I got down behind this rock where I could see. My heart come up to my mouth for I thought they would catch me behind this rock. But they didn't. They went out Laurel Ridge. And they weren't spirits!"

"What kind of lookin' men were they?" Ben asked, doddling his head.

"Mean-looking," Alf told him. "There's more than one man hiding on this ridge. They were after something, too. They were whispering to one another things I couldn't hear."

"Maybe they were squirrel hunters," Ben said hopefully. The automatic shook in his huge paw.

"They weren't looking for squirrels on the ground and behind trees and rocks," Al whispered. "They would have been looking up in the trees!"

"They were down in the arc when we were there, Op," Ben whispered in Op's ear. "We might've come head on with 'em like I told ye."

"But they're the men we want to find," Op told Ben. "Let's go atter 'em! Let's get 'em dead 'r alive!"

"I-gods," Ben said. "But all the experience I've had with this pistol is guardin' the ballot boxes in Honeywell."

Alf's teeth were chattering. "D-d-dewdrops were dripping from their gun barrels in the sunlight. One short man had a big mustache and dewdrops were dripping from the ends. I've been thinking about Julia and Lutie out there in the cabin. We'd better go back. We'd better follow their tracks and see if they go out the ridge toward the cabin."

Op started out the ridge and Ben and Alf followed. Op bent over. "Look at these tracks."

Ben looked at them in the sand with Op.

"A-goin' right out the ridge," Ben said.

Op led the way, following the man tracks like Jerry followed a possum's.

"Here they turn," Op whispered when he came to the path that turned toward Wince Leffard Gap.

"Right toward my place," Ben whispered, doddling his head excitedly. "Doshie and the little young uns there today with Hootbird gone a-huntin' a bee tree."

"Hootbird," Op muttered, "that yellerbelly."

They tracked the men down to the ledges of rocks. Here the tracks left the path. Examining the ground carefully, they could track the men by the broken huckleberry twigs, bent-over pea vine, and disturbed bracken.

"I'm glad they didn't go toward the shack," Ben whispered. "My heart ain't a-beatin' as fast as it did."

"Doshie'd probably scare 'em to death if they did get there," Op said to himself.

Alf looked into the mists while Ben and Op followed the tracks among the ledges on the east wall of Sulphur Spring Hollow, the largest tributary of Little White Oak.

"Let's lissen to see if we can hear," Op whispered. "We might hear their shoes slushin' in the wet."

They stopped and stood still, each man controlling his breath while he listened for sounds. All was silent save the drops of water falling from the leaves as the sun's rays penetrated the sea of white and green.

"They can go faster than we can track, Ben," Op whispered. "Ye're too slow to ketch a stud turtle."

"They're using good strategy," Alf whispered, nervously. "They're up to something. We could go back to Laurel Ridge and—and wait for them at the cabin."

"But they might be a-livin' in a cliff around here someplace."

Op's voice was low and hoarse. "While we can track, we'd better foller. We might slip up on 'em a-layin' on a rock a-waitin' fer the morning sun to clear up the mists."

With Alf peering ahead through the mists, Theopolis and Ben followed the tracks and finally reached Sulphur Spring Hollow. There the tracks turned downstream. Shoes had sunk in the soft sand and tracking was easy for more than two hundred yards. Then the tracks parted, each set going in a separate direction around the slope toward Coonden Hollow.

"What d'ye know about that?" Op said in a low voice.

"Doshie's allus said there's more than one man a-combin' these woods"— Ben doddled his big head. "Doshie talks a lot but she's nearly allus right. She's a smart woman."

They decided, over Alf's protests, to follow three separate tracks until they reached the high ridge finger that formed the east wall of Coonden Hollow. Here the tracks came together again. The three man hunters stood close in a huddle, pondering their predicament.

"The clouds have cleared," Ben said. "They'll be able to see us now."

Op was about to answer that it was true the other way 'round, too, when Alf whispered excitedly. "Look, look over there. There they go! See them?"

Op trained his good eye in the direction Alf was shaking in.

37

"I see the boogers, Ben," Op whispered.

"Don't get too excited, Op," Alf warned. "They might be deadly killers!"

"Shhhh," Ben whispered. "Give me more time to see that my

hardware is ready." His big blunt fingers fumbled with the twenty-two.

"Let's go around this finger to the head of Coonden and be a-waitin' fer 'em as they go over toward the wild-strawberry patch on Shinglemill," Op suggested.

Ben just shook his head.

"This is a dangerous situation," Alf stuttered. "We might be killed. This is Sheriff Ackerson's duty!"

"If the Law can't get these boogers, we can," Op bragged. "Now that I'm shore they're not sperets."

They moved at a faster speed, since they were no longer following the tracks, keeping themselves behind the low tough-butted white oaks that grew from rock crevices. When they reached the head of Coonden Hollow, they turned to their left, to a field with second-growth timber, where corn had once been planted. In this second growth of sumac, sassafras, and hickory, they were careful to tiptoe and not shake the tops of the trees which Op could have reached with his rifle barrel. Then, through holes between the trees and vines, they saw the three men coming.

"Stop," Op whispered. "Better to wait right here and have our guns ready when they turn over the rim toward Shinglemill!"

Alf, Op, and Ben stood about two paces apart. They could see the men coming up closer.

"Yander they are!" one of the strange men shouted when Ben's doddling head shook a sassafras and made a leafy noise.

"Dead 'r alive, boys!" another shouted, as the first man raised a single-barreled shotgun to take aim.

Ben's head doddled and his hand moved jerkily as he started firing. One bullet hit the dirt in front of him. He shot a spray of bullets from the ground straight up toward the sky.

"They're armed," shouted one of the strange men.

"Surrender and we won't hurt ye," Op shouted as he held his

rifle to his shoulder and aimed with his good eye at a man who had started for cover.

Theopolis fired, missing his mark.

"No surrender," came a reply. "Let's go after 'em. They're armed but they can't shoot."

They charged into the second growth in the direction of the three man hunters. Ben's big hand was shaking until he couldn't get it into his pocket to get more cartridges.

"Let's go," Ben shouted as he turned and started running. He ran through the brush like a big horse.

"Stay under the brush, man," Op shouted.

Op fired twice in the general direction of their adversaries and then he turned and followed.

"Dangerous criminals," Op grunted as he ran through the brush, following Ben and Alf. Behind them guns set up an awful racket. Shotgun pellets sprayed the air above them and fell like drops of hard rain onto the sassafras leaves. Two pellets stung Op's neck.

"Go fer the rocks," Op shouted.

Then a rifle bullet sang near Op's ear. Op went to his knees, rose again, and ran faster than ever.

"Yander they go," shouted a voice from behind. "Get 'em!"

"Halt before we kill ye!"

"They're still a-runnin'!"

Shotgun pellets and rifle bullets spatted the green leaves and the bushes. One pellet stung Ben's shoulder.

Then Alf and Ben left the old field for the rocks on the east wall of Coonden Hollow, almost the way they had come. Op was only two steps behind when they reached the protection of the rocks. A rifle bullet hit the first rock and whistled off into space.

"Let's reload and get behind a rock," Op said.

"No time to reload," Ben said. "Let's keep goin'."

They dodged behind the rocks with the men in hot pursuit. Op, while still on the run, loaded a cartridge in his rifle and fired once back over his shoulder. He thought he heard a man yell but he was getting his breath too hard and fast to be sure. Ben was getting his breath like a wheel oxen drawing a heavy log. Alf was in the lead screaming as he went over the finger of the ridge between Coonden and Sulphur Spring Hollow. Here Alf turned up the hill and Ben and Op followed.

"Keerful, men," someone shouted below.

"Did he hit ye, Fatus?"

"Grazed me with that last bullet."

"They're a-trackin' us," Op grunted.

"And we were trackin' them a while ago," Ben wailed.

"Yander they are," shouted a voice among the pursuers. "Let's get 'em! Come on!"

The man aimed and fired, and the bullet marked a tree beside Alf. Ben emptied his pistol wildly in the direction of the men. He didn't take aim and his hand was shaking so he could hardly hold on.

"Let's take our stand," Op shouted. "Criminals!"

"That big un," one shouted, and a rifle barked.

"On the hip," Ben screamed as he went to the ground.

Op got behind a white oak as the bullets whizzed by. Alf jumped behind a rock and started digging a hole in the ground with his hands.

"Keep 'em kivvered," said the men coming down the hill with their guns pointed.

"Up with yer hands, big man!"

Ben lay on the ground with both hands up.

"Drop that rifle from behind that tree! We got ye!"

Op dropped the rifle.

"Feller, come out from behind that rock!"

"He's unarmed," Op said with a trembling voice.

"Come out from behind that tree in the name of the Law!"

"What law?" Op asked, stepping out.

"Jake Ratcliffe's law!"

"Op Akers! Is that ye?"

"Jake Ratcliffe," Theopolis said, "what are ye a-doin' atter us? Fatus Sloane! And there's Tiny Timberlake."

"Well, what are ye a-doin' shootin' at us?" Jake asked Theopolis.

"Thought ye's the men a-hangin' out on Laurel Ridge! I'd like to ask ye the same question," Op said.

"Jake fetched us here to clean this ridge," Fatus Sloane said.

"Ye hit old Ben," Op grunted.

"Are ye hurt, Ben?" Fatus leaned over Ben where he lay on his side holding to his bottom.

"That bullet had a lot of smoke on it!" Ben grunted. "Creased my rind good."

"Who's behind that rock?" asked Tiny Timberlake, the short, broad-shouldered man with the mustache.

"Alf Pruitt," Op answered.

Tiny walked over behind the rock and found Alf lying face down in a little hole he had scooped out with his hands. His entire body was shaking like a white oak leaf in the January wind.

"What's the matter, man?" Tiny asked. "It's all a mistake! We ain't a-goin' to hurt ye."

Alf didn't answer but lay with his face against the ground, shaking.

"Alf's a little nervous!" Op said.

"He's plenty nervous if ye ask me." Tiny stood over Alf's body watching it quiver.

Fatus and Op helped Ben to his feet. There was a hole across the seat of Ben Hammertight's tight-fitting overalls. The hole was about six inches long and looked as if it had been cut with a pair of dull scissors. There was a red mark across his flesh, just a little more than skin deep.

"See if ye can walk, Ben," Fatus said.

Ben took a step and then another. "I'm all right," he said.

"It's just skin deep." Fatus bent over, looking close.

"Who give ye a warrant to arrest us?" Ben asked.

"Jake Ratcliffe brought us to arrest the wild men yer wife has been a-seein' on this ridge."

"Show me the warrants," Ben said.

"I didn't put the warrants in writin'," Jake explained. "I looked into my lawbook and I said: 'Let's go fetch 'em fellers, dead 'r alive. Let's bring 'em in to justice.' That's good as a warrant."

"But, Jake, ye can't read," Op said. "Ye can't read any more'n I can. I've known ye all my life."

"But it's in my lawbook," Jake said. "I can turn to the right place and show ye!"

"I feel like goin' before the Grand Jury and indictin' ye," Ben said. "A-comin' in here from the other side of Sandy River on Snake Blue's premises and a-shootin' me."

"But this Laurel Ridge is in my district," Jake said.

"To hell with yer district," Ben said, shaking with anger. "If I knowed the man amongst ye that fired the shot that hit me, I'd choke his infernal gizzard out."

"Where's *yer* warrants?" Jake Ratcliffe asked Ben. "Ye're out here with a pistol man huntin', too."

"Quit yer gassin' and come over here and give me some help," Tiny Timberlake said. "I can't do it by myself."

Op walked over and took Alf by one arm and Tiny got him by the other. They lifted his face from the hole. Dirt was in his

188

eyes and mouth. His face was as white as a frosted beech leaf and his glassy eyes stared into space.

Op pulled his bandanna from his pocket and wiped Alf's face while Tiny held him in a standing position.

"Ye're not hurt, Ben; quit complainin'," Tiny said. "Here's the man that's gone to pieces, 'r somethin'."

Fatus Sloane ran to the little stream below and dipped his hat full of water and poured it on Alf's face. Alf blinked his eyes and slowly looked around.

"What happened?" he asked. "Where was I hit?"

"Ye're not hit, Alf," Op told him. "We've made a mistake. The men we were atter are huntin' fer the same men we're huntin'. And we started to hunt one another. Jake here, is Justice of Peace of the Tenth District. He fetched Fatus and Tiny to Laurel Ridge to hunt the same man we were atter."

Alf shook himself and blinked his eyes. Then he stood alone, pulled a handkerchief from his pocket, and wiped his eyes again.

"Everything turned black." Alf sighed heavily. "I don't remember what happened."

"We're lucky somebody wasn't kilt," Op said. "Best thing is to ferget the whole affair."

"Somebody come nigh as a pea gettin' me," Fatus said. "Look where this bullet grazed my cheek." There was a long red mark across Fatus's cheek and under his ear. "That's how close I come to the call when we left the old field and went into the rocks."

"I fired that one over my shoulder without aim." Op chuckled.

"Ben," said Fatus Sloane, a tall bean pole of a man with a sharp hatchet face, "if ye go before the Grand Jury and indict us fer man huntin' without warrants, we can go before the Grand Jury and indict you, too. All of us might get fined 'r sentenced to jail. And people in town shore would have a laugh on us."

"Best thing fer all is to go home and ferget it," Op repeated.

"A thing like this is hard to ferget," Ben told them. "I'm a-goin' to remember every time I sit down." He twisted his big neck and looked down under his arm at the long red spot and the big rip in his overalls.

38

"Did you see anybody?" Lucretia met Op and Alf on the cabin porch.

"Yep, we shore did." Op dropped into a chair. "Wrong people, though." Lucretia looked relieved.

"We thought we had the right men," Alf said. "We trailed them for miles, then they tried to take us."

"What do ye mean 'tried'? They *did* take us."

Julia looked bewildered. "This gets more fascinating by the minute."

"Jake Ratcliffe and his men got us," Op grunted. "They thought we's the strange men loose on the ridge. We thought they were. So we met in the woods and shot at one another."

Lucretia burst into laughter. Julia turned her face away from Alf.

"It's not a laughin' matter," Op said. "It's a dangerous thing."

"Not anybody hurt, though?" Lucretia asked.

"Ben went around the ridge with a six-inch scratch on his rind," Op said.

Julia reached over and took her husband's hand. Alf looked as if he might be about to breathe his last.

"Alf went to pieces durin' the battle and dug a hole and put his face in it," Op said.

"Poor Alf," Julia said. "And I encouraged you to go."

"Encouraged me? You practically insisted on it."

"I'm proud of you anyway, Alf," she told him.

"All wimmen love a hero, Alf," Op grunted. "Not that ye was a-lookin' very heroic with yer rear a-stickin' out of that hole."

"Doshie will have something to talk about now"—Lucretia changed the subject quickly—"with Ben shot and everything."

"Doshie," Op said, as if the word didn't taste very good. "Doshie's been packin' 'er lies to old Jake Ratcliffe and he's anxious to do somethin' big so the voters in Looten County'll hear about 'im. He wants to run fer High Sheriff next time, since Sheriff Bill Ackerson can't run again. Jake plans to run against Sop Johnson. But he'll never get my vote. I'll vote agin him a dozen times."

"Dad, why blame it on Jake Ratcliffe?" Lucretia asked. "Both parties made a mistake, seems to me."

"I'm tellin' ye the truth," Op sputtered. "That's why old Jake deputized men and brought 'em in here. He's got big idears. He'd love to wear that silver badge on his coat, but he never will! I'll walk the ridges and up the hollers and work agin 'im."

"Why can't a sheriff succeed himself in Kentucky?" Julia asked.

"One time in office is enough fer most of 'em," Op replied. "They make enough money to last 'em the rest of their lives. Ye'll never see one of the boogers a-sellin' possum hides, diggin' ginseng roots, and a-pickin' berries atter he's been sheriff. I know what I'm talkin' about."

Alf stirred himself slightly. "You mean the sheriff gets good pay here?"

Op laughed. "There's more than one way a sheriff can get it. Protectin' moonshiners, fer instance. Yep, old Jake wants to be sheriff, so he come in here with deputized men to make a name fer himself! And that little puff of hot wind, Doshie, started the whole thing."

"There I agree, Dad," Lucretia nodded. "She's stirred up all this trouble!"

"There's no wild man on this ridge," Op said. "I'm convinced of it now! I feel like a-goin' before the next Grand Jury and indictin' Doshie fer lyin'. Her long tongue got old Ben a nice red stripe across the butt!"

"Are you tired, darling?" Julia asked Alf. He was sitting slumped down in his chair. "You're not so nervous as you were!"

"I'm too tired to be nervous." Alf laughed weakly. "Maybe that's a cure."

Op was not to be outdone.

"I'm as tired as a red fox atter it's circled this ridge all night and up till ten the next mornin'," he said. "And my stummick is empty as a gourd. I want to eat till I push my belly from my backbone."

39

"I'm only a-tellin' you what Little Johnnie Blue told Pap and me about Esmerelda Sutton," Op said, leaning back in his chair on the porch. It was noon and they were resting. "There's not a doubt in my mind she was a witch. And she was the last witch I ever heard tell of around here. Little Johnnie Blue told it like this: There was about fifteen hounds atter the fox. He was a big old red fox, almost the size of a new-born calf. He had a red body and a big bushy tail with a white tip. The old fox was jist a few yards ahead of the hounds. He was barely a-gettin' over the rocks and logs atter the hounds had run 'im about seventeen hours. And the hounds didn't put their noses to the ground to trail 'im, they were too close. They held their noses in the wind and were ready to close in fer the kill. Sweeter Barnhill, Jimmy Overton, Hester Cremeans, and Johnnie Blue were standin' in Pawpaw Gap ready to see the hounds finish the fox. They would've ketched him right before their eyes but then somethin' happened. All of the hounds changed into foxes and the tired old fox was turned into a hound. And the foxes turned tail and fled in all directions. There were so many of 'em the big old tired hound didn't know which one to take atter. But he singled out a fox and got his revenge!"

Lucretia and Julia smiled. Alf put his hands to his sides and groaned with pain.

"What's the matter, Alf?" Op asked him.

"I'm sore as a boil all over from the chase yesterday," he replied. "I can't even move my body without hurting."

"Ye should've chopped wood this morning and got that soreness outten ye," Op said.

"Chopped wood!" Alf groaned again.

"Op, tell us why Esmerelda Sutton turned the hounds into foxes and the fox into a hound," Julia said. "Why would she do a thing like that?"

"Meanness in 'er," Op said. "Little Johnnie Blue said him and the boys looked down from Pawpaw Gap and saw 'er comin' up the road when the hounds were close on the fox. Said she stopped in the middle of the road and said: 'What are we a-goin' to do about it, little brown mouse? Little brown mouse, that fox is tired. The hounds are goin' to ketch 'im. Are ye a-goin' to let 'em do it, little brown mouse?' And she looked at the fox before she started talkin' agin, so Little Johnnie told us. Then Esmerelda said: 'I'm glad ye feel that way, little brown mouse. I'm glad ye want the change made. We'll change 'em.' And that's how Little Johnnie said it happened. When she started walkin' up the road toward 'em, the men took off in all directions. Everybody on Laurel Ridge was afraid of Esmerelda Sutton and that little brown mouse she talked to which no one ever saw."

"Little brown mouse," Alf repeated. "What nonsense!"

"Nonsense? Why, ye ain't heard all yet. Poor old Jake Miller bought a cow from Esmerelda. He wasn't married and Esmerelda wasn't either. She was in love with poor old Jake, so 'twas said, and atter Jake bought the cow she had 'im down in the hog pen rootin' with his nose like a hog. And she had the hogs walkin' around on their hind feet laughin'. Later, when the boys went out to fox-hunt and Jake was with 'em, he tried to stand on his head on the stopper in a whisky jug. Everybody thought Jake was drunk and they laughed at the crazy things he did that night. But he was under the spell. He stayed under it till he took the picture of Esmerelda she'd given 'im up to the Freewill Baptist Graveyard and put a silver bullet through it jist as the mornin' sun was risin' up like a big ember from the east!"

Julia put her head in her hands. "That's the wildest one yet, Op."

"There was never a woman in these parts like Esmerelda Sutton," Op continued. "She was tall and slender. As purty as a green-leafed willow in the early-spring wind. Men fell fer 'er and when they give 'er kisses she put 'em under the spell. Before she could bewitch 'em they had to give somethin' to 'er or she had to give somethin' to 'em. And she was always talkin' to that little brown mouse nobody ever saw. 'Cause of 'er, I remember how my Pap was afeared of mice, especially if it was a brown wood mouse. Pap got so he'd run every time he saw one. Esmerelda had this whole country under the spell."

"Look, Dad, I see somebody coming from the green tunnel." Lucretia pointed.

Op stopped talking. He trained his good eye on the ridge road toward the sty.

194

"He's a big man," Alf said as he watched him walk toward the cabin.

"He's got a pole across his shoulder," Julia said. "He must be going fishing. But where is the water up here?"

"Who is it, Dad?" Lucretia asked.

"That's not Ted Newsome, is it?" Op asked her.

"No, it's not Ted."

"Wait till he gets a little closer," Op said. Then his voice rose with excitement. "Honest, I believe it's Jack. It is Jack! It's Jack!"

Op ran from the porch to meet him.

40

"Hi, Op," said the young man. He was a big muscular boy and broad shouldered, maybe in his middle twenties. His eyes were long and narrow and he had a low forehead.

Jack dropped the pole from over his shoulder. It had a net on the tip end of it and a bag of clothes tied to the middle.

"Where have ye been this time, Jack?" Op shook Jack's big hand and patted him on the shoulder.

"I've been to Iowa, Op," he said. "I've been a-livin' with Fred and Kate Schultz on a farm near Creston. I've had a good place to stay, Op, with a good bed in the granary and plenty to eat and a big team of hosses to drive. But I've missed Laurel Ridge and ye, Op. I've wanted to get back and ketch butterflies in Shinglemill Holler."

"I've missed ye, Jack," Op said.

"But ye know yer old Run-around Jack allus makes it back," Jack said, grinning. "He allus gets back to the butterflies before the spring and summer're over! Ye still love me, don't ye, Op?"

"Yes, I love ye, Jack." Op looked as if he might burst out crying.

"I like to be loved," Jack said. Then he saw the other three who stood on the porch, gaping. "Who are all these people ye got around ye, Op? Who is this purty woman? Are ye married to 'er?"

"Nope, I'm not married agin," Op answered. "Only one wife in this world and one speret in the next fer me. This is Lutie, who says she's yer sister."

"My sister!" Jack was surprised. "I didn't know I had a sister."

"I am your sister, Jack."

Jack said just one word—"Purty."

"I've heard about you for years, Jack," Lucretia said.

"But I never heard anything about ye. Why didn't ye tell me I had a sister, Op?"

"Oh, I didn't see any use of that." Op looked down at his old brogans. "I raised ye, and yer Uncle Will and Aunt Corrinne Day had Lutie. I never thought she'd come back here." A little bitterness came into his voice.

"If Op had raised ye and me together, I wouldn't've been lonesome all the time," Jack said to Lucretia. "I wouldn't've played so much with the butterflies, frogs, and baby-handed moles. I had plenty of playmates during the spring and summer up till late fall." His low forehead came down in a frown. "Had only Op and the dog in the winter."

"Jack, we've eaten, but I'll run and fix you some dinner," Lucretia said. "I want you to meet your cousins!"

"Gee, I got a lot of kinfolks." Jack smiled again. Op picked up Jack's pole with his turkey of clothes and net. He followed Jack and Lucretia onto the porch.

"This is Julia Pruitt," Lucretia said. "And this is Alf. They're your cousins and they've come from Dayton."

Alf stared dumfounded from Jack's face to the butterfly net and back to Jack's face. Julia mumbled her "hello."

"I've been through that town," Jack said. "I didn't know I had kinfolks there. If I had, I'd a-stopped and stayed awhile with ye!"

Alf glanced nervously toward Julia.

"This is yer home, Jack," Op said, almost angrily. "Yer home is here on Laurel Ridge with me. Ye're allus welcome here!"

"But come lonesome wintertimes when the leaves fall and the ridge gets dark and cold I haf to go," Jack said. "I remember the winters here and the snow in big drifts and Op a-wadin' through 'em up around his knees with an ax across his shoulder a-breakin' a path and me a-followin'. I don't like the lonesome winters here without somebody to play with. Summer, spring, and early fall are all right. But never a winter here agin fer Jack." He turned to Lucretia. "That's why I'm called Run-around Jack in Honeywell. I think Doshie named me Run-around Jack." He turned to Op. "Can ye keep yer Run-around Jack, Op? In the cabin? Have ye got too many?"

"Julia and I live over in the smokehouse, Jack"— Alf found his tongue. "We don't live in the cabin."

Op picked up the butterfly net and started inside with it. He smiled. Run-around Jack was home.

"Don't bother the pole, Op," Jack told him. "I'm a-goin' in a few minutes to Shinglemill. I can't wait to get back down there and see every bloom and butterfly."

"Rest awhile, Jack," Op said. "Stay and let's talk. The butter-flies'll keep."

"I'm not tired," he told Op. "I've been on a bus from Creston to Honeywell and I feel cramped. Like old Mike and Kate, my team out there in Iowa, when a rainy spell hit and I had to keep 'em in the barn fer two weeks. I've just got to go!"

Jack stepped down from the porch and got the pole Theopolis had leaned against the cabin wall.

"Go see my friends," he said.

"When will ye be back, Jack?"

"About sundown."

41

"There's a purty one," Jack shouted.

He took off running with his net high in the wind above him. He held the pole with one hand and kept his eyes on a black butterfly that had red dots on its wings. It was fluttering in the bright wind high over Jack's head.

"Purty thing!" Jack leaped high into the wind and swung his net like a baseball bat. The net opened and the butterfly was caught in its center. When Jack came back to earth, he relaxed his net and it closed behind the butterfly.

"I've got ye, purty thing," he said softly. Lucretia, Alf, and Julia watched in amazement. "I'll soon get ye a playmate. I don't want ye to get lonesome."

"Will he kill them?" Julia asked Op.

"Nope, he won't kill anythin'," Op said. "He'll leave 'em in the net until he's through runnin' and playin' and then he'll turn 'em all loose. He jist likes to ketch 'em. He started playin' with the butterflies when he was big enough to walk and he's been a-doin' it ever since. I made 'im a little net when he was about five years old. Later I showed him how to make one. Now Jack makes his own nets from regular twine. He allus keeps a supply ahead."

"It's strange he'd catch them just for the fun of it," Lucretia said. "I know a lot of people who catch them and make displays under glass."

"Jack couldn't stand to see a butterfly under glass," Op said. "When I ust to ketch a possum and start to break his neck with a mattock handle, Jack would run away like a wild turkey. Jack can't kill, he's too gentle. He's got the mind and the heart of a child. A happy child, too."

Jack leaped a cluster of saw brier swinging his net far over to his left side. He scooped down low and came up with a golden-colored butterfly. They could hear his laugh at the cabin. They watched him from the porch until he turned the bend in the ridge road and was out of sight.

"Jack's a-havin' the time of his life now," Op went on. "He'll run over this ridge and comb the deep hollers on both sides. All of this land is his home. He'll hep me some, but mostly he'll ketch butterflies all summer and atter the first frosts he'll take off to a new place in the West. He'll go there and work fer the winter. Jack loves big herds of cattle and hosses."

"What does he do with the money he earns?" Alf asked.

"Jack never thinks about money," Op answered quickly. "He never was ust to money, never had it to play with like a lot of young uns a-growin' up. And he didn't have any place to spend it. He played with pet birds, squirrels, coons, and ground hogs. Jack's had every kind of animal and bird that was not too full of wild nature to be tamed. He's even petted possums as much as they could be petted. But he never had money. And he works fer whatever a farmer will pay him. He works enough to buy his clothes and shoes, twine fer his nets, and bus tickets to travel over the country. He never has any money when he gets home and I give him a little when he leaves."

They could still hear Jack's happy voice in Shinglemill Hollow. Op closed his eyes and listened a moment, the same way he might listen to hounds closing in on a tired fox on a clear summer night.

"He's a-travelin' fast," Op said. "He'll go down into Shingle-mill Holler where the shoe-makes, persimmons, and daisies are in bloom. And he'll go from one end of that field to the other like a man hoein' corn rows. He'll kivver every foot of that holler a-runnin' at full speed, laughin' all the while."

"There wouldn't be any place in Dayton for Jack," Julia said.

"Don't worry, Julia, I never want 'im to go to Dayton," Op said. "That's why I've never told 'im about his sister. People with city ways wouldn't understand Jack. They might even lock 'im up in jail. Here on Laurel Ridge, Jack has his freedom. Here up near the sky is the best home Jack can ever have. People understand him up here. They know he wouldn't harm even—even a butterfly."

"Well, Op, I'm glad to hear you say he's not dangerous," Alf said, getting up from his chair. He stretched his arms above his head, and then bent over experimentally. "Oh, oh, my poor sore body!" he cried.

"I'll get ye a cure for that soreness," Op said. He seemed glad to be able to switch the subject from Run-around Jack. "Poke-berry root. We'll bile her up and put the juice to you. It'll smart ye shore, but it'll fetch the soreness from yer body."

42

The sun had gone down beyond the Allcorn Hills. There was a red patch of sky like where Op had burned a brush pile and the night wind had fanned the embers to a bright glowing red on the breast of the dark earth. Theopolis walked the porch impatiently.

"When Jack told me he'd be back at sunset I expected 'im to be back," Theopolis said to Lucretia. "He was allus back at the time he told me. Jack never lied to me. Somethin' has happened to 'im!"

"Wait a few minutes longer, Dad. He might have found more butterflies than usual."

"But the evenin' dew has dampened their wings," Op explained to her as he walked the floor. "Butterflies are a-gettin' under leaves to sleep fer the night. Jack might be atter some white moths. I've seen 'im chase 'em. And he has followed the lightnin' bugs. But Jack's not much fer a-runnin' and swingin' his net atter the stars are in the sky."

"There comes somebody, Dad." Lucretia pointed. "Out Laurel Ridge from the direction of Pawpaw Gap!"

"It's me, Op," Jack shouted. "Don't worry about me, Op! I'll tell ye what's kept me soon as I get there!"

Op stopped walking from one end of the porch to the other. He could tell Run-around Jack was more excited than usual.

"Op, I've been with Ted Newsome, the feller ye allus useta talk about," Jack said as he walked through the gate. "I've been with Ted Newsome, the speret."

"Tell me about it, son." Op's expression changed to one of pleasure. "Sit down here and tell me all about it!"

Lutie said nothing, but moved closer, listening to every word.

"I was a-swingin' my net atter a butterfly on the north wall of Shinglemill when I come face to face with a man as big as I am," Jack said excitedly, dropping down on the edge of the porch and letting his feet hang over. "He had a rifle in his hand. And I stopped all of a sudden. I said, 'Who are you?' 'Don't ye know me?' he ast. And I said: 'Nope, I don't know ye. I've never seen ye around here before and I've been all over this holler every spring and summer of my life. Who are ye?' And he said, 'I'm Ted Newsome, the speret. I have left my long home fer a walk.'

And I said, 'Where is yer long home?' And he said, 'My long home is in a grave in the Freewill Baptist Graveyard. My home is marked. Ye're welcome to come over and see where it is if ye're a doubter.'"

"What have I been a-tellin' you, Lutie?" Op said, turning to Lucretia. "Tell us more, Jack."

"Op, my legs got awful weak," Jack continued. "My strong legs give down under me and my body shook like a shoe-make leaf in the wind. Fer a minute I couldn't speak. But I opened my net and let my butterflies go free. And they rose up like a bright flutterin' cloud. They went all around Ted Newsome's face. And I almost fainted when I saw his long-bearded face in that cloud of flutterin' golden wings. But the cloud got higher and thinner and spread in all directions and there stood Ted with a big smile on his lips. 'Ted, I've heard Op talk about ye,' I said. 'I've heard 'im tell many a time how ye was bushwhacked over Lucinda Dortch right up there in front of where our cabin stands. While ye held 'er in yer arms, a bullet came from nowhere right outten the woods and drilled ye betwixt the eyes.'

"'That's right, Jack,' Ted said, and then he laughed like he didn't pay it no minds now. 'If ye'll step a little closer and look hard, I'll show ye a spot right betwixt my eyes. I'll show ye the price I paid fer love.' And I said: 'No, Ted Newsome, I won't come that close fer I feel a weakness in my body and a little faint. I'd rather stay right where I am and not move another step.' 'I paid the price of love, but Lucinda Dortch has gone to her long home too,' Ted said. 'She, too, sleeps at the Freewill Baptist Graveyard but I have never seen her speret. She has gone to a different place. We are not in the same world, Jack, and it is just as well that way. Because I have found my love!'

"'Who is yer love now?' I ast him. And he said: 'Lutie Akers, yer beautiful sister, Jack! And ye go back to the cabin and tell 'er I said that I love 'er so much my heart aches fer her.' That's what he said to me, Lutie, honest he did!"

Jack was so excited the foamy spittle flew from his mouth faster than milkweed furze drifting from an opened pod on an August wind.

"And I started back right then. And Ted said: 'Jack, wait a minute. I want to send more word to the cabin. Tell yer Dad, Op, that I'm partial to him, too. Tell 'im I know that he is my friend and that I will see him face to face someday. But not now!' "

"I told ye, Lutie," Op said in a positive tone. "I've been tellin' ye Ted Newsome was a speret! Now will ye believe me? It won't be long till I'll see Ted Newsome face to face. And I've got a lot of questions to ask 'im about some of the old-timers I've had my doubts about. They talked outten two sides of the mouth and I thought they were hypocrites. I'll find out from Ted if they're numbered with the blest! And ye, Lutie, thought Ted was a real flesh-and-blood man!"

"Op, that wasn't the all of it," Jack broke in eagerly. "Ted Newsome told me so much I can't remember it all. But I'll never ferget the way he shook the long blond sunburnt hair on his head and laughed as he talked and made me feel better. I said to 'im: 'Ted, why is yer hair so long?' And he said: 'I've not had my hair cut in a long, long time. Ye don't expect a speret to go to a barbershop and sit in a chair and have his hair cut, do ye? That'd skeer the wits outten the barber.'

"Then I asked him: 'Ted, did they bury ye in boots and ridin' pants? Didn't they put a nice suit of clothes on ye that fastened up and down the back and a collar and tie when ye left this world?' And he said, atter he'd finished laughin': 'Yep, they buried me that way but I've got to keep my best for the company of sperets on Laurel Ridge. We meet and have parties. Once we had supper together in yer cabin until Op came in from possum huntin' and opened the door right easy. We were a-makin' too much noise, all a-sittin' at Op's table. That night I was a-partyin' with the ore diggers and the lumberjacks. I got awful mad at Op over disturbin' us. Ast Op if he remembers? Tell 'im I said fer 'im never to do that agin.' "

"Remember!" Op repeated. "I hope to tell ye I remember that very night. I'll never ferget. Ye tried to laugh about it, Lutie. Now, ye see! I'll never break in on 'em when they're a-havin' another party in my cabin. I'll let 'em have a dozen parties here if they want to."

"What else did he say, Jack?" Lucretia asked.

"He said: 'I don't like the Hammertights. I don't like Doshie. She will never reach the land of the blest. She stirs up too much trouble with her long lizard tongue. She has people huntin' fer me. As long as she keeps runnin' to Honeywell a-tellin' the people about Laurel Ridge, there will be trouble! Doshie's a busybody!' "

"What did I tell ye?" Theopolis said, pointing a big index finger at Lutie. "Ye can't say I've not warned ye about the Hammertights! I've warned ye about that Hootbird, too!"

"Ted said somethin' about Hootbird." Jack talked faster than the wind in the Laurel Ridge pines. "He said: 'That Hootbird is a sneak. Fox hunters had better keep an eye on Hootbird. He's a good shot with a rifle!' "

"So it is Hootbird!" Op shouted. "I hope they ketch that little striped-tail snake. He's the young man a-shootin' the foxes. And he lays it off onto a stranger, a wild man a-livin' in the cliffs. He's caused Jake Ratcliffe to come in here with deputized men and bust old Ben's rind with a bullet till he has to stand up to eat and he has to sleep flat on his stummick yet. He come nigh as a pea a-gettin' old Ben killed. It's that Hootbird a-causin' about as much trouble as his long-tongue mother."

Run-around Jack was concentrating hard, trying to remember more. "Ted said to me: 'Jack, come back and see me. Let's ye and me be friends.' And I said: 'Where can I find ye, Ted?' And he said to me with a big smile on his sun-tanned face: 'I will come to ye, Jack. But if ye bring anybody with ye, I won't appear. If ye come alone, I'll swoop down from the skies. Ye'll never know when and where I'll come. But I'll appear to ye, Jack.' And long atter the sun had set in Shinglemill and I told Ted I'd promised Op to be home by sundown, he said to me: 'Tell yer sister, Lutie, I love her. Tell 'er I'd love to see 'er. And tell 'er,' he said, and he started laughin' agin, 'that I'm a-gettin' awful tired of wild meat and wild berries. Tell 'er I'd like to have a nice basket of table grub.' "

"Did he say that, Jack?" Op asked, his expression one of pure wonderment. "But sperets ain't supposed really to eat."

"Honest he said it, Op," Jack replied. "And I said: 'If Lutie'll fix it, Ted, I'll fetch it to ye!' And he said: 'That's a good boy. But remember not to bring anybody with ye. If ye do, ye'll haf to carry the basket of grub back or eat it yerself. Ye'll not see Ted Newsome, the good speret on Laurel Ridge.' "

Theopolis and Lucretia both stared at Jack in a kind of enchantment.

"And I said to Ted: 'I didn't know sperets had need of grub to nourish their bodies atter the body temple had been sleepin' in its long home.' " Jack raced on. "And he answered me right quick. He said: 'If a speret roves over the ground plane he gets mighty hungry.' I didn't know what he meant by 'ground plane' and I didn't ast him. I knew ye'd be out a-lookin' fer me, Op, and I said: 'Good speret, Ted Newsome, don't hold me any longer. I've got to get back to the cabin.' He laughed out loud and the wind blew his long blond hair: 'I won't hold ye any longer, Jack. Go back to yer father and yer sister. I know ye've been away a long time. But come agin!' And when he said these words I took off a-runnin' like a gray lizard over a hot rock atter a June bug!"

"Poor Ted, if he's on the ground plane," Op said, shaking his head sadly, "he's never reached the land of the blest. He's almost made it. After the ground plane, the next and final step is the land of the blest."

"In the morning, Jack, I'll fix breakfast for Ted Newsome," Lucretia said, "if you'll take it to him."

"I shore will, Lutie," Jack said. "I like Ted Newsome. I'll be a-wantin' to see 'im every day I'm thinkin'."

43

A day later, because Alf still had aches and pains from the fish shoot, Op took him on a root walk in the woods looking for natural remedies.

"Look at the flowering shrubs," Alf marveled, walking up a steep slope where lichen rocks as small as his head to the size of his smokehouse lay in disheveled piles. "These are beautiful blossoms!" Alf pulled a flower from a cluster that grew from the crevice of a rock and held it close to sniff the fragrance.

"Ye know what it is?" Op asked.

"No."

"Mountain laurel some call it, but I call it pizen ivy. Not much of it left around here. A body has to hunt to find it. Little Johnnie Blue and his son Snake tried to dig it all up a long time ago. It will pizen livestock. They wanted to make their side of Laurel Ridge a range fer cattle and sheep. But they couldn't get rid of the pizen ivy. I remember a lot of dead cattle and sheep and even a few hosses a-rottin' under these trees, pizened by this here mountain laurel. When the wind blew, a body had to hold his nose!"

"Was Laurel Ridge named for this?"

"That's right. Alf, ye're a-pickin' up, ye're a-showin' a little sense."

"So beautiful and yet it's poison." Alf stared at the flower. "Why would the good Lord create a blossom so perfect and then fill it with poison? Only good to look at and stay away from."

"Oh, it's good fer somethin' else, too," Op said. "Every weed, flower, or plant was put here fer a purpose. The mountain laurel has the purtiest blooms I've ever seen on any wild shrub that grows among these cliffs, hills, and hollers. And it's good medicine too. I remember when I's a young sprout . . ."

Alf recognized the story-telling tone creeping into Op's voice. He relaxed against the hillside, his face up to the sun.

". . . back when old Al Webb ust to buy the plug hosses at the jockey ground fer a dollar or two apiece and bring 'em out here and kill 'em and skin 'em fer their hides. That's the way Al made a livin'. All the fox hunters kicked on it fer their hounds got so fat on 'em they didn't have wind to run the foxes. Pap kicked on it, too. The smell from the hosses, when the wind blowed toward our shack, nearly run us from Little White Oak Valley. Al got awful close to us with his hosses. Our three hundred chickens that we ust to get eggs from and trade fer groceries went out into the woods a purty piece, too. They had to have a big range to get enough worms, insects, and berries. But they got somethin' else. They got maggots. And a devilish maggot won't die like a worm when a chicken swallers one. He works his way right through a chicken's craw. When our big flock of chickens got maggots, they died in piles. I remember how Adger and me dug holes and toted 'em still a-kickin' and dropped 'em in. They'd have the limber neck, stagger, and fall over. Their red combs and wattles would turn blue. They'd gasp a few times and that would be the end.

"I remember Ma said to Pap atter we'd lost half our flock: 'We got to find a way to save 'em.' 'I'd like to know what would kill a devilish maggot,' Pap said to her. But Ma couldn't rest easy until she figured a way to save her hens. Ye see, we traded them eggs fer things we needed at the store. 'If pizen ivy will kill cattle and sheep, it'll kill maggots,' Ma said. 'Go find and fetch me some, Little Op.' 'It will kill the chickens, too,' Pap objected. 'If it'll kill a yow, a buck, a hoss 'r a cow, ye know it'll kill a thing little as a chicken.' 'They're all a-goin' to die anyway,' Ma said. 'It can't be no worse. Better to finish them in a hurry and get 'em outten their misery.' "

"What reminded you of *this* story, Op?" Alf shook his head.

"So I come right up here where we're a-standin' now"—Op paid Alf no attention—"and I broke me an armload of pizen-ivy limbs with green pods of leaves fresh as mornin' daisies and I took 'em back down home a-runnin'. Ma biled 'em until the water was thick and green. 'It takes pizen to kill a thing like a maggot,' she said. 'We've lost a dozen more purty hens while ye was gone atter the ivy, Little Op.' So we ketched the chickens, and Pap opened their mouths and Ma poured the juice down 'em. Some of the hens were easy to ketch. They were a-staggerin' half dead and their heads were a-turnin' blue. Well, that juice cooked the maggots soon as it teched one. We went to the places where the chickens got the maggots and cleaned them up too. We poured the pizen-ivy sirrup over 'em. And Ma used the sirrup on young chickens atter that. When they got the roup, instead of takin' a broomstraw like she had done to punch the worm from one's throat, she used the pizen-ivy sirrup. Atter we'd discovered this here remedy, Pap run onto Al Webb in Honey-well and give him somethin' worse'n pizen-ivy sirrup. Al didn't bring another hoss out here to skin. We never knew where he took his hosses atter that. But we do know we found a remedy fer sick chickens."

Alf was enjoying the sun and when Op's chattering voice stopped, he sought to start it again, a task which never proved very difficult. "You know about every kind of weed that grows, don't you, Op?"

"Ye're wrong, Alf"— Op took the bait. "I wish I did. I'd be the greatest doctor in the world. Nope, I have only a few of the answers. I couldn't larn 'em all in my lifetime." He stopped to mop his dark, creased brow with his red bandanna. "There's a little weed I'd love to know, fer instance. If I could find that weed, I'd have the answer to the copperhead bite. I'd be able to do away with the black-powder and the black-cat cures. Pap, one time when he's a young man, had the answer if he'd only thought of it at the time. He watched a copperhead a-fightin' with a black snake. Pap said they were quiled up with only about two feet betwixt 'em. Said they put their heads up like a couple of fightin' roosters and let each other have it with their fangs. Said he never saw sicha fightin' in his life. The black snake would fight awhile and then he'd slide away and get a bite of a weed and chew it. Then he'd come back to the copperhead because a copperhead won't run from a snake or any other animal. When the snakes were fightin', Pap went over and pulled up the weed and threw it away jist to see what would happen. When the black snake went back to get a bite of his weed, it was gone. He raced around in little circles a-huntin' fer it, so Pap said. When he couldn't find his weed, he started gettin' sick. His long, black, shinin' body began witherin' right there on the ground. He crumpled himself up and died right there and the ants started workin' on his eyes. Pap said that was one mistake he'd made in his life. He never could get over not a-lookin' at that weed so he'd know and could pass it on down to us. When I walk through the woods I've allus hoped to come upon a black snake and a copperhead a-fightin'. If I ever find that weed, I'll have the cure fer copperhead bite."

44

Op stopped under the tall beech tree where the pea vines covered the dark leaf-rot loam. He sniffed the air like a hound-dog winding a rabbit. He stood for a minute and then he sniffed the air again.

"It's here, Alf," he said. "I smell snakeroot!"

"I wouldn't know snakeroot from ginseng," Alf said.

"Snakeroot's good medicine," Op answered. Then he started wading into the knee-deep pea vine, bracken, lace fern and poke-berry.

"This is the ground that grows snakeroot," he said. "It's a green little plant, grows about six inches high and has a V-shaped leaf."

Op, with a mattock in his hand, peered at the green upheaved floor of earth. "Here, here, Alf," he shouted. "Look beside this old log! Here's all the snakeroot we'll want!"

Op raked away the vines, bracken, and fern, cleaning the ground around the snakeroot down to the dark, smelly earth. Alf stood by watching Op use the mattock as skillfully as he had seen him swing the ax. Op's nostrils worked as he sniffed the fresh, invigorating odors coming from the disturbed loam.

"Can't ye smell it, Alf?"

"I sure can! It smells like a city dump!"

"Not anythin' better fer colds, chills, and fevers than snakeroot," Op grunted, swinging his mattock. "Bile the roots and drink the juice. It's bitter medicine to take but it will do the work!"

Op dug more than a dozen snakeroot stools from the ground while Alf shook the clinging dirt from the roots and put them into the sack.

They crossed the Sulphur Spring creek and started climbing the steep slope. "Alf, look here!" Op pointed with his hand. "Bear's-paw! Bear's-paw!" It was a tall plant, about shoulder high, with a large square leaf. Op stood beside the plant and fondled it like he might a child.

"What's it good for, Op?" Alf asked. "Looks to me like just another weed."

"This bear's-paw is good fer the stummick." Op sank his mattock to the eye down in the soft loam. "And jist one of these will make all the bear's-paw medicine we want."

When Op dug the dirt from around the plant, he lifted the root stool from the ground. Then he took the hunting knife from the sheath and cut the stem. Alf put the root stool in the sack.

"Now, we've got to have ginseng," Op said. "And I know where it grows." Alf followed him up the steep slope to the middle of the high hill where there was a broad flat.

"Oh, a four-prong!" he shouted.

"What's a four-prong?"

"It's four years old," Op explained, scornfully. "A prong fer each year! What did ye think?"

"What's it good for?"

"The heart. It's good to eat raw. It's a great yarb. I use ginseng in my tonic. Look, a two-prong, a three-prong! Here's a whole patch of ginseng!"

"Looks like there's a whole drugstore out here," Alf said.

"These are things ye'll want to know," Op said. "Ye with yer aches and pains and miseries from a little fish shootin'. There's a cure fer every ill right here on Laurel Ridge!"

"And look here, Alf." Op was staring at a small tree with little red berries on its boughs beside him. "Here's a spignet tree."

"You don't say." Alf yawned. Op started digging.

"It'll put pounds on ye," Op said. "I lay up spignet roots in the spring and I chew 'em 'n' swaller the juice in the lean spring months."

"Never heard of the spignet tree," Alf said as he put the roots into the sack. "I'll take cod-liver oil."

"Ye need somethin', Alf." Op was walking the few feet up the hill to the second bluff that extended from the flat to the ridge top. "Sassafrilla," he called down. "Good fer the blood, lungs, and stummick!"

Alf said, "Sounds like an all-purpose Alka Seltzer."

The vine wound around a small butternut tree. Op dug around the main big root. Then he cut the root from the vine with the hunting knife and began pulling it. It was from three to four inches deep in the loam.

"Take hold and hep me, Alf," he said. "This is a wonderful yarb root."

Alf took hold and the two men pulled with all their might, ripping the tough root up from the earth. When they had pulled up the main root with all its small and finer branch roots, it was almost twenty feet long. Op coiled it around his arm like winding a rope. Alf opened the sack, peering in at the tangle of roots and green leaves.

"We're getting a lot of chlorophyll in here," Alf said.

"A lot of which?" Op asked.

"Oh, Nature's green. Chlorophyll." Alf stared up at the green leaves. "That magic substance of living things, transformed by the sun's energy into life-giving nourishment. When you get that green color you're getting chlorophyll content and a deodorant besides, and . . ."

"What'n the hell is wrong with ye, Alf?" Op looked at him in disgust. "Have ye gone crazy? What ye need is a yarb fer yer head! And that's a yarb hard to find."

45

"Let's stop here fer a few minutes, Alf." Theopolis took the mattock from over his shoulder and held it on the ground beside him. "Somethin' happened to me here onct that I'll never ferget!"

"What was that, Op?" Alf was breathing heavily after climbing the steep slope from Sulphur Hollow to Laurel Ridge. They had added to the bulging sack some yellow root ("fer bellyache and sore mouth"), life everlasting ("good fer the asmie"), boneset, toe-each, and calmus.

"Right here is where I climbed on the Devil's back and rode 'im home," Op said.

"Oh, good Lord!" Alf stared at Op standing there with the coffee sack filled with herbs over his shoulder and the mattock in his hand. He looks like some sort of prehistoric man, Alf thought.

"I don't care whether ye believe it or not," Op told him. "I know I'm a-tellin' ye the truth. I climbed on the Devil's back right here one night and he took me home. I'll tell ye just how it happened.

"It was in October and I'd come out here a-possum-huntin' with old Jerry the night before," Op explained. "It might've been two nights before. I'd fetched along a quart of 'simmon brandy. It was a dark night when possums love to stir. There wasn't a wind to shake the dead leaves on the trees and skeer 'em. The air was hot-like and felt like rain. Jerry had treed one possum up a bull 'simmon tree. So I took an extra snort of brandy and scaled up the tree atter it. Throwed 'im down and Jerry sulled 'im. Out Laurel about another hundred yards and old Jerry treed one of the biggest possums I ever saw up a little pawpaw bush. All I had to do was shake 'im from the bush. I put 'im in the sack and I felt purty good atter gettin' that possum. Then I took a real big snort of brandy.

"The next thing I woke up right about here where we're a-standin' and I was flat on my back and my eye sockets were filled with water. But my clothes were dry. That's the reason I say I might've come out here a couple of nights before the Devil carried me home. I might've been here that long. I know it had poured rain some time atter I'd laid down or my eye sockets wouldn't have been full of water. And that's a sign that I'd never moved till I'd woke up. The wind on this ridge had dried my clothes atter the rain. Old Jerry was a-layin' beside me when I rose up and the water run down my face. The moon was shinin' and poor Jerry looked like a mud dauber, he was so thin in the middle. The possums were a-jumpin' around in the sack. I got up on my feet, wiped the water from my eyes with my shirttail and looked up at the thin little moon above Laurel Ridge. I didn't feel bad at all. I felt purty good. Old Jerry barked and ran circles all around me when I come alive agin. I picked up this very mattock I'm a-carryin' now, put the possum sack across my shoulder and hadn't walked five steps till I met somebody. I thought he was a fox hunter at first!

"'Howdy, Op,' he said to me. 'Where do ye think ye're a-goin'?' 'I'm goin' home,' I told him. 'Ye've not been there for three days,' he said to me. 'How do ye know?' I ast him, suspicious-like. 'Ye've not been fox huntin' that long, have you, Plack?' I thought he was old Plack Rivercomb who hunts the fox here on Laurel Ridge. 'I'm not Plack Rivercomb,' he said to me. 'Op, look me over. I've never fox-hunted in my life. Several of the fox hunters are my boys and I'm with 'em a lot. Ye know, Op, I take keer of my own. Climb on my back and I'll give ye a lift. I'll take ye home.' I wasn't a bit skeered right then. I thought he was the speret of one of the big timber cutters that had gone on before. But when I looked him over right there in the moonlight, I knowed he wasn't the speret of a man."

"How did you know?" Alf asked amiably.

"Ye never saw the speret of man with a pair of horns above his ears that come out about two feet from the side of his head and bent back like oxbows, did ye?" Op said. "I never saw such horns. How he managed to get through the brush with that pair of horns was a mystery to me. I'd thought when he first spoke to me he was wearing a dark suit of clothes that needed pressing, for the legs of his pants were like big, round, dark-black oaks. But when I looked him over more keerfully I saw he wasn't wearing a suit at all. His skin was somethin' like a bearskin, only the hair was longer. And when I looked at his feet I saw he had the cloven hoof. Whether he was wearin' steel shoes like the giant oxen on Laurel Ridge ust to wear I'll never know. But he was made in the image of man. He walked standin' up and not on his all fours. He had shoulders broader than my cabin door and a big unshaven face somethin' like a bear's. He had a full set of teeth that looked like small white handspikes. He had mule ears he could twitch in the direction of any sound.

" 'What kind of a speret are ye?' I asked, lookin' 'im over. 'I've never seen ye before on Laurel Ridge.'

" 'But I've been on Laurel Ridge many times before!' he said. 'I was on Laurel Ridge before ye were born. And I'll be here atter ye're gone. I'm a speret ye've heard more about than any other speret on Laurel Ridge. I'm the Devil. Get on my back, old Op, and let's get goin'.' 'No thank ye, I'll walk,' I said, nice and polite-like. 'No, I'll take ye home, Op,' he insisted. 'If ye don't ride on my back, ye'll be a sorry speret one of these days.' Then old Jerry, who had whined and barked, inched a little closer to smell of this giant Devil. Old Jerry must've thought he was another harmless speret like so many he'd seen when we hunted at night on Laurel Ridge. But the Devil kicked at Jerry with a mighty hoof that whistled as it cut the air, and if Jerry hadn't been quick on the dodge, he'd've kicked his head clean offen his shoulders! Jerry took off around Laurel Ridge a-runnin' and a-barkin' as I'd never heard 'im before. That's the only time he ever fersook me. And I've never held it against 'im.

" 'Get on my back, Op,' the Devil said, speakin' plain as I ever heard with a voice as big as the roar of waters in April down at Sandy Falls. 'I don't have time to fool too long with ye. I've got business to do. Ye know I'm a busy speret. I never sleep, I go day and night and have to be in a thousand places at once. I'm nowhere else tonight but right here. Ye're not a-gettin' my split personality. Ye're gettin' all the charm I can turn on one of my prospective subjects. I saw ye here sleepin' with puddles of dark rain water in yer eye sockets. Saw ye drinkin' my brew from the 'simmon. So I want to do somethin' fer one of my own.' 'But I have my mattock and my sack with two possums in it,' I said, thinkin' fast. 'That won't add too much to the load I'm able to carry on my broad shoulders,' he said. And he took my mattock in his hand big as a coal scoop, with hairy fingers big as sticks of stovewood. He took the possum sack in his other hand. I leaped upon his back like a ground squirrel. I took him by the horns and swung my weight up to his shoulders. Put a leg over each shoulder and a hand on each horn. And he started around Laurel Ridge with me."

"That's enough, Op," Alf said. "I don't want to hear any more."

Alf started walking around Laurel Ridge, and Op followed with the sack across his shoulder and the mattock in his hand.

"No matter what ye want to hear, I'm gonna finish. It happened right where we're a-walkin' now. This is the way we come."

"You carry these tales too far," Alf said, walking faster. "I've heard enough. It does something to me."

"What do ye think it did to me that night?" Op answered. "Don't ye think I was nervous? But I thought I'd better ride. I didn't want to take any chances. When a man's old body is planted back on this earth and his speret leaves the old clay temple and journeys on into the next world, he never knows where he's goin' to land. I had to play along with 'im, don't ye see, Alf?"

"I expect so," Alf murmured.

"Now right along here was where the Devil started trottin' with me." Op pointed at the path. "He jogged up and down so I thought he was a-tryin' to throw me off. But I locked my legs around his bull neck and gripped his big horns fer dear life while the fire streaked like lightnin' from his feet. That's the reason I've often wondered if he wore steel shoes like an oxen on his cloven hoofs. And while I held onto his horns and he trotted, there was a great rumblin' among the leaves still a-hangin' on the tough-butted white oaks. I thought all the leaves were fallin' from the trees. Then, suddenly, the Devil changed his pace. He started rackin' like one of the hosses I'd seen young men and wimmen ride around this ridge when I was a boy. 'How do you like yer ride?' said the Devil to me. 'I love the rackin',' I said. When I said this, he changed to a slow pace. And dark clouds started rollin' over Laurel Ridge and hidin' the moon and stars. It suddenly got dark as charcoal and all of Laurel Ridge began to tremble. I could feel it on the Devil's back. All of a sudden the lightnin' flashes cut the dark, thick air. They danced over the Devil's horns till I thought, onct, I'd have to let go.

" 'How do ye like it now?' the Devil ast me. 'I don't like it 't'all,' I said. And he laughed and it sounded like the thunder that was jarrin' Laurel Ridge to its foundations. I heard trees a-splinterin' on both sides of me as the Devil took off in a gallop. I thought he was a-runnin' to beat a great storm that was at our heels. I could hear the rain behind us but I couldn't look back to see. The fire was flyin' in all directions, rain fallin' behind, yet the Devil was gallopin' ahead of the storm. And I was a-ridin' as comfortably as I'd ever ridden anything in my life, with my legs locked around his bull neck and my hands ahold of his horns. He took me full speed right up in front of my cabin and stopped so suddenly his big feet skid twenty feet on the ground, and streaks of fire shot from them. Old Jerry ran from the cabin barkin' and growlin'.

" 'Get away from me, ye mongrel!' the Devil shouted as he kicked at 'im agin. 'Don't try to bite me! I'll kick yer head clean from yer shoulders.' 'If ye kick that dog, I'll dehorn ye,' I said. I would have done it too. I had my knife from my pocket and I'd've really worked on one of his horns. 'Wonderful, Op,' the Devil said. 'That's the way I like to hear ye talk, especially to anyone who has done ye a favor. Allus be that grateful and ye'll be my favorite speret someday. I'll call ye home. I've got a great need fer ye. Get down offen my back, friend!' Well, right there I climbed down offen his back. Right in my own front yard.

"And the Devil gave me my mattock and my sack of possums. He smiled, a-showin' his full set of big white teeth. He looked down at me right kindly, and fer a minute I thought he was gonna pat my head. Good thing he didn't, he'd a probably crushed it. I didn't thank the Devil fer my ride. To hell with
218

him, I thought, that's a friendship that can't do me no good. When I got my gate opened, I looked back to see if he was still standin' there grinnin' his big horse-whinny grin. But the Devil had gone. And with him had gone the thunder, lightnin', splinterin' of trees, and the great roar of the storm among the white oak leaves. The sky was clear agin and the moon and stars were a-shinin'.'"

"That was some ride," Alf said, looking Op in the eye. "Don't guess you were able to do much sleeping after that."

"I turned the hungry possums loose, went into the cabin, shelled my rags off down to my shirttail and underwear," Op said. "I went to bed and slept like a log. Got up next mornin' and thought so much about my ride on the Devil's back that atter breakfast I walked back out Laurel Ridge to see how many trees the lightnin' had struck and what the storm had done. Not a tree was split by lightnin' and the 'simmons and pawpaws were all a-standin'. And I decided to myself the Devil was a big bluff. Jist a big wind. If I ever got on his back agin, I would shore dehorn 'im!"

46

A few evenings later somebody pounded on the cabin door.

"Come in, Alf," Op shouted from his favorite chair. He had made the chair and had woven a seat in it with hickory thongs. He had sat on it while the thongs were green and had shaped the seat perfectly for his bottom.

"I'm not Alf," shouted a familiar voice. "I'm Hootbird!"

"Jist a minute, young man." This time Op jumped up.

"Old Hootbird," Jack said, shaking his head. "I ain't seen 'im in a long time."

"I wish I could say the same." Lucretia laughed. "I made the mistake of being polite to him when I first came to the ridge."

When Op pulled the door open, there stood Hootbird under his ten-gallon hat and hanging on to his rifle. Behind him Op saw a broad field of stars stretching above the Allcorn Hills. Hoot's face was hidden in the shadow of his wide hatbrim, and Op couldn't see his expression.

"How are ye, Hoot?" Op stood blocking the doorway.

"All right, Op," he replied gruffly. He peered around Op into the room. "How are ye, Run-around Jack?"

"All right, Hootbird," Jack said.

"Are you a-findin' many butterflies?" Hootbird asked him. Then he let out a little wild laugh. "I saw ye a-goin' around the ridge road a week ago yesterday at about noon. Ye had yer turkey of clothes and a butterfly net on yer pole."

"But I didn't see ye, Hoot," Jack said.

"Not many people do see me. But I see and hear a lot of people."

Lucretia, who hadn't spoken to Hootbird, sat very still over her sewing. Hoot hadn't seen her.

"Have ye come fer somethin', Hootbird?" Op asked.

"Yeah, I've come fer somethin' all right," he said. "But instead of my geetar, I brought my rifle. And I've got another piece of hardware on my person."

"Then tell us what yer business is, Hoot." Op felt half inclined to shut the door in Hootbird's face. "We're not a-interested in yer armament, Hootbird."

"Ye've come to see me, ain't ye, Hoot?" Jack said hopefully.

"Not at all," Hootbird replied. "I'll see enough of ye before the summer's over. I've really come to see Lutie. Where is she? Has she gone to the woods?"

"I'm right over here, Hootbird," Lutie answered. She stopped sewing a button on Jack's shirt and looked toward the door. "No, I'm not in the woods."

"Ye have been in the woods, there's no denyin'," he said. "Ye've been meetin' that strange man under the Wince Leffard Gap cliffs. I know because I heard geetar playin' and singin' the other night and I left my bed and crawled up there on my belly like a snake. I got so close I could jist about reached over the wall of dirt and teched either one of ye with my hand. If I'd a had my rifle with me, I would've shot a few times back under the cliff. I couldn't see but I know Lutie's voice. And I can even tell ye what he played and sung—the Hoot Owl Song. I've come to tell Lutie that no decent woman'll meet a man in the woods at night. I won't be cuckolded in love no longer. I won't be a bonehead."

"That's Ted Newsome, Hootbird, ye're a-talkin' about," Jack broke in. "I met him in Shinglemill Holler the day I got here. I've been a-takin' 'im a basket of grub every day. He's not a man, Hootbird. He's a speret. And he don't like ye none. Ted Newsome thinks ye're a-killin' all these foxes around here."

"I'm not a-killin' 'em either," Hootbird shouted angrily. "He's the one a-killin' all the foxes. And he's got old Op here a-thinkin' he's a speret. He ain't no more speret than I am. He's a real flesh-and-blood man. And he's a-sparkin' with Lutie most every night, that's what he's a-doin'."

"What business is that of yours?" Lucretia dropped her sewing basket and stood up angrily.

"What right have ye to say that Lutie ain't decent?" Op asked. His voice hissed like the tongue of a bull black snake. "I don't like to hear that kind of talk, Hoot!"

"I jist want to tell Lutie that we're through," Hootbird said, craning his neck around Op. "I've come to tell 'er that I don't love 'er no longer. I want 'er to know that our love is as cold as the ashes where that man built his fires to cook the foxes."

"My love for you has always been that cold, Hootbird," she told him. "In fact, we never did begin, so how could we be through?"

"But I was in love with ye, Lutie, until I saw the handwritin' on the wall," he said. "I was in love with ye until strange things begin to pop around here. I could tell there was another man in the picture. I had to carry hardware to pertect my life."

"Ye're skeery, Hoot," Op said. "Ye're afeared of yer shadder. Ye imagine things."

Hootbird's ten-gallon hat waggled back and forth as he talked around Op at Lutie. "Call 'im Ted Newsome if ye want to, but that's not his name. I don't know what it is, but I do know he's a real man and Lutie knows he is, too. Maybe Lutie knows how he got here and why he's a-hidin' out. Maybe Lutie knows what he's done!"

"What are you talking about, Hootbird?" she asked, moving closer to the door. She carried a shirt clutched in one hand. "Why don't you go on back to Wince Leffard Gap where you belong? It's none of your business who I go with. Let him be a man or a spirit. But keep your nose out of my business. You're like your old long-tongued mother! You can't stop blabbing off at the mouth!"

"Ye keep my mother's name outten this," Hootbird shouted.

"You leave this place and don't ever come back," she shouted at Hootbird. "You little jellyfish!"

"I don't believe what ye say, Hootbird," Op said. "I'm right here in this cabin with Lutie all the time. I don't believe she meets anybody in the rock cliffs at night."

"Not only in the rock cliffs at Wince Leffard Gap," he said, "but I've heard them down in the deep hollers among the pea vines. I've heard that damned old geetar playin' and his singin' and I've heard 'em a-laughin'. Love-makin' in the woods, that's what it is! One night when the skies were clouded and I couldn't see my hand before my face, I heard the singin' up near the arc and walked near 'em as I could on my all fours like a terrapin. I hate to believe all of this about Lutie but I know 'er voice!"

"If ye're through with Lutie, Hootbird, I'm happy," Op said. "I'm glad ye're through with 'er. Now go home and leave us alone. Stay away from here! Don't ever step on this porch agin!"

"But a father ought to know about his daughter," Hootbird told Op. "A father ought to know when his daughter goes at night to the rock cliffs, the hollers, and the ridgetops. I'm a-doin' ye a favor, Op, by a-tellin' ye! Ye're the one ought to know who she's with!"

"If she was with ye, Hootbird, I'd be worried," Op sputtered. "I'd have cause to be a worried man. Because I wouldn't put anythin' past ye. I wouldn't want ye with Lutie at high noon in this cabin much less on a dark hill at night. But when she's with Ted Newsome, I can sleep in peace."

"Because Ted's a happy speret, Hootbird," Jack spoke up. "First day I got back to Laurel Ridge I went down in Shingle-mill a-ketchin' butterflies. Ted appeared to me. I run onto 'im face to face and I trembled in the legs when he told me who he was, Ted Newsome the speret. I'd heard Op tell about Ted all my life but that was the first time I'd ever seen 'im. He must've dropped right down from the skies!"

"Poor simple-minded Run-around Jack," Hootbird broke in. "Op, ye and Jack are two of a kind. Ye don't know what is real and what ain't. Ye've lived so long by yerself out here that ye imagine the woods are filled with the sperets of the long departed. Ye're both addled, that's all. But all the trouble started when Lutie came back to the Ridge. She's the one!"

"Lay everything on to me, you little coward," Lucretia stormed. She had been standing there trembling with anger listening to all that had been said. "Just because I won't have anything to do with you! I've not forgotten how you acted the day I went to see a picture show with you. I slapped your face once and I can do it again!"

"Go home, Hootbird, and leave us," Op said. "I'm a-tellin' ye my last time to leave this place. Ye might not even get home atter the unkind things ye've been a-sayin' about a good speret. If ye're bushwhacked on yer way home tonight, I won't even bat an eye. If I was ye, I'd be afeared to step into the starlight on Laurel Ridge atter the talk that's come through yer lips here this evenin'."

"Lissen, Op, there's one more thing I want to say," Hootbird said, stubbornly, "before I'll be on my way through yer world of sperets fer home. I want to tell ye I'm gonna get that man who's loose here on Laurel Ridge. I'll work with the fox hunters, with Snake Blue, with the High Sheriff of Looten County. I'll help get 'im! We might find 'im a-layin' on a bed of leaves asleep. We might find 'im in his rock-cliff den. But we'll get 'im. Ye wait and see! I won't be cuckolded in love. We've got some good rope plowlines down at our barn too, and I'll help swing 'im to an oak limb over Laurel Ridge! I've got the tree picked out on this side of the arc. It's a big oak, Lutie!"

"Nothing you say could surprise me, Hootbird," Lucretia cried out. Op was surprised to see she was close to tears. "Maybe you'll capture Ted Newsome. Maybe you'll hang him. But you won't do it alone. He's a better man than you are!"

"I say he is," Op said. "Begone, Hootbird! Leave before I lay these big hands onto yer shoulders. They might work themselves up around yer bird neck!"

Hootbird stepped backward on the porch when Op took a step forward with his big blunt fingers spread.

"Remember I'll help get that man, Lutie," Hootbird blubbered as Op closed the cabin door in his face. "He's been loose nearly four months. He's a-gettin' tamer. He might even run out of cartridges fer that army rifle of his. We'll get 'im, Lutie. And it won't be long. . . ." His voice grew fainter along the ridge.

Inside the cabin, old Op watched Lucretia fighting back the tears. Run-around Jack sat at the table in utter confusion. Op wanted to say something to Lutie, maybe even to pat her shoulder, but he couldn't bring himself to do it. Tonight, watching her storm at Hootbird, he was finally sure that Lutie was his and Beadie's own offspring. She had the Akers spirit and she'd showed it aplenty. That was enough for him.

But what he couldn't understand was why she'd gotten so upset when Hootbird had talked about hanging Ted Newsome. "Lutie—" Op cleared his throat, feeling hot and embarrassed— "ye know ye needn't worry none about Ted. They kin hist his speret up to a dozen trees and it won't bother him 't'all."

Lutie sat down in the chair, took the sewing back on her lap, and burst into tears.

47

Op was first to hear the strange sound. He had stopped hoeing tomatoes in the garden and was looking back to see how far behind Lucretia, Alf, and Julia were. Jack had taken his butterfly net and basket and had gone in the direction of Shinglemill Hollow. Ted Newsome, the good spirit on Laurel Ridge, was appearing to Jack daily. On one day, Jack had taken him two full baskets of food. Julia had remarked that Ted was becoming a pretty well-fed spirit.

Op looked in the direction of the sty. When Alf saw Op standing with his cupped hand behind his ear, he stopped hoeing too.

"I hear somethin'," Op said. "It's like a swarm of wild bees in the distance."

"It's a motor humming," Alf told him. "I hear it too. And it's on Laurel Ridge!"

"It can't be," Op sputtered. "Never was an automobile on this ridge!"

"It's an automobile all right," Julia said.

"It's a-comin' out Laurel Ridge," Op said softly, unbelieving. They waited a minute in silence as something emerged from the green tunnel near the sty.

"It's a jeepload of soldiers!" Alf was surprised. "Wonder what they're doing up here?"

"I'd like to know." Lucretia's soft voice trembled.

"Civilization is coming to Laurel Ridge." Julia smiled. "Things are certainly happening around here."

"Yep," Op said, "the wrong things."

"It's the military police." Alf peered at the jeep. "Look at the MP written there on the side."

Op looked at the jeep but he couldn't read the letters.

"Reckon they're atter ye, Alf?" Op said. "Who are ye?" He turned suspiciously on Alf. "What have ye done?"

"I've not done anything," Alf said. "You're still suspicious of me, Op! I can't understand it! After we've been on the ridge all these weeks."

"But it keeps a-goin' through my mind that Sheriff Ackerson and his deputies were out here to see ye," Op said. "And funny things been a-goin' on around here ever since ye come. A body should never get tied up with strangers."

The jeep pulled up at the garden gate and stopped. The driver, who had a silver bar on each shoulder, got out of the jeep. There was a soldier riding beside him and two in the rear seat holding rifles.

226

"Is this the residence of Theopolis Akers?" the driver asked politely.

"Yep, this is where he lives." Op walked slowly toward the gate with his hoe in his hand. "I'm Op Akers."

"I'm Lieutenant Edward Cox of the military police," he said. "I'm looking for a man named Private Rodney H. Bohannon."

He took a little card from the files in a small box and gave it to Op.

"No need to give it to me," Op said. "I wouldn't know my own name if I's to meet it in the big road."

"Let me see it," Alf said as he walked up and took the card.

"Have you seen this man around here?" Lieutenant Cox asked. "Do you know him?"

"Never heard tell of 'im," Op said. "Not any Bohannons on Laurel Ridge. Never heard of that name in Looten County."

"He was granted a sixteen-day furlough from Fort Eustis, Virginia, to his home in Dayton, Ohio, last March 19th. He was to report back to Fort Eustis, Virginia, on April 4th. He's never reported. He's taken a long furlough and the Army wants him."

Alf handed the card back to Lieutenant Cox and then he looked at Lucretia. Julia was watching Lucretia too.

"What makes ye think he's on Laurel Ridge?" Op asked.

"Because the description of a man loose on this ridge fits Private Rodney H. Bohannon," Lieutenant Cox explained. "He's six-feet two-inches tall, has blue eyes and blond hair. Has a scar on the left knee and a square-set jaw. Never saw him myself but that's the description they gave us."

"Who told you he was up here, Lieutenant?" Op asked.

"Sheriff Ackerson in Honeywell," the lieutenant answered pleasantly. "The MPs in the Dayton, Ohio, district haven't been able to pick him up. They've combed that section for him.

227

And while we have no right to go to Ohio because we work eastern Kentucky with our headquarters at Morehead, this AWOL has been transferred to us. We have one hundred and six men to pick up in twelve counties of eastern Kentucky. We've got twelve in Looten County alone."

Over Lieutenant Cox's shoulder Op noticed the three soldiers in the jeep talking in low tones to one another. They looked at the cabin and then over at the thin stream of smoke coming from the stovepipe stuck through the smokehouse window.

"Have you ever seen a man around here that fills this description?" Lieutenant Cox asked Alf.

"I never have," Alf replied. "I've been hearing about him but I've never seen him."

"We've got an old long-tongued blatherskite named Doshie Hammertight who goes to Honeywell every day," Op said angrily. "She carries all the news to Sheriff Ackerson. Maybe ye'd better go ask her some questions."

"Sheriff Ackerson told us this morning that this whole section was up in arms," Lieutenant Cox directed his remarks at Alf. "And he said a man filling this description had been seen by one Hoot—Hootbird Hammertight several times. They said whoever was loose on this ridge was a good shot and that he carried a rifle. According to our records, Bohannon qualified as an 'expert rifleman.' If he had shot at Hootbird Hammertight, as his mother claimed, we don't see how Bohannon ever missed him."

"Don't pay any attention to Hootbird Hammertight," Op said. "He's a bigger liar than old Doshie, his mother, and that's goin' some! He's been a-hangin' around here tryin' to go with Lutie. We had to run 'im off night before last."

"If Private Rodney Bohannon is hanging out on Laurel Ridge we'll get him," Lieutenant Cox said, "even if we're a little slow about it. If you see a man of this description, inform Sheriff Bill Ackerson down in Honeywell. He'll get in touch with us. We'll
228

be here in Looten County for a few more days. Remember the description."

"There's a speret here that meets that description all right," Op said.

"A what?" Lieutenant Cox looked doubtfully at the old man before him.

"A speret," Op repeated. "It's Ted Newsome."

The soldiers in the jeep turned to listen. Lieutenant Cox looked as if he didn't think he'd heard right.

"That's who Hootbird has seen if he's seen anything at all," Op said. He trained his good eye on Lieutenant Cox. Theopolis's face was somber.

"Who is this Ted Newsome?" Lieutenant Cox asked.

"He's Ted Newsome," Op said. "Been dead thirty years." Then he repeated the story of Ted Newsome's death and of his spirit that had come back to the ridge.

The soldiers in the jeep didn't bother to hold in their laughter. One of them circled his head with his hand and nodded toward Theopolis.

"I'm not off in the head either," Op said, looking toward the soldier. "I saw what ye did. I know the sperets of men long dead and gone come back to this ridge. It's a fine place and they won't leave it. Not them that's numbered with the blest. If ye lived on this ridge as long as I have ye'd see plenty. Ye'd see things that would make yer hair stand straight up!"

Lieutenant Cox didn't trust himself to speak. Lucretia's face was blank. She looked into space over the Little Sandy River Valley beyond Laurel Ridge.

"Lutie knows I'm a-tellin' you the truth," Op said. He was proud of Lucretia, who never laughed or doubted when he spoke of Ted Newsome. "Lutie's seen Ted Newsome. He gathered wild flowers fer her. He's been right here to see my daughter, I tell ye!"

"Now just a minute," Lieutenant Cox said, turning to Lutie. "I want your daughter to tell me where this spirit came from and where he went. Do you know where he lives?"

"No, no, I don't," she replied, hesitatingly. "First time I saw Ted Newsome was—was down at the spring when I went after water." Lutie seemed uncertain, her eyes on the ground. "He was sitting on the big rock down there and he dipped the buckets into the spring for me. He carried the water up the path and he set the buckets on the porch. When I turned around he had disappeared. He disappeared like the smoke coming from that flue on the Laurel Ridge wind! He comes from nowhere and then stays awhile and disappears right before my eyes!" She ended with a big smile.

Lieutenant Cox looked troubled, as if there was something he definitely didn't understand. The same soldier in the jeep circled his head again and pointed toward Lucretia. "Like her old man," he whispered hoarsely. "Batty people."

"I heard ye. Ye think I'm deef!" Op pointed a big calloused forefinger at the soldier. "We're not batty people either. Be keerful how ye talk, young man. Somethin' can happen to ye before ye leave this ridge. That car can turn over. Ye can't insult a speret and get by with it. Woe be unto ye unbelievers!"

"Thank you, Mr. Akers," Lieutenant Cox said hastily. "Sheriff Ackerson never told us about Ted Newsome the spirit. It's all very interesting information." His tone was polite, his face without expression. As he closed the gate behind him, he shot one more curious glance in Lucretia's direction. Alf and Julia, standing a little to the side, also looked at Lutie wonderingly. Only Op watched the retreating jeep bounce toward the green tunnel.

"An automobile on Laurel Ridge. If that don't beat all!"

48

After breakfast, Alf walked outside the smokehouse to breathe deep of the morning air on Laurel Ridge and to get his vitamins from the rays of the early morning sun. Op, disgusted with the slow way Alf, Julia, and Lucretia had hoed the tomatoes, was out working early in the garden. He was rehoeing them, heaping the dirt around the plants and cutting the little weeds they had left in their rows. Beyond the garden palings, Alf watched Jack leave with a basketful of food and a butterfly net. Jack was pretending there was a butterfly above him and he'd reach up with his pole to make a catch. The net would swish the wind.

So he's going to feed the spirit Ted Newsome, Alf thought. I know Ted Newsome's no spirit. There's somebody on this ridge. Why not see who it is by following Jack? Won't let Op see me. Go through the hole where the palings are loose.

As Alf started to tiptoe across the garden, Op looked up, saw him, and quickly looked away. He's a-followin' Jack, Op thought, looking down at the tomato plant he was hoeing. I don't want Alf to know I saw 'im. I want 'im to go and see Ted Newsome. Alf is a city man. He's an unbeliever. And he wasn't balanced in the head when he come here. But he's beginnin' to look more like a man now and talk more like one. He's not a-gabbin' so much about the adam bumbs as he did. He's a-gettin' so he can use the ax and mattock better and he don't holler and shake when he jumps into the cold water in Red Bird Holler. Yep, Alf's been convinced about a lot of things. Now let 'im see fer himself that there is a speret on Laurel Ridge.

When Op looked up again, Alf had disappeared through the

hole where the garden palings were loose. If he had gone through the garden gate, he would have passed right by Op.

He thinks he got by without me a-seein' 'im. Op smiled. I can see 'im even now outten the corner of my eye. I ust to hunt from the corners of my eyes when they were both good. I could almost see behind me. And I could hear a black snake crawlin' over the green weeds.

Op had just finished the row of tomatoes when he heard a rifleshot ring out. Then he heard Alf let out a scream. Julia ran to the smokehouse door.

"Was that a shot I heard?" she asked Op. "Was that Alf's voice? Where's Alf?"

"I don't know about Alf," Op said. "I know I'm a-hoein' his row over in the garden."

"That was Alf's scream all right," Julia shrieked as she ran from the smokehouse. "Alf! Oh, Alf!"

"What's the matter, Julia?" Lucretia shouted from the cabin porch.

"Poor Alf, Lutie," she shouted as she ran down between two rows of tomatoes.

Julia stopped suddenly. She seemed to be holding her breath. Laughter came from the north wall of Shinglemill Hollow. Loud laughter on the wind blew over Laurel Ridge and rustled the leaves on the oak in the corner of the garden. Lucretia heard it too and came running toward the garden gate.

"It's Alf, Lutie," Julia said. "Somebody shot at Alf!"

Then Alf came running around the bend on Laurel Ridge with his hat in his hand, fighting to get his breath.

"Alf," Julia screamed. "Have you been shot?"

"No," he grunted as he came up to the garden palings.

He held to the palings and breathed hard and fast. His face was flushed. He breathed like a lizard panting in the sun. Julia put her arm around his trembling body. Op came over and stood on the other side of the fence.

"I saw him with my own eyes," Alf grunted as he got more breath.

"A speret won't do that," Op said slowly. "A speret don't shoot at people."

"It's time you were coming to your senses," Julia spoke sharply as she held on to Alf.

"He's a real man," Alf mumbled. "He fits the description! He's blond, big, looks like a prize fighter. He's who"—Alf got a half breath—"they're after! That Bohannon fellow!"

"Why did he shoot at you, Alf?" Julia asked.

"I followed Jack to see who he was. He was eating the breakfast Lutie prepared for him when he saw me."

He stopped talking and got a long breath.

"When he saw me," Alf panted, "he reached down and got his rifle. I started to run. I thought I felt the wind from the bullet on my left ear. I let out a scream and he laughed like a maniac."

"You know anything about this man, Lutie?" Julia asked. "This is no longer a joke."

"Only what I've told you," Lucretia replied quickly.

"I'll go take a look fer myself." Op started through the garden gate. "I don't believe Ted Newsome would do that. This feller must not be the real Ted Newsome."

"No ust to go now, Op." It was Run-around Jack with an empty basket and his butterfly net. His voice was full of sadness. "Ted Newsome's gone. Alf slipped around there and disturbed 'im."

"I'll say I disturbed him, Jack," Alf said. "And if Ted Newsome's a spirit, he's one that's badly in need of a haircut and a fresh change of clothes!"

With his hat still in his hand, Alf walked through the gate

and across the garden toward the smokehouse. Julia walked with her arm around him and they went into the smokehouse talking together.

49

After supper, Op and his two children walked up to the smokehouse door and he rapped on the puncheon boards. They watched the door open slowly to a width of approximately six inches. Two eyes peered into the dark.

"Oh, it's you, Op," Alf said, opening the door wide. "Come in!"

"Who did ye think it was?" Op asked, friendly-like.

"Well, you never can tell around here who it might be," Alf said. "You remember it was Sheriff Ackerson and his three deputies one morning."

"Come in and sit on our bench," Julia invited them.

"I thought ye might be mad over what happened today," Op said as he dropped on the bench. "Thought we'd come over and talk to ye awhile."

"No, we're not mad," Alf said. "Where there's a lot of smoke there's bound to be some fire. And I nearly got burned. I know there's a real man hiding on this ridge."

"Or a spirit," Julia added, "getting mighty fat on Lutie's good cooking. What about it, Lutie?"

Lucretia laughed uneasily and looked away.

"We've talked it over and we never heard of the name Bo-hannon around Dayton," Julia said. "Of course Dayton is a big place. We don't even know the names of all the people who live on our block. But we never knew of Lutie dating anybody by that name."

"But we don't know everybody Lutie's dated," Alf added.

"What are you driving at, Cousin Alf?" Lucretia asked. "I came down here to help Dad when he was blind and the Red Cross sent for me."

Lucretia got up from the bench to go.

"Now just a minute, Lutie!" Alf spoke in an apologetic tone. "I'm not accusing you of anything. But all this spirit business on Laurel Ridge is a lot of nonsense, and you know it as well as we do! What confuses Julia and me is your pretending to believe in such foolishness."

"Watch how ye talk, Alf," Theopolis warned him. "I've had to warn ye too many times! Lemme ask ye this—don't the speret leave the body atter we wear out these old clay temples of ourn?"

Alf didn't answer Op. There was silence for a minute.

"Answer me, Alf," Op said. "Doesn't the Good Book tell us that? Don't ye believe in the Good Book?"

"But I don't think they're back here pestering us," Alf replied stubbornly.

"I think they're anyplace and every place they want to be," Op told him. "Why wouldn't they be back?"

"Let's don't get off on the spirits, Dad," Lucretia begged him.

"But Alf is an unbeliever in sperets," Op said, as the wind blew through the crack and the yellow flame in the oil lamp bent low. "This Ted Newsome might not be the Ted Newsome I ust to know. I don't know why he's a-totin' a rifle around and a-shootin' at people fer fun. And a-screamin' with laughter when he makes somebody run. That's strange actions fer a speret. It's got me vexed. And why won't he appear to me, his old friend? But when ye tell me, Alf, that ye don't believe in sperets, I know better. Remember, I'm the seventh son of the seventh son and I can show ye mighty soon! Do ye believe me?"

"I do not," Alf said, looking Op straight in the eye. "I don't believe that stuff and I never will."

"It's been a long time since I've raised the knockin' sperets," Op said. "I ust to raise 'em over there in my cabin. But they got to follerin' me around so I had to say: 'Good speret, Red Jacket, go away and take the other sperets with ye. I won't bother ye agin.' And Red Jacket, the speret, went away. I couldn't go to sleep at night fer 'em a-knockin' on the head of my bed and all around over the cabin. I'd get up and light the lamp and they'd still knock on the footboard of my bed. I've had 'em to knock on my hatband, and on my ax handle. They became sich a bother I swore I'd never raise 'em agin. But, Alf, looks like I'll haf to show ye how bad ye're fooled."

"Where will you show me there's a knocking spirit?" Alf asked.

"Right in this smokehouse."

"Bring on the sperets, Op," Jack said. "I know ye can. I ust to hear 'em a-knockin'. I know Op can do it."

"How will we know there's a spirit in here?" Julia asked.

"Ye won't have any doubts when I'm through," Op told her. "I'll have Red Jacket to climb up the cracks of that wall over there and come back down with eyes like balls of fire!"

50

"Shall I blow out the lamp, Op?" Julia asked, smiling.

"If ye want to," he said. "But ye don't haf to. If the smokehouse is darker, his eyes will shine brighter."

Julia got up and blew out the lamp. It wasn't entirely dark in the smokehouse, for there were light stripes of many different sizes over the floor and walls where the moonlight came through the cracks and windowpanes.

"Now ye jist sit still a few minutes till I call Red Jacket and the sperets," Op said. "Old Red Jacket ust to be a Indian Chief. But he's a speret now and a good one. Sit still while I talk to 'im and in a few minutes ye'll hear 'im a-climbin' that wall over there by the stove. And if ye wait long enough ye'll see 'im come down with eyes like balls of fire."

There was silence except for Op's hoarse whispers. A minute or two went by. Then a few more. Op continued to whisper. Then there was a step on a log that sounded like someone trying to climb the wall, and his foot had slipped.

"That's 'im," Jack said, nervously. "That's the speret. That's Red Jacket!"

There was another step up higher on the wall that sounded like the slipping of dead bark from a log.

"I hear something," Alf said. "I certainly do!"

"Oh, be quiet," Julia whispered. "Listen carefully."

There was a pawing on the log and then another step.

"I'm a-gettin' outten here," Jack shouted. He opened the door and took off toward the cabin.

"Come on, Red Jacket, good speret," Op croaked. "Show the doubters that ye're real!"

There was a step high upon the smokehouse wall. Alf jumped up just as there was another loud scratching sound from the same place. He just said, "Excuse me," in a very low voice and walked out. Lutie was close behind him. She didn't say a word.

Julia called after them, "Come back, it's only a cat or something."

Alf stood outside screaming at his wife. "Come out of there, come out of there this minute." He sounded hysterical. Julia sat still looking Op directly in the eye for a moment. Alf shouted again, his voice breaking in the middle. Then, reluctantly, Julia walked out of the smokehouse door. Op sat alone in the smoke-house, smiling at the darkness.

"That's enough, good speret Red Jacket," Op said softly as he got up from the bench. "Ye've showed the doubters!"

When Op stepped out into the moonlight he heard Jack say: "Alf, did Red Jacket come down the wall with eyes like balls of fire?"

"I don't know, Jack," Alf admitted. "I didn't stay long enough to see."

51

When Op walked over to his cabin, Alf, Lucretia, Julia, and Jack were inside.

"Do ye have any doubts now?" Op asked.

"I know I heard something," Julia said. "But it might have been a—a woodpecker."

"I wouldn't sleep in that smokehouse tonight for any amount of money." Alf shook his head. "You're going to have to let us stay with you tonight, Op. I know you're crowded but I'll sleep on the floor. I'll sleep anyplace until daylight!"

"Ye're welcome to stay with me, Alf," Op told him. "But the sperets won't hurt ye. Ye can go back over there, ye and Julia, and sleep and not any harm will come to ye."

"Op, I'm so confused I think you might be a spirit yourself." Alf smiled faintly. "And I'd just as leave not sleep in that smoke-house." Op noticed Alf was fidgety and quick-moving again, the way he'd been the first day he'd come, months back, so full of adam-bumb talk.

"Nope, I'm not a speret now, but I will be," Op told Alf. "I'm still a Laurel Ridge flesh-and-blood man. I usta be the only one up here."

"I don't understand you, Op!" Alf looked Op over from head to foot as he stood there in the yellow glow of lamplight. "I've never seen a man like you! I've never even heard tell of a place like Laurel Ridge! I've had enough!"

"Oh, calm down, Alf," Julia said. "How do you know it wasn't a woodpecker or a big lizard or something?"

"Alf, ye're too skeery," Op said. "Will ye be afeared to stay here in my cabin with Lucretia and Julia? I'll take Jack with me and we'll sleep in the smokehouse tonight."

"No, ye won't take me over there, Op," Jack retorted quickly. "Ye skeered me to death when ye ust to raise the knockin' sperets. Ye promised me onct when I cried ye'd never raise 'em agin. I won't go over there in that smokehouse with ye! I'm afraid of 'em as much as Alf."

"Then will you and Alf sleep together in my bed and let Julia and Lutie sleep in Lutie's bed?" Op scratched his head. "Won't be comfortable but I can't think of anything else."

Alf just nodded unhappily.

"I'll sleep with ye, Alf, before I'll go back to the smokehouse," Jack said. "That speret will keep a-knockin' fer hours. I remember too many nights. Get old Red Jacket to knockin' and he won't stop!"

Op stopped at the door, looking around. "Be the first time anybody ever slept in the cabin when I wasn't in it. Wonder what Beadie would say?" He looked at the others almost apologetically. "I'm sure old Red Jacket didn't mean fer ye to spend sich an uncomfortable night."

52

When Theopolis awoke at five the following morning, he looked through the crack above Alf's and Julia's bed. The lamp was shining through his cabin windows. In the early twilight that came to Laurel Ridge from the light streaks in the east, the yellow glow of lamplight looked good to him. In the unlighted smokehouse he fumbled for his clothes and shoes as he had done every morning when he was going blind. He remembered it well. That was before Lutie came to him from Dayton.

Op walked down the path across the garden, breathing deep of the fresh early-morning Laurel Ridge air as he had done winter, spring, summer, and autumn for many years. The blowing wind felt fine in his lungs. He walked through the garden gate that creaked on its rusty hinges. Then through the paling gate of his own yard. These two spots of earth, his yard and garden, in the great green wilderness of Laurel Ridge, made up the center of his universe. Technically they might belong to Snake Blue. But the imaginary deed which Theopolis Akers held for all of Laurel Ridge was a thing of the spirit, more valid by far than any mere scrap of paper.

When he reached his front porch, he heard voices from within. He rapped gently on the door and Alf opened it.

"Good mornin'." Op greeted his guests cheerfully.

"Good morning." The four voices seemed ragged, cheerless.

"Did everybody have a good night's sleep?" He felt awkward entering his own cabin in this strange way.

"Did everybody have a good night's sleep?" Alf repeated sarcastically. "Everybody in this cabin rolled and tossed all night!"

"What?" Op was surprised. "I slept like a log over in the smokehouse. Waked at my usual time, five o'clock. Didn't have a timepiece but I knew it by the light streaks in the east this time in July."

"We've been up since two o'clock," Lucretia said. "We've had breakfast and washed and dried the dishes."

"We couldn't sleep, Op," Jack said. "That knockin' speret Red Jacket knocked on everythin' in this cabin last night. I heard 'im a-knockin' on the footboard of our bed and I punched Alf in the ribs and he jumped and I said: 'Lissen to Red Jacket on the foot of the bed. He's knockin', Alf!' And Alf said to me: 'Lay down, Jack, and go to sleep.' But then Alf heard him give a big knock and he come outten the bed and took all the kivver offen us."

"Dad, it was like a woodpecker drilling for worms," Lucretia said. "Remember how that one scared me when I first came here last April? And I spilled a pot of beans on the floor? Well, the drilling was like that last night. It seemed to jar the whole cabin."

"I slept all right," Julia said, looking at Op. "I heard something climbing these walls but it sounded like a rat, not one of your spirits."

"There's not a rat in this cabin," Op protested. "I don't have 'em here. I never kept one, atter he come in from the woods, more than a night. Old Jerry always got the rats. Ye didn't hear a rat, Julia. Ye heard Red Jacket and his angels. But I had nothing to do with his comin' here. I opened communion with 'im last night fer the first time in several years. I did it jist to show you unbelievers. And now these sperets've come back to the cabin jist like they ust to come. They feel that they're welcome onct more. And they are!"

"I heard knocking last night," Alf said. "I know I'm of sound mind. And I wasn't dreaming. I heard knocking on the footboard and headboard of our bed. I lay and tossed and turned until I ended up rolling on the floor."

"I know ye heard the knockin' too," Op said, pleased to be agreeing with Alf. "Ye don't haf to tell me that ye're in yer right mind. I know ye are now. I've been tellin' ye I could raise the knockin' sperets. Last night atter ye all took off from the smokehouse, Red Jacket came down the wall with eyes like balls of fire. I wish ye'd a-stayed to see 'im. It's somethin' ye'd never ferget as long as ye live!"

A few days back, even the day before, Alf would have scoffed at the old man and then changed the subject. Now he just sat there staring across the table out of tired eyes. "Op, we've had enough of this spirit world on Laurel Ridge," Alf said finally. "Right there at that table, while we were drinking black coffee about two hours ago, we came to a decision. Julia and I figured we've had enough of Laurel Ridge. We're going back to Dayton this morning."

"What, ye mean to tell me ye're a-leavin'?" Op was genuinely surprised. But there was just the suspicion of pleasure in his voice too. "Don't tell me ye're a-quittin' Laurel Ridge for good?"

"Yes, we're leaving, Op," Julia said. "Alf has finally had enough."

"Julia's decided we'd better leave," Alf said. "The life's too hard on her up here."

"*I've* decided? Alf, you've done some deciding yourself," Julia protested. "You've gone to bed and dreamed of big snakes. You've had nightmares about drowning in Sandy River. You've jumped out of bed over there in the smokehouse and flattened your nose against the wall and I had a time getting the blood stopped. You've come back from taking a bath in Red Bird Hollow shivering and shaking. You've complained about your sunburns and your calloused hands. And yesterday you ran scream-

242

ing from the smokehouse because of Red Jacket, the knocking spirit—"

"But there's one thing ye've gained, Julia," Op broke in to stop their quarreling. "Alf will go back to Ohio a different man. I haven't heard 'im talkin' much lately about the adam bumbs and a lot of that foolishness. He come out here a-talkin' crazy about the world a-goin' to be destroyed by fire. He even said all the graveyards would be destroyed. I never heard sicha crazy talk in my life. I was afeared to take 'im to Honeywell, afeared he'd start that crazy talk down there. People in Honeywell and Looten County wouldn't understand it. They'd think Alf was teched in the head! Now, Alf's a-goin' back to Dayton a better man. He's not been here but two months. If he'd stay a year he'd be a well man."

"Alf's not as nervous as when we came," Julia said. "I'll admit, Op, something up here has done him good."

"I've never had time to think of the country's welfare," Alf broke in. "I've had to carry water and cut wood for our stove. I've tramped these hills with Op gathering greens and berries. I've chopped wood. I've been too busy with the little things close to me to worry about the big ones further away."

"But ye didn't take yer yarb tonic, Alf." Op frowned. "If ye'd taken all the roots and juices I told ye to, then ye'd really be a different man."

"We've been trying to persuade Lutie to go back with us," Julia told Op. She looked at Op carefully to see the expression on his dark, weathered face.

"Well," Op said slowly, "well. . . ." His face didn't change. "I ain't hardly thought of that. It's up to Lutie." He turned to her.

"I want to stay here with you, Dad," she told him. "I don't want to go back. I'm staying on Laurel Ridge!"

243

"But I can see well enough now," he said thoughtfully. "If ye want to go, it will be all right with me. Jack may stay with me fer a time, maybe till fall. Then old Jerry and I will be here together. We'll get along all right. We've done it before."

"But I'm not going, Dad." Lucretia's words were positive. "I'm staying here."

"What is it that's holding you, Lutie?" Julia asked. "Could it be the good spirit on Laurel Ridge? Or maybe it's just the fresh wind and the pretty clouds that keep you here?"

Lucretia answered very politely: "It's getting daylight, Julia. You said you'd pack when daylight came. I'll heat the coffee for Dad and fix him some breakfast."

"I'll fix my own breakfast," Op said. "Ye hep 'em pack."

53

Theopolis had eaten his breakfast and was on the porch sitting in his favorite chair when Alf walked up with a suitcase in each hand. There was a smile on his sun-tanned face. His hands were no longer soft and white and he seemed to fill out his shirt better. He set the heavy suitcases on the ground beside him. Julia, Lucretia, and Jack were walking up slowly saying their good-bys.

"Well, I feel pretty good to be on my way back to Dayton," Alf said, smiling. "I've got to admit it."

"I believe ye do," Op said. He was smiling too. "I know ye'll like it better when ye get back where ye growed up."

Julia smiled at Op. "You've done a lot for Alf, Op, despite the cold baths and the knocking spirits."

"I ain't done nothin'," Op said. "But I want to warn ye that it might not be farewell to the knockin' sperets. Red Jacket might knock a few times on yer hatband as ye go around Laurel Ridge this mornin'. And he can find ye in yer nice home in Dayton, same as he can on Laurel Ridge. He can even knock in yer office at Wright Airfield!"

Alf and Julia smiled at Op's warning. Standing in the bright morning sun and thinking about Wright Airfield and their house in Dayton, Red Jacket, the knocking spirit, faded like a bad dream.

"Julia's about convinced me it was a woodpecker," Alf said.

"Come and see us in Dayton," Julia invited vaguely.

"Doubt I'll ever get that far away," Op called after them. "Got everythin' right here."

Op watched Alf carry the two heavy suitcases into the green tunnel and disappear. Julia's laughter came floating back to them.

"There goes a good riddance," he said, turning to Lucretia and Jack. "I never was as glad of anythin' in my life as I am to see 'em go."

"Dad, I'll bet Julia and Alf will get in touch with the Law when they get to Honeywell," Lucretia said. "About Ted New-some's shooting at Alf yesterday."

"Let 'em get in tech with the Law," Op said. "Who cares who they get in tech with! They're yer cousins, Lutie. They're no akin to me. I didn't bring 'em here."

"I didn't either," Lucretia said.

"But they followed ye here. Be keerful about the letters ye send away. Don't bring any more people in here like 'em. When I think about Alf, I say to myself: 'It's a sight what kind of a weaklin' man will strike a purty woman's fancy and she'll up and marry 'im.' Julia's a plump and purty woman. And one with a little spunk, too."

Then Op pulled a calmus root from his pocket and bit off a chew.

"Alf thinks he said good-by to the knockin' sperets," he said, laughing and chewing his calmus root. "A woodpecker, eh? Old Red Jacket is now knockin' on his hatband. He's not to the arc yet. I'll see that he has a time gettin' away from Red Jacket!"

"Ye want me to take breakfast to Ted this mornin', Op?" Jack said.

Op thought a minute. "Yep. Fix breakfast fer 'im if he's a flesh-and-blood man or a speret, don't matter which. Whatever he is and whoever he is, I like 'im better than Hootbird Hammertight."

54

"Lutie, I've been a-doin' a lot of thinkin' since Alf and Julia left here," Op said. He pushed his chair back from the breakfast table. It was the morning after Alf and Julia had left the ridge.

"What've ye been a-thinkin' about, Op?" Jack asked.

"A lot of things, Jack," he replied mysteriously.

"About Alf and Julia?" Lucretia asked.

"Yep, I've been thinkin' about 'em too," Op said.

"What is it, Dad?" Lucretia looked at him sharply. "What's troubling you?"

"I can't figure things out," he said. "I know Jack is real. I know he's my son. He allus has been. But I'm not so positive ye're my daughter!"

"Dad, are you starting that again?" Lucretia seemed truly annoyed. "I've been living in this cabin since last April and still you wonder whether I'm your daughter. Why else would I be here?"

"I know ye look a lot like Beadie," Op mused. "And Beadie

was my wife and ye say she's yer mother. But why didn't ye never come back to see me before? Why did ye wait until ye were a woman grown?"

"I've explained all of that to you, Dad," she told him. "You know why I came! You know why I spent my own money so you could see again."

"But why ain't old Corrinne and Will Day been down here to see ye?" he asked. "If they raised ye and thought so much of ye, looks like they'd get down here to see how ye was gittin' along. Ye've been here almost four months."

"But, Dad, I hear from them every week," Lucretia said. "I wish you could read the letters they write me."

"And then yer city cousins come down here and they were a-goin' to stay and live on Laurel Ridge," Op persisted doggedly. "Where are they now?"

"Back in Dayton," Lucretia replied. "You know that as well as I do. I don't suppose you believe they were my cousins."

"I'm not so shore." Op took another sip of his hot red-sassafras tea. "A lot of things've happened since ye've been here, Lutie! Things that never did happen before. And ye wouldn't go back to Ohio with Alf and Julia when they begged ye."

"Are you trying to run me away, Dad?"

"Nope, I'm not a-tryin' to do that. I jist want to be shore about ye."

"I'm Lucretia Akers! I've told you a hundred times before!" Lucretia's temper was rising. She got up from the table. "And I'm not leaving here! I'll show you I won't leave until I get ready!"

"If I jist knew ye were my little gal young un that left here twenty years ago," Op said. "I wish I had some way of knowin'."

"Well, I am," she retorted. "I positively am!"

"Ye believe in Ted Newsome, don't ye, Op?" Jack asked. The loud talk was confusing him.

"I'm not so shore about 'im now."

"I'm shore about 'im, Op," Jack said. "I like 'im. And ye would too, Op."

"That's jist it," Op said. "He can appear to Lutie, Hootbird, you, and Doshie but never to me. He can slip around the cabin when I'm gone and see Lutie. Why can't he come when I'm here? And why does he haf to tote a rifle? I'm beginnin'," he complained, "to have my doubts!"

"Dad, if you'll come back sometime with me to Dayton, I'll prove to you that I'm Lucretia Akers, your daughter," Lucretia said.

"I'll never go to Dayton and ye know I won't," Op told her. "The proof will haf to be right here in Laurel Ridge."

"Op, I know Ted Newsome is a happy speret." Jack plucked at Op's arm. A new light came into his eyes as he sat there remembering. "He's full of fun. He laughs all the time he talks with me. Sometimes he looks sad and worries some. But mostly he laughs. He asts about ye every mornin' when I take 'im breakfast. I walk around with 'im and talk. I told 'im about how Hootbird come here accusin' Lutie of bein' a bad woman and a-runnin' the ridges at night. Ted Newsome didn't like it at first. Then he smiled and began to laugh and laugh. Don't doubt Ted Newsome, Op! He's a real happy speret and he's shore fond of Lutie!"

Theopolis got up from the breakfast table, patting Jack on the shoulder absently. He pulled a calmus root from his pocket and bit off a chew. Then he walked outside the cabin and faced into the morning wind. The stars had set in the sky, and Laurel Ridge was filled with early-morning light. Over the Little White Oak Valley and the Little Sandy River Valley white clouds rolled like August milkweed furze. Beneath there was still darkness in the deep valleys. He got his long-handled gooseneck hoe from under the cabin floor and went to the garden.

55

When the sun was up and shining on patches of clouds over the valleys, Op stopped digging long enough to watch Jack walk out the Laurel Ridge road with his food basket and butterfly net. He watched Jack turn the bend toward Pawpaw Gap and then went back to his hoeing.

The last clouds were going up in thin white wisps toward the sun when he heard Jack scream on the other side of the cabin toward the sty: "They got Ted! They've got Ted!"

Op dropped his hoe and ran toward the cabin. When he reached the front gate, Lucretia came from the cabin with a wild look on her face.

"Where? Where?"

Theopolis ran inside the cabin to get his rifle.

"Out by the arc!" Jack ran up, trembling and breathing hard. His face was flushed and sweat streamed from it.

"Who's got Ted?" Lucretia cried.

"Hootbird, Ben, Doshie, and the fox hunters," Jack answered. "A whole crowd of mean, mad people. A lot of 'em I didn't know. I didn't try to find out. When I saw they had 'im, I run here to tell ye! They've got a rope. They're goin' to hang 'im!"

"Come on, Dad, hurry." Lucretia wept openly. "We've got to do something. We've got to."

"Go fer the Law, Jack," Op said as he ran from the cabin with his rifle. "Run faster'n a fox! Go the Sulphur Holler road to Six Hickories so they won't see ye! Get Sheriff Bill Ackerson and his deputies! Get 'em in a hurry, Jack. Tell 'em they're a-hangin' a man—'r a speret."

"All right, Op," Jack said.

Jack turned and was off toward the green tunnel. The sod

flew from his big heels like dirt flying from the pounding hoofs of a fleeing horse. He was out of sight before Theopolis and Lucretia entered the tunnel. When they got beyond the sty, they heard the cries and curses of a crowd of men near the arc.

"Come on, Dad," Lucretia cried, clinching her hands.

"Stop cryin' and save yer breath," Op grunted as he ran with all his might. "Ye might need it!" She stopped crying and ran faster, her bright skirt swirling about her knees. Op was a few steps behind with his rifle in his hand.

"Hang a man 'r speret on Laurel Ridge, will they!" he muttered as he ran.

They raced onto the long straightaway over the blighted nuts that had fallen from the tall, bushy-topped hickories. The shouts grew louder as they approached. Where the ridge road turned to go around the arc, they reached the milling crowd.

56

"Stop it! Stop it!" Op shouted hoarsely. "Don't ye tech Ted Newsome! He's Ted Newsome, the speret, all right," Op panted as he trained his eye on the captive. "Only his hair is a little long."

"Ted," Lucretia wept.

"Lutie," he said, lifting his head to look at her.

Ben Hammertight had both of his big hands clenched on Ted's wrist and had twisted his arm behind his body. Plack Rivercomb was gripping the other wrist. Both men were standing behind Ted who was bent forward looking at the ground. When he tried to free himself, they twisted his arms.

"I told ye, Lutie, I'd get Ted Newsome," Hootbird shouted down from the big oak. "I even told ye this would be the tree!

Ye remember, don't ye, Lutie? I told ye he'd run out of cartridges! He won't thump any more on that old geetar either."

Hootbird was climbing the body of the oak. He was almost up to the big limb that grew over the Laurel Ridge road. Hootbird had one end of two rope plowlines they had tied together attached to his waist. He was taking it up to lay the rope over the limb while Penny Shelton was tying a noose in the end that was on the ground.

"He'll never kill another fox," Penny spoke savagely. "I'll tell ye that!"

"This ridge will be at peace agin," Doshie cackled. "I'd walk a hundred miles to see 'im hang. He's tried to kill my Hoot!"

"Don't climb another step, Hoot," Op said, raising his rifle. "If ye do, I'll fetch ye down from that tree. Ye'll tumble out like a squirrel!"

Lucretia ran toward Ted Newsome.

"Ketch 'er there!" Ben shouted.

Jimmy Torris grabbed at Lucretia as she ran past. Hawgie Cawhorn ran in front of her. He caught Lucretia in his arms and folded them around her.

"Where do ye think ye're a-goin', Miss?" he said. Hawgie looked like he was prepared to enjoy his part in the hanging—clutching this pretty blond girl.

Lucretia kicked Hawgie's legs and tried to bite his arms.

"Let loose of 'er, Hawgie," Op shouted.

"I won't do it," Hawgie told him. "I'll slap 'er face if she bites me again!"

Op was standing back with his rifle raised to his shoulder.

"Do somethin' with Op!" Hootbird squealed, looking down the barrel of Op's rifle. "He might shoot me."

"Help me hold this woman, Doshie," Hawgie pleaded. "Do somethin' besides stand around and talk!"

Lucretia was still struggling to get loose. She was kicking

251

Hawgie's legs and biting his arms. But Doshie got her by one hand while Hawgie held her by the other. They held her between them too far away to bite and kick.

"Don't a one of ye make a move toward that rope," Op threatened again. "I'll blast ye if ye do!"

Men stood under the oak with grim and determined faces. They were hunters Op knew, and some men he didn't know. They were beardy-faced men, wearing tight-fitting pants and brogans. They were armed with rifles and many had holsters on their hips. They had come dead serious and determined to catch the man shooting their foxes. Op understood their anger. Many's the time he'd said to others: "Ye don't fool with fox hunters if'n ye know what's good fer ye."

"I feel like blastin' the old man," said a small man with a black mustache.

"No, don't shoot Op," Jimmy Torris begged, as pairs of mean eyes looked strangely at Op. "He's been our friend! He never kilt a fox. He jist don't realize this man's a criminal!"

Ted Newsome stood still. When he moved, he writhed in pain because of the way Ben Hammertight and Plack Rivercomb were holding his arms. His long blond hair fell down on the shoulders of his tattered, faded, khaki shirt. There were holes in his shirt and in his khaki pants. The blond beard on his face was over six inches long, and dirty. His face was scratched and there were spots of blood on his beard. One sleeve was gone from the elbow down and his sun-tanned arm was bruised and bleeding.

"How can ye fight fer that awful lookin' thing, Lutie?" Hootbird said, looking down from where he held onto the tree. "If he's not a wild man, I never saw one!"

"He's not Ted Newsome either," Turkey Maddox said.

While Op kept his good eye trained on the crowd that faced him, a tall, unarmed man quietly left the crowd and walked out the Laurel Ridge road in the direction of Honeywell. Op didn't notice him go, since he was watching the mean eyes in the crowd and at the same time glancing up the oak now and then to see that Hootbird was not inching up toward the limb.

"The noose is finished, boys!" Penny said.

"Take it up, Hoot!" shouted a squat, broad-shouldered man Op didn't know.

"Yeah, take it up!" Others took up the cry, keeping one eye on Op.

Lucretia kicked Doshie's leg and Doshie let loose of her hand and screamed.

"Hold onto 'er, Hawgie!" Plack Rivercomb shouted.

"Ted," Lucretia wept.

The prisoner tried to free himself again. He was a disheveled-looking human being. Op couldn't tell if he were young or old. Only his blue eyes were bright and clear.

"Ye ain't a-gettin' no place," said big Ben Hammertight, as he twisted on Ted's arm.

Just then two arms went around Op from behind, pressing his arms down to his side. In the struggle, Op dropped his rifle. The tall man had walked out the ridge, crossed over on the Little White Oak side, and had slipped around behind Op.

"Now, go on with the hangin', men," he said. "I've got 'im!"

Hootbird let out a yip of joy and started climbing up the tree with his rope. The men closed in to hold Op and help Hawgie with Lucretia.

Hootbird climbed up to the big limb and sat down. Then he untied the rope from his waist and dropped it over the limb. Penny reached up and pulled the end down until the noose went up.

"The rope is ready," Penny said.

"Ye got any confessions to make?" Ben asked Ted.

Ted Newsome didn't speak.

"Boy, this is what I've been lookin' forward to fer weeks," Hootbird said as he came sliding down the tree. "Ye'd a-had me, wouldn't ye, Ted, if ye hadn't run outten cartridges! I heard that rifle snap. I knew it was empty! And now, I've got ye!"

Ben and Plack led Ted up to the noose. Lucretia screamed to the top of her voice. Op's long powerful arms had three men down at once, but there were plenty of others to hold him. There were curses of mad and violent men in the struggle.

"The old feller's a wildcat!"

"We don't want to hurt ye, Op!"

"Swing 'im up with the other one!"

One of the men came over and put the noose around Ted Newsome's neck.

"All right, boys," Hootbird called as he pulled the rope over the limb and tightened the noose. "Come on and hep swing 'im up!"

"Jist a minute, Hoot," Plack said. "Wait till we get his hands tied behind him. We want to hang 'im proper-like."

Plack and Ben crossed Ted's tired arms behind him and tied a bandanna around his wrists.

"Any confessions?" Plack asked again.

"Yes," Ted replied.

"All right, let's hear 'em," Ben said.

Lucretia sobbed loudly where they held her.

"I'm not really Ted—" But he didn't have time to finish.

Plack, Ben, Turkey, Penny, and Hootbird had hold of the rope and were pulling it tight.

"I'll send every last one of ye to jail," Op screamed from the ground. "This won't be the end of this hangin'—" Someone put a hand over his mouth.

57

"Lissen," Penny Shelton said in the sudden silence. "Be quiet, everybody!"

"It's a car," Lucretia whispered. "It's a car! It's a car!"

Ted Newsome stood with his hands tied behind him ready to swing. The rope was pulled around his neck tight enough so that his tongue was out and his eyes bulging slightly. He balanced on his toes.

"It might be down in Honeywell," Doshie said.

"It's a-pullin' up Seaton Hill it sounds like to me," Penny said nervously. "Boys, let's slacken this rope!"

"It's on top the ridge beyond the arc," Hawgie Cawhorn said. "It might be them soldiers back here!"

"I pray to God it is," Lucretia said as she kicked at Hawgie's shin, but he held her at his long arms' length. She tried to bite his hand again.

"They're a-comin'," Op shouted. "There won't be a hangin' now! It's the soldiers!"

The jeep rounded the curve from the arc on two wheels. Jack was in the back seat between two soldiers. Lieutenant Cox locked all four wheels and slid up to the crowd before he could stop.

"What's going—what are you—?" He jumped from the jeep, taking in the scene with wide, unbelieving eyes.

"They're a-tryin' to hang Ted Newsome," Op said.

"But that's not Ted Newsome," Lieutenant Cox said as he pushed his way through to the men holding the rope. "You people are *crazy*. You could all spend the rest of your lives in jail for this."

The soldiers jumped from the jeep, and Jack with them.

"It's Ted," Jack said. "Ted Newsome, the good speret!"

Lieutenant Cox peered at Ted's face through the beard. "He's nothing of the sort. He's the man we've been hunting." He looked at the beard again. "At least I think he's the man."

"I met 'em a-comin' up Seaton Hill," Jack said to Op. "That's why we're here this soon! I told 'em what was goin' on. We come all the way on two wheels."

"Let me loose, ye scoundrels," Op shouted. "Free me!"

When the men turned Op loose, some started running. They went over the ridge and down under on the Artner side. Op took a few threatening strides after them, his long hair hanging down wildly over his face.

Lieutenant Cox slipped the noose from over Ted's neck. He left his hands tied.

Hawgie Cawhorn turned Lucretia loose. She ran toward Ted.

"Private Rodney H. Bohannon," Lieutenant Cox said.

"Th-that's right, sir." His voice was shaking and his Adam's apple was working up and down under the beard.

"Just a minute, Miss Akers," Lieutenant Cox said, as Lucretia reached for Ted. "I'm afraid this man is my prisoner."

"How'd ye get the name of Ted Newsome?" Op broke in angrily.

"I got the name from a tombstone in the Freewill Baptist Churchyard," he replied.

"AWOL since last March 19th?" Lieutenant Cox said.

"Yes, sir."

"Why would a man with a record as good as yours do a fool thing like this?" Lieutenant Cox asked. "Why would you come here and take an assumed name and play the part of a spirit?"

"It was the best way, sir," he replied. "And I had a good time doing it. The chow was the roughest thing, sir!"

Turkey Maddox started for down under the way the others had run.

"No ust to run, Turkey," Op called. "Sooner 'r later I'll get ye too."

There were whispers among the fox hunters. Ben stood back, doddling his head and looking with his beady black eyes at Private Rodney H. Bohannon.

"Lieutenant, I've got a question or two to ask this man," Op said.

"All right, Mr. Akers, ask them."

"How come ye to look so much like the Ted Newsome I ust to know," Op said as he looked Private Bohannon over.

"Just a coincidence, Op." The face tried to smile behind the dirty beard. "I guess I chose the right name from all the ones I looked over in the cemetery."

"But how—how did ye know the right story of Ted Newsome and Lucinda Dortch so's ye could repeat it to my son Jack, and take 'im in the way ye did?"

"Lutie told me all about Ted Newsome, Op, so's I could play my part better."

"And ye knew Lutie in Dayton?" Op was getting angrier with each question. The spittle flew from his mouth as he pushed his face up close to Ted's.

"I certainly did," Ted replied.

"But why did you follow her down here?" Lieutenant Cox asked. Leaning shakily against the tree, Hootbird looked on with his mouth open.

"She tried to help me, sir," Private Bohannon said.

"Tried to help you go AWOL?" Lieutenant Cox shook his head in confusion.

"Tell him, Rod," Lucretia said. "Tell him everything!"

"Tell me what?" Lieutenant Cox asked.

"I killed a soldier, sir," he confessed, looking at the ground. "I didn't mean to. He got nasty with Lutie in a tavern and I hit him over the head with a bottle."

"So that is why Miss Akers brought you here?" Lieutenant Cox said.

"That's right, sir," Private Bohannon admitted. "She thought it would be the perfect place to hide till we decided what to do."

"Now we're a-gettin' someplace," Op sputtered. "It wasn't my eyes at all that brought ye to Laurel Ridge, was it, Lutie?"

"Dad, I came here and found you nearly blind," she said. "It worked two ways."

"I wondered why ye ever come here at all," Op said. "Now I see through everythin'."

"Bohannon, there's something I don't understand." Lieutenant Cox chewed on his lip, thinking aloud. "If you had killed anybody, I'd have the record. I wonder if you just *think* you've killed him."

Lucretia's face lit up with hope. Her mouth opened but no words came out. Tears flowed from the depths of her eyes.

Bohannon's bearded face was all confusion. "But—but I hit him awful hard and he lay still. His buddy bent over him and felt his chest and—and said, 'He's dead, you killed him.' Then Lutie and I ran for it."

Lieutenant Cox scowled at his prisoner. "Well, I don't like deserters much but I prefer 'em to murderers. I've got reports on a lot of bar fights around Dayton but no murders. You didn't kill him, Bohannon. I'd know about it if you had."

Bohannon staggered back against the tree in amazement, his hands still tied behind him. Lutie just cried and cried.

Old Theopolis scratched his head. "I jist don't understand it. More things happened on this ridge this mornin' than all the other days of my life strung together." Then he saw Doshie, Ben, and Hootbird huddled together under the tree. Op bristled like a dog. "But I understand about ye varmints! Ye'd better be a-thinkin' about what the next Looten County Grand Jury will do! Ye've almost hung an innocent man." He stopped and
258

scratched the back of his turkey-red neck. "Least I think he's innocent."

"Private Bohannon will have to come with us," Lieutenant Cox said. "Desertion's a serious offense."

"What'll be my sentence, sir?" Bohannon asked. He turned and looked at Lieutenant Cox over Lucretia's head.

"I'm not sure. Maybe four to six months in the stockade on a work detail," Lieutenant Cox told him. "And I think you'll be fined about six months' pay! But this is a mighty confusing case."

"Why, that's a light sentence! Lighter than I could have hoped for." He looked down at Lutie. "Only six months! And it won't be as tough as my four months on Laurel Ridge."

Hootbird picked up his rifle and sneaked off into the woods and over the Laurel Ridge. Big Ben and little Doshie walked away silently, Ben's long arms swinging back and forth, gorilla-like, his hands plucking nervously at his knees.

"Don't ferget the Looten County Grand Jury," Op called after them. "It's somethin' fer ye to be thinkin' about."

"Get your belongings, Bohannon," Lieutenant Cox said.

"I've got 'em," he said. "No more cartridges and I lost my rifle in the chase this morning. Only thing's my guitar in the cave in Shinglemill Hollow. But it's not worth going after."

"That's another thing," Lieutenant Cox was suddenly reminded. "Where'd you pick up this guitar?"

"It was one of the few things I brought with me, sir. We left Dayton in a hurry and I had the crazy idea I could pretend to be a wandering ballad singer and hide out in these hills." He laughed and looked embarrassed. "I guess I was kind of panicky."

Lieutenant Cox just shook his head.

Jack said, "Best friend, except Op, I ever had. I'm glad he loves Lutie. Ain't ye glad, Op?"

"Anybody's better'n Hootbird Hammertight," Op muttered.

"Op, you've been my friend." Rodney Bohannon reached fondly for Op's arm. "And I've been your spirit." He laughed his gay loud laugh.

Op turned and glared at Bohannon. "Why, I think ye're another unbeliever! Ye're not good enough to be Ted Newsome's speret! He's ten times the man ye are." He shook himself free of Bohannon's hand.

Then Op walked up to Lutie. "I can see ye're a-goin' with this man. Ye did a lot fer me up here, cleaned the cabin and all. But since I got my sight back I'm better off by myself. Allus have been." His tone was gruff and there was no doubting he meant what he said. But out of his one good eye he looked at her kindly. "Ye do look like Beadie. That's the best thing about ye."

Then he turned and walked out the ridge.

Lutie started after him. Then she stopped and watched his figure grow smaller along the ridge. He meant it. She knew he was better off by himself. But at least he realized she was his daughter. Ye look like Beadie, he had said. . . .

Lieutenant Cox cleared his throat. "We've got to take you back, Bohannon. Come along!"

The mouth behind the beard asked: "You got room for two, Lieutenant?" He looked at Lutie hopefully. "You can come back for your things later." Lucretia nodded, still looking after her father.

The Lieutenant took off his cap and scratched the back of his head. "It's against regulations but it isn't every day that we stop a hanging. We'll give you a waiver."

Then Run-around Jack spoke up. "I'll be a-goin' back to the cabin fer my net now. Lots of butterflies up and about." He looked uncertainly at Rod and Lucretia, not knowing what to say. He laughed happily, the same loud, affectionate laugh he gave while jumping through the brush after butterflies. Then, natural as the seasons, he just left.

Cox looked after Jack and muttered, "Wait until I tell them about this day. Nobody will believe it. I'll end up in a psycho ward." He shook his head. "All right, come along now."

The little jeep sagged on its springs as they all climbed in.

Theopolis Akers—six feet tall and broad-shouldered—took his time walking around the Laurel Ridge road. A small green-shelled hickory nut fell from the interwoven branches high above his head and sent up a little wave of yellowish dust beside him. He chuckled to himself for he thought of the night three years before when a hickory nut hit him on top of the head. He thought somebody had knocked him on the head to rob him. He lay there for hours and when he came to his senses old Jerry was still beside him, bored but patient. He had felt in his pocket to see if he had his one-dollar bill. It was still there. He struck a match and looked around him and found the big hickory nut in its green hull.

Biggest hickory nuts in the world on Laurel Ridge, Theopolis thought. And they're all mine.

About the Author

Jesse Stuart—a poet, short-story writer, and novelist of the Kentucky Hills—is one of America's best-known and best-loved regional writers. Although still a young man, he has written fifteen books, taught school, lectured extensively, and traveled abroad. In a non-fiction work, *The Thread That Runs So True*, he describes his experiences as a teacher and principal in various schools in Kentucky and Ohio. One of his most successful novels, *Taps for Private Tussie*, was a Book-of-the-Month Club selection in 1943.

All of his work, in prose or poetry, has for its setting the Kentucky hill country he knows so well. He lives there today, in Riverton, Kentucky, with his wife Deane and daughter Jane. When he is not on the road lecturing or busy at his desk writing, he can be found working in his fields. He has written literally hundreds of short stories and published them in the country's leading magazines. His astounding energy, his wry humor, and his wealth of colorful experiences have made him one of the country's most sought-after lecturers.